D.C. STONE

EVERNIGHT PUBLISHING ®

www.evernightpublishing.com

INTIMATE HONOR

Copyright© 2022

D.C. Stone

Editor: Audrey Bobak

Cover Artist: Jay Aheer

ISBN: 978-0-3695-0604-7

D.C. STONE

DEDICATION

This one is for all our furry soldiers, companions, and family members.

D.C. STONE

INTIMATE HONOR

Blue Empire, 3

D.C. Stone

Copyright © 2020

Prologue

Juliette Graham stared down at the two pink lines and the room began its ride *a la* merry-go-round. The *thump, thump, thump* of her heart hammered out a staccato rhythm, the organ driving a beat that would make many rave disc jockeys proud.

The pounding moved to her head, and with the spinning room, her meager breakfast of a bagel with her favorite strawberry cream cheese threatened to make a reappearance.

Boom, boom, boom.

"Juliette!"

She blinked at the positive pregnancy results and turned toward the door as if she moved through a room of water where the current wanted to drag her under. The pounding didn't originate from her head at all, but instead from a petite young woman on the other side.

"Juliette, if you're having second thoughts, we need to discuss this quick. Your case is next and court is about to be called into session."

Second thoughts? Especially now?

Her plan had always focused on finding the love of her life, marrying said person, opening her own veterinary practice, and raising a family. She hadn't asked for any of the other stuff. Things that had made her wish more than a time or two that she'd made a different decision.

Or just died.

She quickly but carefully wrapped the little stick in a brown paper towel found in most public restrooms across America and washed her hands in record speed. Then she unlocked the women's restroom door and met the frantic, doe-eyed gaze of her domestic violence advocate, Sunny.

Kid not, that was her name. Sunshine "Sunny" Floret. In layman's terms, Sunny Flower. With a name like that, it was amazing she surrounded herself with such darkness and violence in her career choice. Domestic violence wasn't a pretty thing on any given day. And Juliette's story was more horrid than most.

But she'd live to tell the tale. And now she had even more of a reason to get through this. She tightened her grip around the stick in her pocket and placed her other hand over her stomach as if to shelter the tiny being that was a part of her now.

Juliette appreciated everything Sunny had done for her, especially since she'd been unable to escape Manuel's abuse on her own, and for that, she'd forever be grateful.

Despite the turmoil rolling in her stomach and the secret she held, Juliette presented her best smile and tossed her long, curly red hair over her shoulder with practiced ease. The thick weight landed just below her bra strap. The hair, along with her bright green eyes, was a product of her father's Scottish ancestry. Unfortunately, in Georgia with the hot, summer sun bearing down six months out of the year, her very fair skin took the most abuse.

"I'm not having second thoughts. I just needed a few minutes to collect myself."

Sunny arched a thick brown brow and looked at Juliette's hand. Their gaze reconnected in an instance and she tried not to squirm.

"Juliette," Sunny started.

"I don't want to talk about it. I'm fine. Let's get this done."

This being attending the hearing where she'd get her name changed to Samantha Eagen, obtain a new social security number, and start a fresh life away from Manuel. But first, she had to have her whole sorry life put out for all to see.

Okay, maybe it wouldn't be for all. But for whoever would be in attendance within the courtroom. A handful of too many people who would look at her with sad eyes.

Pity eyes.

"Things change if certain circumstances..." Sunny took a deep breath and shook herself as if pushing away her train of thought. She dropped her head to the folder she held, a one-inch binder that covered twelve years of hell. Twelve years of ultimate terror compacted on a short court document describing Juliette's life. The constant worrying of what would set Manuel off. The wrong piece of clothing to put him in a rage. An innocent smile at a stranger to bring out his demon. The lash of his belt because she hadn't said the right thing in front of his colleagues. And that didn't even begin to describe what would happen at night when he felt the need to assert his dominance, as if she hadn't already been completely brought to heel.

Even now, after six weeks of being hidden at a safe house, weeks of having fear live like a breathing being in her veins, she still struggled with constantly checking over her shoulder, looking for him … for his approval or disdain. To prepare for what would come. She genuinely feared he would come to the courthouse and rip her out of what she wanted to rebuild.

Her life. Her company. Her confidence.

Instead of continuing with what she knew would be an uncomfortable line of questioning that could yank everything away from her—freedom, safety, and security—Sunny gave her a bright smile and held out her free hand. "Ready?"

Juliette smiled and took a deep, cleansing breath. "Yes."

Chapter One

I firmly believe that any man's finest hour, the greatest fulfillment of all that he holds dear, is that moment when he has worked his heart out in a good cause and lies exhausted on the field of battle—victorious.

—Vince Lombardi

Christopher Gonzalez had always been a firm believer in keeping two feet on the ground, or inside an airplane, as was the case with his job. His sanity—or insanity with his current predicament—came into question when he agreed to jump out of a perfectly good aircraft and embrace the lethal whip of air against his face.

He sat back from the loading deck as the tail of the C-130 Hercules opened and revealed the dark sky. They were several thousand feet above the ground, which spread like a black sea of nothing, just beckoning with the kiss of death. Despite the wind rushing against the thin layer of the plane, the only sound he heard was his heartbeat, which sped as it always did before a jump. Adrenaline spiked high in his veins, and in his arms, his military working dog, Delta Alpha, shifted.

He lowered his head, knowing that despite the oxygen mask, his partner, affectionately also known as Dumb Ass, would hear him. If not his voice, then at least he'd pick up on the low timbre of vibrations through Chris's chest.

"Right here, buddy. We'll be on the ground soon. I don't like this any more than you do." He let the feral grin take over his face. "But just think of the fun we're going to have in a bit."

Dumb Ass wasn't stupid, not by a long shot, and those dark-brown eyes filled with years of intelligence and training glanced from the opening cargo bay to his face. The anxiety in his dog's expression and the shifting of his doggy brows reflected back at him. Chris continued to stroke the long brown and gray hair Dumb Ass's ancestors gave him from their German Shepherd breed. After a few minutes, anxiousness melted out of his body.

The light above the doors switched from red to green, their sign that the mission was a go. His team, the rest of the Special Forces unit that made up the six badasses who would take down their assigned mark—or capture him, whichever came first—lined up along the side of the plane.

Chris tilted forward to hook the straps of his body harness to the dog. He double-checked DA's bite mask, making sure the supply of oxygen still flowed, before checking his own. Despite what many thought, at this high in the air, both man and animal still had to take in a steady supply of oxygen or risk hypoxia. It was why his team had been strapped to nothing but one hundred percent oxygen for forty-five minutes pre-jump. It was also why none of them smoked or did drugs. They kept in shape because despite being part of a Special Forces team, his team went above and beyond that call ... a lot. And jumping out of perfectly good planes was just one of those beyonds.

Rising from the folding seat attached to the hull of the aircraft, he grunted. The bulk on his back and front made him feel like he weighed close to five hundred pounds. Which, now that he thought about it, with a hundred and five in his rucksack, and another ninety-five on the front from his dog, he supposed it was about right.

His knees cracked. "You're going on a diet when we get back to base," he said to Dumb Ass, unknowing if the dog understood the words. It wouldn't surprise him if he got some of what Chris said, because yeah, his partner was pretty damn smart.

"Aw, my feelings are shattered," Captain Joe "Squirrel" Ford answered in his lazy southern drawl. "I've been trying to maintain my feminine figure." Squirrel wiggled his brows and cut a hand down the side of his frame, *a la* Vanna White.

Chris snorted a laugh and shook his head. The captain always had a way with his dry wit. And out of all on the team, Squirrel was the least of them who'd be considered feminine in any way. Bulky, much like a human-size version of the incredible Hulk, he looked like he could crush someone's head between his biceps like a watermelon under pressure.

In stressful situations or under fire, the humor was often welcomed. But right before jumping out of an airplane, Chris wasn't so sure he could appreciate it as much. "Not quite what I had in mind for a feminine figure there, Cap'. Dumb Ass here is either putting on weight or my damn knees are going out." He shifted again, making sure DA's legs were free to move but not close enough to kick out and nail him in the balls. Not again. Happened once before. Lesson learned. Took one time of him losing his breath at several thousand feet in the air when the oxygen was thin and the pain of being nailed before it became a habit to make sure both he and his dog could breathe and move easily.

One time was enough.

Stepping into formation, Chris stood second in line. They needed to be ready to work from the moment they landed. It wasn't about him as much as it was about DA's sense of smell. The dog could root out a bad guy, or a treat, in less time than any other canine he'd worked with. And seeing as they'd been partnered together for close to two years, they had learned to read each other better than other teams. His dog's training and intelligence, combined with Chris's skills behind a rifle, had led to their spot on this elite crew.

Squirrel glanced back as they got in position. The captain, shrouded in green from Chris's night-vision goggles, and always leading his men, even when they hated it, winked at Dumb Ass before scuffing the top of his head with affection. "Time to live," was all he said before he jumped. Chris's heart lurched into his throat and his balls hid in his stomach, as it always happened, before he followed three seconds after. He pushed off the plane, and for what seemed like endless seconds, time stilled. No movement, no sound. Even the catch in his breath alerted him he had quit breathing. Just stillness, a peace in the sky where you were wrapped in the comfort of nothingness, like a heavy blanket on a cold night.

The peace never lasted. Dumb Ass jolted at the same time the air disappeared from beneath Chris's body. He tightened his grip around his dog and tucked his chin to his chest, pulling DA close with one arm to protect him as his instincts from training took over. He stretched his body as much as he could, trying to slow their descent. He fell faster than the typical one-twenty, and he'd heard rumors of people who had gotten up to two-hundred miles per hour, but that was a speed he'd leave for those who wanted to take that chance. He was in no way ready to push that bar. Jumping out of planes was where he drew that line.

He choked on laughter with that thought. His dog wiggled and fought to turn his face against the wind. The world rushed to meet them from below in different shades of false green.

Chris shifted into the wind to slow their fall and looked around, making sure they wouldn't collide with others or interrupt their landing. In his ear, his team communicated in low, almost silent tones. An announcement followed, relaying the aircraft had gotten away from the landing zone without incident.

They'd been falling in the air for about two minutes, which, from his calculations in his goggles, and from the time on his watch, told him he was only seconds from needing to pull. As if jumping from the plane wasn't bad, the jerk in which he and DA would soon experience was worse. More so, the landing would be a bitch.

Shit, he was getting too old for this. Even in his mid-thirties, he felt each landing take another year off the age of his knees.

A low murmur in his ear told him Squirrel had ejected his parachute successfully. Chris braced and squeezed his eyes shut as he pulled on his cord, knowing he flirted with death doing this job. If this parachute didn't work, at least he had the reserve. If the reserve didn't work, well, then his team would have fun scraping him off the dangerous jagged mountains of Afghanistan for the next couple of years.

Two to three seconds pulsed by with an agonizing slowness before his chute caught and whipped him and Dumb Ass up in a hard jolt. He gritted his teeth against the jar and slowly relaxed his hold on his dog. The Shepherd turned his head into Chris for a moment, taking the comfort he needed before looking back out. Not needing night-vision goggles, DA's gaze roamed, searched, and hunted, his little doggie brain in full combat mode now with the scary part over.

That thought almost caused Chris to laugh again, but he choked it down. They were operating in full blackout mode. And being only three hundred meters or so off the ground in enemy territory, he needed to concentrate and land as quietly as possible. They were vulnerable in the air. Sure, no one expected an attack from above, but anything could give them away. The whisper of a command, the glint of a gun, the paleness of skin under the moon.

He glanced above to the dark ceiling. It was a new moon stage, leaving the very early-morning sky a deep empty pit with nothing but the blaze of stars. They winked like sequins on a dark velvet gown. He didn't have time to relish in the beauty of things you didn't see back home. He had to brace for landing. His feet touched first before he curled his body over his dog and rolled, coming to a hard and very painful stop. Before he could register any injuries or how much that fucking hurt—because it did, right on down to his bones—he unsnapped Dumb Ass from his harness, ripped off both their oxygen masks, and grabbed his M4 Carbine from where it had been strapped across his chest between him and his canine. Had he not been able to get his dog off in time, he still had the familiar and reassuring weight of his M9 on his thigh.

Dumb Ass stood still beside him as one by one, each member dropped with almost complete silence, low murmured commands whispering over the com-sets in their ears. Only he and DA didn't focus on anything other than what could be hiding out in the darkness. They, as the military-working-dog team, acted as a big part of perimeter security. If it had to be compared to anything, a kind of early warning system. With his dog's low growl, one could consider the sound a deterrent. When his partner gave a good grumble, no one could resist pissing right where they stood.

It was *awesome*.

Mini clouds of white air puffed in front of his face, the effects from the jump still skittering through him. It took a bit for his body to calm and, unfortunately, time didn't afford them that opportunity. They landed on the edge of a village where a local tribe leader to Al Qaeda was suspected to be hiding. Tayseer al-Libi had earned a spot on the top twenty of America's Most Wanted Terrorist list, and the mission handed down had been straight to the point: capture by any means necessary, even death. Intel on the plans al-Libi prepared to do included shocking images of dirty bombs he'd set off in the region, chemicals that caused big blisters to cover every inch of exposed skin until they popped. The aftermath had shown women and children, men of all ages with what looked like sores of acid eating them from the inside out. And the next stop on al-Libi's list: the United States of America.

It was bad enough this activity, this disgusting display of power in the wrong hands, happened in some far-off place where civilization still struggled to root. To bring it to his nation's front door? *No fucking way.*

Stashing the heaviest of their gear in a shallow grave, a place they'd come back to when all was said and done, the team moved forward. The only sounds surrounding them were the small clicks of their gear and the slight shuffling of feet. Dumb Ass brushed against his side, the Shepherd's training absolute.

The village sat in a canyon where two majestic mountains collided. Houses made of brick and stone faced away from the rise of caves inside the mountain, easy trails leading into each, an underground escape hatch for what hid inside this place, and a way for the terrorist organization to escape the seeing eye of the good 'ole US of A.

On the other side of the village sat a network of

farms designed to feed and provide income for the community, grass so green and plants so lush that even under the cold climate in this portion of Afghanistan, it was still a surprise to see.

His team had landed to the east, needing the shortest and most direct access to the main house. A dog barked in the distance as they slid over the short two-foot concrete wall, and Chris tensed, his attention darting down. He didn't need to worry, though. Pride swelled inside him as Dumb Ass dismissed the sound with a flick of his alert ears.

The team divided, subtle whispered commands coming through his earpiece like a well-trained concert. Three split to the back of the house, while the rest of them with Squirrel moved to the front. Chris gripped his partner's collar, keeping him firmly by his side for what came next.

This was what all those extra hours prepared them for...

A breeze kicked up and brought the scent of deep forest and green life, something that tickled his senses to an old memory. One he couldn't quite fully picture but knew had occurred when he'd been a little boy. These small breaks in his attention had been occurring lately, some memory triggering his mind to put together the whole picture. He didn't know what it was, only that he'd been happy, in New York City, and riding a carousel. His childhood prior to being adopted had been anything but sunshine and roses. But for the life of him, he could never fully put it all together.

He shook his head, bringing himself back into focus. The mission needed to be his entire world right now, otherwise, his lax attention could cost the life of one of his brothers, or even his own.

A few seconds of utterly agonizing silence ticked

by before two explosions rocked through the village. With the entryways at both the front and back blown to pieces in splinters of wood, they entered the dark house.

****

Three hours later...

"Goddammit, Crack, I need that air support. And I needed it yesterday!" Squirrel's voice barked through the headset and Chris grimaced as he ducked another bullet. The damn things seemed attracted to him like bees to pollen. He dodged behind another spiked boulder and tried to catch his breath. Air sawed in and out of his lungs, puffed in circles, and threatened to freeze midair to fall in droplets to the ground.

The mission had *initially* gone off as a success. Tayseer al-Libi had been asleep in his room, and while they had taken down a few of his lieutenants, the bloodshed had been minimal. Hog-tying the SOB went smooth, and just as the thought of how easy it'd been ... things went to hell in a handbasket from there. Some silent alarm was apparently initiated, and hordes of tribal militia swarmed out of the caves above. Effectively cut off from getting to higher ground, they'd been forced to retreat away from their gear and into the canyons.

Stuck out in the middle of the White Mountains, a more apt location should have been Antarctica for all the ball-freezing cold surrounding them.

To be honest, when he didn't have to dodge those lead-wasp stingers, the mountains were beautiful. Set in eastern Afghanistan, the range was known not only for being an important area for the Taliban insurgents, but it was also lined with some of the most striking natural caverns formed by limestone streams. Even with the remnants of bombing left over from the good 'ole US of A's strike to pull Bin Laden out of hiding, nature's true painting could not be described using words alone. Bob

Ross would have even had a hard time capturing the beauty in one of his paintings.

The range surrounding his team bottomed out with a lake so blue it hurt his eyes. The fish inside probably weren't clean enough to eat, but hell, when the bright, pollution-free sky mirrored off the crisp surface, one could almost believe they were sitting on a lake back home, basking in the sun, relaxing with the birds chirping nearby, the sound of the wind whispering through trees.

Almost—that was, if you ignored the acidic-burnt scent of gunpowder, temperatures that threatened to have your balls receding inside your body, and bullets flying over your head. Yeah, it could be considered a torturing kind of paradise.

Right.

"Crack!" Squirrel's voice boomed seconds before the ground shook with another aftershock of an explosion.

"I'm on it, Captain. Trying not to get my head blown off before the party's started."

"Come on, Princess," Sergeant Davis, the squad's leader drawled. "Having a few holes in your head would actually be an improvement."

Chris snorted and risked a peek around the rock before tightening his hand on his dog's leash and darting out from the hiding spot. He had to get to the top of the range, or at least at a higher elevation, in order to contact one of the big birds in the sky. Big birds meaning one of the planes hovering some couple of thousand feet above, a far distance from the hell engulfing below. He jutted over rocks, jumped across ledges—not an easy task when worrying about a hundred and fifty pounds on his shoulders when he had to pick Dumb Ass up, the M4 in his hand and the M9 strapped to his leg, and *still* carrying the radio pack. The handgun would be like taking a baseball bat against a bowling ball in this godforsaken hell, but if he was that close to anyone to have a need to use it, then he was too close to the enemy. A place no one wanted to be.

Coming up on a higher cleft, he dove to the ground just as the *zing* of a bullet whooshed by his head. *Too fucking close.* Chris dropped the pack and dug for the satellite radio, their only hope for getting a ride out. Earlier, when this whole mess began, the radio sergeant took a knife to his thigh. Chris didn't want to think too hard about how it had been his knife used, nor about how al-Libi apparently had gotten the one-up on him. Dumb Ass hadn't liked the show of aggression at all and chomped right through the calf of the SOB who had a few tricks up his sleeve.

Good dog.

With the Taliban coming down from the caverns and the bullets echoing through the ranges, it wouldn't be too much longer until every bad guy in the area—and proceeded to join their comrades—knew that a battle was underway with the United States military.

Goddammit, it was supposed to be a quick in-and-out based on the intel. He had one week left of his yearlong deployment and then blessed-be, he would be flying home for some R&R. This wasn't something he signed on to do for the pay, nor something he did to assert power over anyone. This was about doing what was right, and growing up outside of New York City, the missing towers from the skyline served as a reminder that some people needed to be stopped.

"Cobra 93, this is Crack coming in under fire. Request assistance for immediate extraction and medical emergency," Chris said, pressing the mic. Sweat, despite the frigid temperatures, popped out underneath his uniform. Yet another damn thing he would have to worry about if they didn't get off this mountain range. If he stayed stationary too long, the moisture would freeze and he'd run a risk for hypothermia. When trying to keep his ass, and his team alive, being worried about his body's temperature was the last thing he needed.

"Crack, this is Cobra 93. We're three miles out perpendicular to your location. Coming in hot. Request secure landing-zone."

The snap of gunfire had muted to almost the sound of popcorn in a microwave. A good sign for holding the enemy back. A bad one should they decide to regroup. And there was no doubt they would. Only a matter of time out here in a field where the bad guy could gather forces faster than rabbits mated.

"Cobra 93, LZ secure and in visual. Winds 250/8, Activity 4 north with small arms on east and west ridge lines. Report final."

Chris whipped his head away from the battle, something that made the hairs on the back of his neck stand, and forced himself to watch the horizon for the C-130 coming in. Landing the hunk of metal in a hot zone where enemy forces were breathing down their spines wasn't the best-case scenario, but it was the only one they had. The ranges and high winds whipping through left the fighter jets with hardly any options and the risk for friendly fire too great. With the four-engine turboprop aircraft holding its own defense system, and the quicker of the larger aircraft, as much as it pained him to do this, if he wanted to get his team out of here—and he did— and get medical help to those needing it, this was their only, albeit risky, shot to do it.

Had Max Carletto, the radio sergeant, and al-Libi not suffered serious wounds that couldn't be ignored, they might have tried to hump it to a more secure location. But as it was, Max stood on his last leg, literally. In addition, no way could the guy, no matter how tough he was, make it the ten or so miles they needed to hike.

A glint reflected the sun and Chris narrowed his eyes as the C-130 came into view over the horizon. Adrenaline, a separate kind from the gunfight, surged. Landing a billion-dollar plane out here, where it was vulnerable to surface-to-air missiles, not to mention any IEDs they may have missed during their quick sweep, fell on his shoulders. Not only did his team rely on him to get them out of here, but the pilot and his aircrew were betting on him to have done his job right.

"Cobra 93, Crack LZ, 240/10, LZ secure as it's going to get. Cleared to land."

"Crack LZ, uh … seems pretty short. Provide confirmation of distance," Captain stated warily.

Despite the situation, Chris couldn't resist the instinct to fuck with him. "Roger, Cobra 93. Distance confirmed. Make a hard right at the end, center for immediate take-off. Going to be really close to those cliffs, which jut off into a deep space of who-the-hell-knows. If you're not able to do that, take the Guadalupe exit off Highway 101, make a right at the light, and return to the airstrip."

Silence ticked by so long Chris thought the pilot might be one of those uppity kinds who didn't know a joke when they heard one. They were rare, but it would really suck for this guy to be one when they needed the ride home.

The radio crackled. "Ro-ger, Crack. Google for a drive-thru liquor store. Next stop, Southern California, I'll keep that in mind."

Chris snorted.

Seemingly moving too damn slow to stay in the air for a hunk of metal its size, the aircraft lowered inch-by-inch in the sky. He held his breath during the last few seconds as the plane hovered over the ground, then it touched down. The ground shook with force as the pilot tossed the engines in reverse, attempting to stop the progression with the short field they had available.

Chris moved, pack back across his shoulders, down the cliff with his dog. Not only did he act as an STS, and a pseudo-air traffic controller, but he also had to be the ground crew and get the plane turned around and ready to take off at a moment's notice. He was pretty sure the pilot and each of the aircrew had puckered assholes right about now. Especially seeing the telltale sign of smoke coming from caverns, the Taliban's announcement that they knew they were there, and they wanted reinforcements to move in.

A ticking time bomb had begun.

From the sound of gunfire, which had increased, Chris wasn't too far off the mark for the clock either. He rejoined his team at the bottom of the range just as the tailgate to the C-130 slammed down and the Ravens—flight crew and plane security—whooshed out in a startling pop of gray flight suits, each taking a knee once they cleared the wingspan and focusing their attention on securing the plane.

Chris still talked to the pilot. "Cobra 93, cargo moving up now. Coming from your six, SF team, and two injured. Providing 180 to you."

"Cobra 93, copy," the pilot responded, his voice sounding as if he were sitting back enjoying the same lazy day Chris dreamed of earlier.

He dropped to a knee next to Squirrel and scanned the horizon. Each second the plane stood on the ground, the more of a risk it drew, a big gray bull's-eye sitting in the middle of mountains. "Pilot knows it's hot. What's the ETA on the rest of the team?"

Squirrel glanced over. "Nice job, Crack. ETA two minutes and this plane could not have come any sooner. And look at you, no extra holes. It's been a good day."

Chris resisted the urge to roll his eyes … barely. The entire operation had been one clusterfuck after another. He'd be glad to put this behind him, as he was sure they all would. They still had to get through takeoff, though. And that would be a risk in itself.

Distant sounds of gunfire grew closer and the radio traffic in his ear more excited as the team with the injured came up on the landing zone. Chris rose and braced for the switch that would overtake the somewhat peace they had. In the space of seconds, this area would be heavy under fire. Like turning a light on.

As if on cue, two members broke out of the clearing, carrying Sig, aka Max, between them, making a beeline for the plane. He rushed to provide cover and started counting bodies as they made way for freedom. Squirrel took up point next to him and one by one, they fired shots. His world narrowed until all he focused on was his teammates, the rushing of bodies to get to the plane, the occasional popping of a head behind a rock, his partner's weight against his leg, and the steady squeeze—five pounds of pressure against the trigger.

When the last body rushed past, Squirrel slapped his shoulder. Chris dropped back and contacted the pilot again. He kept his gaze forward, weapon at ready, but for the most part knew Squirrel would let nothing get between them and the plane.

"Cobra 93, Crack LZ, cargo secure. Coming up on your tail, plus one. Cleared for departure. And we need to do this fast."

The crackle of the corresponding transmission came through mumbled as the power of the engines kicked up, preparing for takeoff. Would be a quick ride, but one they had to do if the sounds of impending doom coming down the mountain didn't speak volumes. Squirrel picked off one figure after another, his rifle never lowering as the bodies began to grow in numbers.

Chris grabbed the back of Squirrel's pack and hauled him up. Dumb Ass brushed against his leg and Chris gave him the command to get on the plane.

He turned and time seemed to slow. The plane's engines dropped to a low whisper. Dumb Ass had turned around on the loading dock and headed back toward him. What the hell was he doing? Chris shouted at him to halt, but his damn dog wasn't listening. Explosions vibrated through the ground, shaking his exhausted legs until they threatened to crumble.

Chris looked over at Squirrel and while the captain yelled something, he couldn't make out the sound. Panic crossed his commander's features before a dark ball of fur cut off his vision. Air whooshed out of his lungs as the sky exploded in dust and debris. Pain slammed into his skull, rocked through his chest. His leg and back screamed in agony. His vision dulled around the edges as explosions continued to pummel the ground around him. Bullets whipped overhead and Squirrel's face filled his vision, his eyes wide and terrified.

A heavy weight lay on his chest and Chris shifted to grab a full breath of air, but the body held him fast.

"Are you hit?" Captain asked.

He blinked, couldn't think of an answer. Everything moved in slow motion. What the hell had happened? Warmth spread across his stomach and moments later, the weight lifted from his chest. He sucked in precious air with a hard gasp.

He glanced down. Davis took a limp Dumb Ass in his arms, his eyes full of sorrow just as the world tilted.

"Dumb Ass?" Chris shouted after Davis.

Squirrel kneeled in front of him, wrapped Chris's arm around his shoulders, and heaved him up. Pain pulsed in a steady wave and nausea swirled in his stomach. His vision wavered but the rest of the team surrounded them, fighting back whatever the hell was happening. He couldn't think, couldn't tear his gaze off his dog, his unmoving partner as they were swept into the cargo hold of the plane.

Flight crew rushed up and darted around, readying for takeoff. Chris was tossed into a seat and buckled in for the ride. His heart pounded to the beat of techno music he hadn't heard in over a year as the plane started to move, bouncing over rocks and holes on the makeshift runway. In front of him, Davis leaned over DA, pressing something to his dog's side, the white gauze soaking crimson fluid faster than Chris could keep up.

He ripped at his buckle and fell to the ground, intent on crawling over to the Shepherd. Pain knifed up his legs from landing on the unforgiving hull. He tumbled forward and coughed. The taste of iron filled his mouth and he spit it to the floor.

"Easy there, Crack. You're hit. Seems you *didn't* escape those holes," Nate, the team's medic said in his ear. With the assistance of Squirrel, who at some point joined him on the ground, they laid him out next to his dog, barking orders to one another over his head. He didn't comprehend any of it. His sole attention was on his partner at his side.

He squeezed his eyes shut as the pilot gave the vehicle equivalent of flooring it, then the nose tipped and—*thank fuck!*—they were airborne.

Reaching out, he grabbed a limp paw and looked into those same intelligent brown eyes now fading in life and full of unspeakable pain.

"Dumb Ass," he choked and fought the sting behind his eyes. "What the hell did you do, buddy?"

Ford chuckled from beside him and Chris glanced over to find Squirrel's worried expression, but strength and will behind his gaze.

"He saved your ass, Crack. *Hoorah*," Captain said. "All in a day's work."

Chapter Two

So many days passed in a blur. If someone had asked him, Chris wouldn't have been able to give a definitive answer. Two weeks, maybe? It was hard to say as the narcotics they kept pumping through his system made his mind fuzzy and his reactions slow. A predicament no Spec Ops soldier wanted to find themselves in. Not when a delay of a second could mean the difference between life and death. Even sitting up in bed within one of the biggest military hospitals in Germany didn't lower his risk assessment any. He had a hard time letting his guard down.

Chris squeezed his eyes closed and pushed out a shaky breath. Pressure sat like a coiled spring in his chest, tightening with each tormenting second. He didn't want to hear the words, wished like hell he hadn't. And he craved, not for the first or second time in as many days, to switch roles with Michael J. Fox and star in *Back to the Future* so he could erase the last few weeks. What he wouldn't give for a time travel machine.

"Did you hear me, Sergeant Gonzalez?" his commander asked, tone hard and cold, yet still holding a trace of pity. The words battered against his pounding head with the staccato of a fully loaded M60.

Chris cracked his eyes open and for one, two, three seconds—yep, he counted those bitches out, the room spun before his commander filled his vision. The man stood tall and proud in his dress blues, metals gleaming in an array of colors and in as many rows. He was surprised he didn't fall over face-first. Silver birds winked from the top of his shoulders and the sun from the late afternoon's rays glared off the rank as it disappeared behind Germany's horizon.

"I heard you, Sir." Chris swallowed and grunted as he tried to shift. Agony speared along his leg, sending his nerves on another roller coaster of excruciating pain. He winced, feeling like a two-bump chump stuck in this bed, wrapped in the thin material of Ramstein's military hospital and recovery gown. The base's hospital name was printed in big, black letters across the bottom, a subtle reminder that it was government property—that *he* was government property—and to not remove either from the premises without permission.

"Where is he?" Chris asked. Seeing as the topic was on Delta Alpha, he didn't think he needed to be much clearer on who he asked for. His partner, his closest companion, his wonderful idiot of a dog.

Colonel Barber shifted and glanced out the window, his brows drawn with displeasure. Everyone took Dumb Ass getting hit hard, some worse than others. Then there was Chris, and his reaction moved to a whole other level.

They trained military working dogs—MWD—to handle all kinds of combat and friendly situations. Some acted in law enforcement roles, some in recovery, many in drugs and explosives. Then you had the elite of the group, the ones who trained harder to fight faster, respond quicker, and were worth more than many a soldier on the field. MWD policy had changed drastically from Vietnam when they were abandoned on the field and left to fend for themselves in a strange country far from home. Now, they served as one of the US of A's strongest resources in fighting the war against drugs, crime, terrorism, you name it.

And his damn multi-million-dollar MWD had jumped between him and several bullets, then took the brunt of a LAW rocket impact only a few feet away.

Chris's jaw tightened.

"He's across base at a facility for the MWDs. They are wondering what you want to do. It's up to you, Sergeant."

Chris blanched and stared at Barber. His jaw worked, but no sounds came out. Up to him? His wonderful idiot of a dog, his partner who had saved his life. And now they were giving him the choice to either put him down or medically retire him and take him as his own. Was this guy serious?

"Sir?" he croaked. "Is there really a question?"

Barber turned back to Chris and pinned him with a stare that no doubt sent many boots quivering for cover. As the commander for their unit, he had to be the baddest of bad in order to lead the best and toughest.

"Taking on a military working dog is no easy task, Gonzalez. Taking one on with the injuries Delta Alpha has, even with the suspected emotional trauma, and if things go downhill? They don't let anyone adopt these animals. Only individuals such as yourself who are trained to deal with them are given the opportunity. But something to keep in mind … what's going to happen when you pick up a new canine? Who's going to care for Delta Alpha while you are off on another mission? These are all questions you need to ask yourself, son. I know you've been with your partner for a while and we all love that dog, but you need to make sure you're thinking this situation through, not just acting on emotion."

A tendon in Chris's jaw snapped. "So, Delta Alpha won't be able to come back? That decision is already made?"

Barber shook his head. "I'm sorry. No. He's been diagnosed with PTSD. There's no way we can be sure how he will act in another combat situation, or worse yet, if he'd turn on his handler."

Chris wanted to argue, the urge so strong his chest heaved. He knew his damn dog, understood he'd never turn on him. But guaranteeing they'd stay together wasn't something he could promise. And putting Dumb Ass in that situation with another handler wasn't something he could risk.

He looked out across the darkening blue and pink sky. He'd decided seconds after Barber walked in. The darkening colors hinted at that lost memory again, but he couldn't grasp a hold of the thought before it skittered away. "I'll adopt him."

"Are you sure?"

Chris nodded and swallowed again. "He put his life above mine. He's been my partner for two years. I'd be a fool to thank him by putting him down."

"Some may say," Barber said, his voice low and soft, "that it'd be an act of kindness."

"No," he snapped and winced as the sound echoed back with a sharp pain to his temple. He turned to Barber. "I'm sorry, but no. I'll take him home, get him better, and depending on when I'm cleared to come back, I'll let you know my plan."

Barber's eyes widened slightly as if surprised. Chris blinked. The guy hardly ever showed anything on his face. If he hadn't witnessed it, he wouldn't have believed the guy had the capability to show anything else other than control.

"Your plan?" his commander asked, his words slow, as if chosen with care.

Chris blew out a slow and steady breath. This probably wouldn't go over too well. He would have rather waited until he was healed and able to stand on his own two feet than laid out in a hospital bed in a gown that gave everyone a show each time he tried to stand. "Yes, on whether or not I'll be returning to duty."

Barber's eyes narrowed and Chris rushed on. "My time in service is coming up in just over two months."

"And?" Barber asked, shifted slightly, stood taller, and took on that badass don't-you-shit-me expression.

Fuck. "I'm not real sure if I'll be coming back, Sir."

Barber stabbed his fingers through his short black and white hair, a move so unlike his steely commander, and so unneeded, seeing as his hair was so short there wasn't anything to run through. "What … what the hell is happening here?"

Chris blinked again at the rise in tenor. "Sir," he started, cleared his throat, and winced as he shifted on the bed. Not the time nor the place he wanted to have this talk, but hell, he needed to be upfront. "My time in service is coming up. I haven't made my decision to re-up."

"You're coming up on sixteen years. Four more and it's a guaranteed pension. What do you mean you're *thinking* about it?"

Chris shook his head. He searched for the right words. He didn't know what he wanted, didn't know what to say. He'd built his life in the military, had become a man in it as well. He dedicated his existence to serving his country, and that enthusiasm was founded on not seeing what happened in the City again. He didn't know what decision he would make. But he knew one thing, he needed time to think. He told Barber as much.

Barber let out a heavy breath and searched the room as if he'd find the answer somewhere within the bland, white walls. "All right, son. You go home, take care of Delta Alpha, and get yourself better. We'll talk. Don't call anyone else. You call me, you hear? You decide to jump ship, you can damn well tell me first."

Chris nodded and Barber walked out of the room. The weight of the decision rode heavy on his shoulders— too heavy for the impact it'd have on his life. The military was all he knew, all he'd been for so damn long. He didn't identify with anything else, but he didn't think he could see himself continuing with everything that had occurred.

The mission scratched like glass shards in his brain. It had gone wrong, so wrong. He couldn't figure out why either. Their communication was locked tight. The only other members who would have known something was within a dotted black line up to the President, and he didn't want to think, couldn't believe it'd be one of them. If so, then the whole system was flawed.

He shifted again and a screaming pain lanced up his leg. Clenching his teeth, he breathed through it. In, out. In, out. The world around him spun, a drab ride for a merry-go-round, not nearly as fun as he remembered back home when he'd been a boy and his life was full with his brothers. Laughing, joking, their lives inexplicably changed forever … and in the best way possible.

Whipping the thin sheet from the bottom half of his body, he stared at his bandaged thigh. He'd taken a high-velocity round in the thick muscle. A few centimeters to the left and it would have clipped his femur. The doc said he'd been lucky. Luck had nothing to do with it. His partner was proof of that. And his dog had taken triple the number of bullets in a body a third of his own size. At six-foot-one, two hundred pounds, he had the frame that should have taken those hits.

He clenched the sheets, worried about his partner all over again, wanting to be able to get out of the damn bed and go to him, let him know he wasn't alone. Chris didn't know the vets taking care of Dumb Ass, wasn't familiar with this base's facility. Instead, he felt like a worthless fool stuck in this bed. And now he had to find someone back home to help him with DA. He hoped the vets here would have an idea, but that plan would most likely result in him having to travel hours to their nearest contracted vet facility. It would be better to have DA close, in his home town, around people who would grow to be familiar to him.

"You know," a low voice drawled, "the nurses here would give you something to take care of that."

Chris snapped his head up at the unfamiliar voice. He hadn't heard anyone come in. That never happened. Being in Special Forces, you had to be aware of your surroundings. When you weren't, you ended up in the hospital, or worse.

He frowned at that thought, the four white walls around him screaming about pot and kettle meeting black.

Chris glanced at the guy's sleeve, identified his rank, and then read the name across his right breast.

"A hazy mind is a soldier's weakness, Sergeant Fusko."

Fusko raised a brow and crossed his arms over his chest, widened his stance, and stared at him as if he had all damn day. Well, dammit, he did, but that wasn't the point.

"But you're not a soldier, Sergeant Gonzalez."

The pulse in Chris's throat pounded and his face heated. "Your point?"

"You're an Airman."

Like he needed it spelled out. Who the hell was this guy? "I don't give a shit which branch of the armed forces you're in, every single one of us are soldiers.

Now," he rushed on, uncaring about his language or attitude at this point, "you'll have to excuse my manners, and my mouth, but I'm not having the best damn day. I've asked the nurses to stop feeding me those damn meds, so do you mind telling me what you want?"

Fusko nodded. "I'm here about Delta Alpha two-niner."

The air rushed from Chris's lungs and the pulse beating furiously in his neck seized. He studied the sergeant for a few moments, stalling to get his voice back. The guy looked calm, no tension in his gaze, his body relaxed, but shadows danced beneath his eyes as if he hadn't slept for days. He could understand. Been there. Lived that. Got the medal to prove it.

"What is it?" he asked once he recovered enough to draw air.

Fusko looked out the window.

And didn't that just get his heart pounding again? He clenched his hand into the sheets and tried to rein in his temper. It wouldn't do any good biting this guy's head off. He wanted to, wanted to demand answers, something.

Instead of saying anything, though, Fusko grabbed a black chair sitting against the wall, whipped it around, and straddled it by his bedside. Only once he settled did he bring his attention back to Chris. "How much do you know?"

"He took three rounds. Just got notified that I have two options: adopt, or he's put to sleep."

Fusko nodded, his lips tight. "It'd be for the best, Gonzalez."

"Chris. Just call me Chris. You're taking care of my damn dog, right?"

The sergeant nodded. "In that case, call me Mike. I've been with him for the past week. It was close when they brought him in, but seeing as we're the closest major military hospital to the action, we've got state-of-the-art equipment. He's being taken care of by the best."

Chris rubbed a hand across his face, wondering when he'd wake up. This had to be a dream. No, a nightmare. Never in his thirty-three years did he think this shit would happen. Sure, he knew it was a possibility, especially doing what he did. But getting shot happened to other unfortunate souls, not him. Not Dumb Ass.

"I'd appreciate it if you'd give it to me straight, Mike. I'd like to know how Dumb Ass is doing." Chris winced. "Sorry, that's a team nickname for Delta Alpha."

Fusko chuckled, the action allowing crinkles to pop up next to his eyes. Laugh lines, he realized. Such a rare thing to see in his line of work.

"Do I want to know the story behind that one?"

Chris rubbed his hand across the top of his crew cut and gave a small laugh, the first in weeks since he'd been hurt. How could he explain that his partner, being as smart as he was, could also make some of the silliest decisions, and often did them with the team there to witness?

"Well," he started and cleared his throat. "Dumb Ass is known for getting wedged in places. Despite his training, he seems to always find himself stuck in barrels, holes, behind couches, you name it. It's nothing that happens when we're on a mission, but more when it's just the team hanging out. It's almost like he wants to make everyone laugh and does something stupid." He shrugged. "I know it sounds ridiculous, but hey, when we're together as much as we are, it's hard not to notice even the slightest shift in behavior."

Fusko grinned. "It doesn't sound ridiculous at all. Who knows if that's really what he is doing? These dogs are smarter than we give them credit for, and we give them a shit-load of credit. And hey, if you get some laughs out of it, can it be all that bad?"

Chris shook his head at the same time Fusko did.

"Right," Mike answered. "So, back to your question." His lips tightened. "He's doing okay considering everything he's been through. You know he took three bullets to his body, but miracles upon miracles, none of them hit any vital organs."

"That's good. But if they didn't hit any organs, and are strictly muscle wounds, then why am I hearing he can't return to duty?"

Fusko sighed, and the sound tugged at something in Chris's stomach. That something bubbled with unease and spread as the silent seconds ticked by.

"Well, it's not something formally recognized in the world of veterinary medicine, but he's been diagnosed with PTSD."

Chris scrunched his face in thought. "I just heard the same thing from my commander, but I don't think it really penetrated then. I thought soldiers only got PTSD, but you're telling me my dog has it now?"

Fusko lifted his arms from the back of the chair and held out his palms. "I know, it sounds weird. It is. And it's something getting a lot of attention. To be honest with you, Delta Alpha isn't the first, and I'm sure with the ongoing war and campaigns, he won't be the last. I've got some questions that should help us settle the matter. But I won't lie, even if you give me different answers, the ones you think I want to hear, and I get it, Chris, you want your partner back. But they won't likely change the decision made. It's a done deal, and it's all from what we've witnessed and compared against his medical file. Okay?"

He swallowed hard. How could this be

happening? Dumb Ass trained to deal with stress. They all did. But even as the thoughts went through his head, he knew the possibility. This *was* happening. His dog was affected by post-traumatic stress disorder. Hell, even the hardest of soldiers suffered from it.

"All right, what questions?" he asked.

"Before we begin, I want you to know your answers will help his recovery, should you choose to adopt, okay?" Fusko paused. "You are adopting, right?"

"Fuck yes," he answered without missing a beat.

Fusko chuckled and asked, "Has Delta Alpha ever been anxious before? During missions, in training, at the range?"

Chris shook his head. "No. Never. He's one of the calmest dogs I've worked with."

"How many is that?"

He thought back on his sixteen years in the military. He'd crossed-trained into K-9, becoming an Air Force military cop two years after he'd signed on. Another two years after that he'd gone over to the "dark side" of Special Ops. He'd held a dog every two to three years before being moved to a new unit. "Six."

Fusko nodded. "Has he ever reacted to bullets, explosions, flashing lights?"

Again, Chris shook his head. "No, never. He's always stayed right by my side. This was the only time he didn't follow a command."

Mike lifted his brows. "Are you talking about when he ran off the plane before the explosion?"

He clenched his jaw and breathed through the memory. "Yeah."

"All right, did he ever wake disoriented, like he'd been in the middle of a nightmare?"

God. Chris closed his eyes and the enormity of the situation hit. Fusko was asking him questions about

Dumb Ass's past, but instead, what he really did was tell him everything his dog was going through. The thought of his goofy, strong, and intelligent partner going through this absolutely killed him. "No." He sucked in a breath. "Are you telling me that's what's happening?"

"I'm sorry, but yes, it is. Look, he needs time to heal, not just his body but also his mind. He will have to be retired. There's help for him out there. First thing will be getting him back to where you plan to be for a while and securing him that help. The vet should be able to assist in smoothing things over for him and making his life comfortable. Being here, especially on a base where the aircraft are constantly going in and out, where he jumps at every sound, it isn't helping him."

"Shit." Chris pulled his gaze away and fought against the rise of emotions inside his chest. It felt tight, tighter than when Dumb Ass landed on him. So much responsibility, yet so much debt. He had to help him. He owed him.

"How soon can he get out of here?"

"He's cleared to travel now. It's just a matter of getting your doc to give you your travel pass. You'll be flying back on military charters, and it'd be a good idea to sedate him before he flies. Are you okay with that?"

Chris laid his head back on the pillow. "I'm good. What do I need to do first for him?"

"Get him a vet. It'd be better to do it before you leave here. He'll need to continue recovery at a place that is familiar, somewhere he can settle and adjust. You don't have to board him at a vet, but I recommend doing that for the first few weeks once you get to where you're going."

"Wait, you just said he needed to be in a familiar place. Is keeping him boarded at the vet's really going to help?"

"He's still recovering from bullet wounds, and even though I know you could take care of him, it's best to leave this kind of trauma to a vet. Do you have someone in mind?"

He thought back on Nyack, a place he'd rarely been home to in the past sixteen years. His mind visually went through the town. He couldn't picture a vet's office, much less know one. "I don't, but my family still lives there. Perhaps they'll know of one, or I'll do some searching."

Fusko gave a clipped nod and stood. "Okay, then. I'll check in with you tomorrow and we'll start getting both of your travel arrangements in order. When you're up to it, come on over and say hi to Dumb Ass."

"Yeah. Sure."

Chris watched Fusko turn and reach for the door. He called out, "Hey, Fusko?"

Mike turned and glanced over his shoulder.

"Thanks. I mean that."

Fusko smiled. "Anytime."

Moving slowly and carefully, Chris reached to the side table and grabbed the phone. After a quick chat with the base operator, the familiar tone of ringing came down the line. It sounded so close, yet he was so far from his family. This was his life, the one he'd signed for. Growing up with his adopted brothers, they'd been as close as any bond without blood could get them, but he'd left it all at the young age of seventeen, and with Pop's permission, joined the Air Force. Started his career. Met a new family.

The ringing abruptly cut off and Dwayne's voice rumbled down the line, so sure, a little out of breath, and with a familiarity that had the air in his lungs seizing. "Yeah?"

"Dwayne," he choked out and felt his world

tumble. They were so damn far away…

"Chris? Where are you? I thought you were out of touch for a few weeks."

"I'm—" His lungs quit working, the tightness in his chest, the pain, and stress of it all sending him into a coughing fit.

"Chris," Dwayne said, his voice sounding worried.

He tried to answer, but once he started coughing, he couldn't quit. Rivaling a smoker's hack, he grimaced as pain shot through his back.

"Chris!" Dwayne shouted.

He tried to breathe steadily, the pain in his lungs excruciating. He pulled in air with a slow, measured inhale, then blew it out. The wheeziness didn't sound healthy at all. "Give me a second."

He took another deep breath, tested his voice by clearing his throat. Best to just get this over with. His brother would probably flip. And he didn't want to think what reaction he'd get from Ma. "My team was attacked," Chris said.

"Shit, you okay?"

He coughed. "Peachy."

"Don't be an ass. Seriously? Where are you?" Dwayne asked.

"Ramstein."

"That's Germany."

"No shit, Sherlock."

Dwayne sighed. "I don't know how long it'll take me to get there, but I'm sure I'll know in a few hours."

Chris tried to sit up, but pain spiraled along his legs again. "What?" he barked.

"I'm coming to you. Ramstein, right? That's what you said?"

"Just like that you're going to drop everything

and come to Germany?" he asked, not hiding the sarcasm in his voice. He loved his brother, but seriously?

"You're family, asshole."

"Look, I'm sorry. They've given me some really good drugs and I'm a bit loopy at the moment." No need to tell him the truth and let him know that his world was damn near falling apart, that *he* was falling apart.

"Tell me what you need."

Loyalty and pride swelled in his battered body. This was Dwayne, his brother who'd drop everything and help. "For you not to get on a plane. I'm coming home."

"You're coming home?"

"Didn't I just say that? Now, pay attention and keep up here, bro. Dumb Ass is coming with me. He's hurt." His voice cracked.

"Hell, Chris," Dwayne said, "how bad?"

He took a deep breath. "Bad. Look, I called you first because I need you to tell Ma and I know you'll be able to keep her calm. I also need a favor."

"What's that?"

"Get my place open. I've got someone from the unit coming by to make sure Dumb Ass will have what he needs, and I wouldn't normally bother you with this…"

"Consider it done. Anything you need. What else?"

"He jumped in front of me, the dumb ass." As the memory of the attack and the implications of what his dog had done rushed through his head, Chris's breath exploded out of his chest and his eyes stung.

"Who did? Who jumped in front of you? And what were they doing? Why?"

"I can't talk about it now," he answered, his voice rough and broken. "When I get home, you'll hear all about it. We'll be there in a week." He hung up the phone, slammed his head back on the pillow, and fisted his hands, fighting to get stronger, needing to be resilient.

For himself.

For Dumb Ass.

Chapter Three

Samantha Eagen, formerly Juliette Graham, sat back on her haunches and took in the day's work. As the weeks had passed and the distance between her and Manuel lengthened, she found she spent less time looking over her shoulder, waiting for him to jump out from behind a corner to drag her back south. She'd been able to settle—as much as she could in close to two months, get her license in the State of New York and a loan needed to get running, and outline a plan for the rest of her life.

Time counted down with the equivalent of a pay-to-use vacuum cleanser until she opened her own practice, her dream, something she'd worked toward for the past eight years, despite the minor—or major, depending on how you looked at it—hiccup. Heat from the sun shining inside sweltered around her and stifled the air into an almost suffocating noose. Yet, she couldn't be more elated.

Tomorrow, she would unlock the doors and officially open *Paws and Claws Veterinary Care*. Over eight hundred miles from where she had learned that trust could be shattered in an instant, and away from her nightmare of a past, she was finally achieving her dream. Nothing, not the ninety-five-degree heat, the eighty percent humidity, nor the dwindling balance in her checking account could sour her mood.

She did it.

She'd escaped her nightmare only to start living her dream.

Tossing the paintbrush in the black bin, she wiped beads of sweat from her forehead and grimaced as she came away with a streak of cream-colored paint on the back of her hand. The walls had taken four days to paint. Four days of blistering heat, long hours, and exhausting work. But looking at the soft colors, the light baby-blue line leading along the waist-level molding, and the airy facility, she didn't regret it. It'd been four days well spent, and she finished just in time. She had to double-check to make sure the rooms were stocked, the floors and counters clean, and then she'd be ready for business tomorrow morning.

A long time coming—this dream—and it was one she'd see through.

Sam pushed off the floor, taking care not to touch anything, seeing as her hands were covered in paint, and turned toward the main counter, looking for a rag she could wipe her hands with. The gray tile-covered counter separated the back of the facility from the wall of windows and the main entrance. Just outside was the town of Nyack, and activity in the small village bustled with energy.

People walked up and down the sidewalks along Main Street, peeking inside window displays, and as they passed *P&CVC*, gazed inside with open curiosity. It didn't bother her—*much*—she understood being the pseudo-newcomer that people would be curious. And seeing as she was over a day's drive from Savannah, she was as outsider as an outsider could get.

And yet another thing she wouldn't change.

It would take time for her to assimilate to the community. People here didn't look at her with pity and sympathetic eyes. They also didn't turn their heads away from what they knew was wrong in her life. Kids waved at her through the glass, police officers tipped their hats before helping little old ladies cross the street, and many stopped and introduced themselves. A town that bustled with being alive and happy to live. They looked out for one another and even when things got a little more on the rowdy side at night with the college kids swarming the local pubs, it was a town she felt safe in. Not completely, but she had hope she'd get to that point again one day.

Hope.

At least she had that now. After years of living in the shadows and darkness of fear, she could finally breathe again.

She grabbed a water bottle sitting on the counter and took long gulps. Besides getting her practice in order, she had to start planning what to do with her ever-changing body. She had a baby in there, a tiny human life that reminded her each morning of its presence as she expelled whatever dinner she'd eaten the night before. It'd been a game of seeing how fast she could make it to the bathroom before morning sickness set in, and one she was bound to win. She'd started setting her alarm for a few hours before she needed to get up, that way she could nibble on some crackers and head off any oncoming nausea. For the past week, it'd been working. But she still found the need to eat smaller meals more frequently, otherwise, that morning sickness turned into all-day sickness.

The blue phone on the counter shrilled, and she jumped, wrenched back inside her shop and away from the possibilities of happier memories. It took her a few seconds of staring at the phone, its ring unfamiliar, seeing as she'd purchased the thing last week and it hadn't made a sound yet. The shop wasn't open, and while she'd gotten fliers out and around town, she didn't expect immediate acceptance from this wholesome, happy community. About the only person who knew her business phone number was the local pizza delivery place down the street. She stared at the phone as it continued to ring. What if it was someone looking to test the waters and make an appointment? She needed word to get out, and with the bills piling up, she needed it fast.

That last thought broke her out of her musings and she picked the phone up, wincing as she caught the smear of cream against the dark-blue handset. In her long thoughts, she had also forgotten to wipe her hands.
Crap.

"Hello, Paws and Claws. How can I help you?" she answered, resting the phone against her shoulder and reaching for a rag. Static crackled down the line and she waited for a beat before trying again. "Hello?"

A deep throat cleared. "Um, I'm looking for Paws and Claws."

She wiped her hands and grimaced at the mess. "You've got her. This is Samantha. What can I do for you?" No matter how many months it'd been, it still felt weird to use her different name.

"I'm looking for the vet," the deep voice asked. She liked the sound of his voice. Low, raspy, almost as if he didn't use it much.

"This is her. How can I help you?"

The deep voice cleared his throat again, and the sound came through as if he were in pain. "I have a problem I need a vet's help with."

Sam brought her brows down and scowled for a moment at the phone. This guy sounded out of it. "As I said, I'm the vet. I'm Doctor Eagen. The only vet there is here. What can I help you with?"

"Oh," he said, sounding … surprised? She scowled more and tossed the rag on the counter, turned, and leaned her hip against it.

"What can I do for you, Mister…?" she asked, growing a little impatient. She hated the older thought process some had, thinking a woman couldn't do a man's job. Maybe presumptuous for her to think that based on one comment, but she couldn't help it. She'd dealt with the same old-school approach for years.

"The name's Chris. Let me first just say I'm sorry, but this isn't something I'm used to. And you've caught me off-guard. I'm feeling my way around without a flashlight in the dark, if you get my point."

She lifted a brow. Something he wasn't used to? She didn't get it. "Okay, I get that," she lied, trying to move this along. "Let me see if I can help you out. I take it you have an animal that needs to be looked at?"

"Yes, a dog."

"Okay," she said and nodded even though he was on the phone. Maybe it was a new puppy. Good for him, she loved puppies. "How old is your puppy?"

He made a strangled sound suspiciously close to a smothered laugh. She straightened her shoulders and stared at the doggie calendar on the wall. Her gaze moved over the month of August. Three puppies sat on the picture, a white, black, and brown lab, tugging on red yarn in a wagon. *Cute.*

"He's not a puppy," the attractive voice said through laughter. "He's full grown. Delta Alpha is five years old."

"Five?" she asked, then continued, skipping over the dog's odd name. "When was the last time a vet saw him?"

"He's currently under medical care here in Ramstein."

Her eyes widened. "Germany?"

"Yes."

Geesh, obviously a talker. "Um, Mr. Chris? I'm in Nyack, New York, not Germany. You know, the United States of America?"

He sighed, and it came out sounding tired, full of

exhaustion. Immediately, her heart went out to him and his dog, but she didn't know what she could do.

"I get that," he said. "Look, I'm not doing this right. Let me start over. I'm an active-duty military working dog handler."

Sam's brows shot sky-high at this piece of news.

"The name is Chris Gonzalez, but please just call me Chris or Gonzalez. When people put a Mister in front of my last name, I look for my pop.

"About three weeks ago, my team was on a mission—classified, can't say where—but what you need to know is Delta Alpha took three shots as he tackled me to the ground. They are medically retiring him and I'm bringing him home. I realize we haven't gotten off to the best of introductions, Doctor Eagen," he said, and her cheeks heated with embarrassment, "but you're the closest vet to where I live, and I want him close. I owe it to him to not leave him in a place that is going to take me hours to get to."

Her heart thumped erratically, and she curved her body over the phone as if to protect him. His words held immense pain when he explained all he'd been through, but his voice grew soft when he talked about his dog. Sweet. A little terrifying since he talked about a military working dog—something she had no experience in—but still … sweet.

"Okay," she said when he grew silent. "I take it you're coming home to Nyack?"

"Yeah."

Shit, shit, shit. She really wanted to help but had no idea where to start, or where she could begin to understand how to treat a military dog, and further, while she could use the business, the added stress on top of everything else, including her pregnancy, she didn't know if she could manage. She sighed. "Look, Chris—"

she started, but he cut her off.

"Please, Doctor Eagen."

Her heart clenched. "I don't think I'm the right vet for you. I'm not even open yet, and I have no experience with military dogs."

"You're not open? But my brother said your shop was on Main."

"It is. But I don't open until tomorrow. And that isn't the point. I'm sorry, I want to help you, but I don't know how much help I can be seeing as I know absolutely nothing about military dogs."

"I do."

"You do what?" she asked, feeling like this conversation spun in circles, taking everything out of her. How could it be so difficult to communicate?

"I know plenty about them. Look," he said, and let out another heavy sigh of exhaustion. "I haven't been home in years. I know you don't know me, don't trust me, so all I can give you right now is my word that I will do most of the work when it comes to getting DA better. I just need you to monitor his care and help me come up with a game plan. I'm flapping my arms out here in the dark and have no clue where to start. All I know is you're there, you're close, and pardon me, Doc, but you just sound right. You have openings and I have a need. I won't be in your hair, and outside of the initial business between us, you really won't have to deal much with me."

"How do you know I have openings?" she asked, somewhat disappointed in that last statement regarding her dealing with him. Also, strangely enough, she kind of enjoyed this weird conversation.

"You haven't opened yet."

"And?"

"Do you have a full house?"

"No," she whispered, hearing the hope in his voice, the pleading.

"Doctor Eagen."

"Samantha," she said before she could think better of it. Why? Why did she do that?

A pause, then, "Samantha. That's nice," he said, and her stomach took a tumble. She hated to admit it, but she liked the sound of her name coming from him.

"That's not the point, Chris. I don't know if I could help you. Military dogs are in a whole other group of care."

"Not Delta Alpha. You'll be fine. He just needs some attention. I'll tell you all you need to know before I leave him in your hands."

She rubbed her eyes. Dammit, she could use the business, but an MWD? She had no clue where to begin. Sure, they were the same animal she treated on a daily basis, but they were trained to kill, could be violent, and were a hell of a lot scarier.

"Does he bite?"

"On command," Chris answered, and she heard the smile in his voice. She couldn't help but match it. "But if it makes you feel any better, I'll bring his muzzle. Although I doubt you'll need it. He's injured pretty bad."

God. Her heart. *Rip*. She was such a sucker. "When?"

"We leave tonight. He'll be medicated for the trip. We land at JFK tomorrow afternoon."

"You said he took three bullets?"

"Yes," Chris answered, his voice soft, almost intimate.

"Is it a good idea for him to be flying?" she asked, matching his tone.

"We're flying military available space. Not commercial. So yeah, we'll be able to give him a little bit of extra attention."

"Okay. I'll need his medical files before he gets here."

"You got it. Email or fax?"

"Email. You have a pen?"

"Got one," he answered. "Give it to me."

Again with that damn stomach tumble. She recited her email and waited until he repeated it twice. "Okay, Chris, what time should I expect you?"

"We land at JFK around three, customs, travel time, I'll say shoot for the latest six, maybe seven. You okay with that?"

"That's fine. I live above the shop so I'll keep a lookout. Do you have my address?"

"Dwayne gave it to me, so yeah."

"Dwayne?" she asked, her heart skipping a beat. Who was Dwayne and how did he know her?

"He's a detective with Nyack PD. Also my brother."

Her scalp tingled with her rapidly calming pulse. "Ah. Okay. Well, you have my number, if you … you need … um, anything." *Really, Sam?*

The smile returned to his voice when he replied. "I do. See you tomorrow."

"All right, Chris. See you."

"Later," he said, and the line went dead. She set the cordless back on its cradle and stared at it for a few minutes. Her stomach took another tumble as her cell phone rumbled across the counter, signaling an incoming email. She had connected it directly, so that way she could make sure she kept up to task with anything. Seeing as everything was business-related, especially as no one from her previous life had her new email, or any way to contact her, and seeing as her first business was one Mr. Chris Gonzalez, she knew the email was from him.

She scooped the phone off the counter, swiped the security key, and took a breath, then went to her office to fire up the computer. She needed to figure out all she could about dealing with an MWD.

Chapter Four

Forty-eight hours after Chris spoke to Samantha Eagen, with her smoky voice and southern accent still stuck in his head, he waited at the side of the airport entry door. Despite the late hour, the loud flight line had a steady stream of traffic coming in and out. He sat off to the left without ear protection and got the full force and beauty that harbored the largest airport in New York City. His duffle hung on his shoulder and his pack was strapped to his back. They had shipped his gear and to both the base and his house in Nyack. All that remained was Delta Alpha, who was being unloaded from the belly of the Globemaster they had flown on from Germany. The typical nine-hour flight had ballooned into twelve with a stopover in New England so they could refuel.

Needless to say, the wind proved to be a bitch when combined with their load.

His wounds throbbed in a steady beat that matched his pulse, and he was sure the bandages needed changing, but he couldn't focus on any of that.

Dumb Ass had been down for the count for most of the flight, not tranquilized, but medicated enough to where he rested fitfully. Chris had checked on him a few times and the crew had allowed him such after hearing their story. It would have had been hit-or-miss if DA was awake, and even when he was, his dog's eyes stared at Chris like he saw straight through him. The entire situation sucked.

He shifted the duffle on his shoulder and adjusted his grip on DA's bag, one that carried the basic necessities they'd need for the next few days—food, meds, his Kong, and a muzzle. His head pounded a fierce rhythm that rivaled the sounds of the aircraft landing and taking off. His mind went through the mental list of to-dos again: get through customs, get a rental, let Dumb Ass out of the crate so he could relieve himself, get to the vet's, get a phone, and get some sleep—in that order.

"Gonzalez," a deep voice called.

Chris snapped his head up at a flight member approaching, ear protection firmly in place around the guy's head. "That's me."

"Your cargo, the MWD?"

Chris lifted his eyebrows, not liking anything about his partner being referred to as cargo. "My dog … yes?"

The guy tossed his head toward another set of doors. "Customs stated he'll be waiting on the other side. Can't go through the processing line with you. Said it's standard operating procedure even with military dogs."

Chris cursed under his breath and held his temper in check. The guy at least held an apologetic look, as he should, seeing as he had been present when Chris was told he'd be able to take Dumb Ass through the line with him. As it was now—with a quick glance through the glass on the entrance doors—the long line hadn't moved much in the twenty or so minutes he'd been standing there.

"Damn it. Did they say exactly where?" Chris asked.

The guy tightened his lips and tossed him another look full of apology. "Sorry, man, I feel for you. The guy said there will be a cargo door on the other side and all the animals from various flights will be sitting there."

Chris sighed and really hoped the sign reading DANGER, MILITARY WORKING DOG—DO NOT TAMPER WITH ANIMAL would be enough for little kids and curious people passing by not to touch his dog.

"Gotcha," Chris said, and with another chin lift, pushed inside and waited in the customs line for his turn.

Another hour later, he walked into the main baggage area and headed toward the lone crate waiting next to a large set of brown cargo doors. No one stood around the crate, and there wasn't any movement inside, but that didn't calm his nerves. His stomach turned with unease and sadness at DA left alone in a strange place, especially with all he'd been through. He didn't like having his dog out of sight.

As he crossed baggage carousel after carousel, Chris eyed other passengers in the area, some from his flight in battle dress uniform, some from other commercial flights. His steps faltered. Now that he looked closer, DA's crate sure as shit got lots of attention. Sure, people weren't approaching, but they stared at the big red and black lettering. And seeing him walking across, still in his desert fatigues, he could only imagine the picture painted. But whatever they thought, this wasn't a hero's welcome home, nor was it happy times.

The last carousel just before he reached Dumb Ass had a crowd surrounding it, waiting for their bags to come out. Chris adjusted his path and went to move through them, his focus entirely on getting to his dog before he heard a little voice chirp up from close to the ground.

"Hey mister, you in the Army?" a tiny voice asked at about two octaves above what his head wanted to accept. He winced and glanced at the kid. Dark-blond curls went in every direction, and tired green eyes, yet full of mischief looked up at him.

"Air Force, kid."

"Were you in the war?" the kid asked, and Chris fought back a growl as pain lanced through his temples.

He inched through the crowd and tried like hell to be patient.

"Was, yes. Now I'm home."

"Welcome, soldier," one older gentleman said from his other side.

"Thank you for serving, young man," another said, and Chris sighed under his breath.

"You're a true hero," an older lady said on his other side.

Chris shifted, taking it all in but still returning to DA's crate, from which he'd yet to see any movement. Beneath his breastbone, his heart thumped against his chest. An animal traveling abroad normally was hard. With three bullet wounds and the stress of being shot, there was no saying what kind of shape his dog was in.

"Thank you. Excuse me, please."

More thank yous murmured through the crowd and while he nodded to a few of them, he disregarded the rest and pushed through. Finally at the crate, he dropped to his knees, ignoring the wrenching pain through his back and the undoubtedly torn stitches in his leg—*because yes, I felt that*—he palmed the grated opening of the door and ducked his head to see inside.

Delta Alpha lifted weary eyes up his way, his gaze jumping between Chris and behind him, as if trying to determine if they were safe or not. As he lay on his side, white bandages stood out starkly against his grey and brown fur. They'd shaved nearly half his body and wrapped the gauze thick around his wounds. The holes were healing, which spoke to how physically healthy his partner was. But the most severe of his dog's injuries were the ones you couldn't see. Delta Alpha shook so severely, it was amazing the whole crate didn't move. His brave and strong dog reduced to quivering in fear at an airport showed how hard the situation was on him.

"Come on, big guy," Chris said and opened the front of the crate. DA shrank back and Chris refused to let any sign of disappointment show. His dog would know, would sense the shift. Most likely, he already felt the undercurrent of Chris's anxiety. Forcing himself to take a deep breath, he tried again. "Delta Alpha, come," he commanded.

His dog whimpered and crouched on all fours, still looking outside the crate as if some threat would come up behind his partner.

"Fuck," he breathed and dropped his bags off his shoulder and back, then slid his ass down on the ground, his legs spread wide in a V, the crate sheltered between them. Chris touched his forehead to the top. He kept his eyes closed, trying like hell to get control over his impatience and anxiety. Perhaps waiting until the baggage claim area cleared out would be the best bet, but they were late. And he was exhausted, they both were. He was supposed to be at Paws and Claws hours ago. With the sun set, no phone, and still in need of getting a car, getting the hell out of New York City, and doing the thirty-minute trek after that, they didn't have time to wait.

He took another breath and tried again, reaching with both hands, letting DA sniff him before he gently ran his fingers through the thick fur of his dog's neck. He spoke in soft undercurrents, encouraged him to be strong, to ignore everyone else, and to act like the true hero here, the one he'd proved to everyone he could be.

People bustled by, despite the late hour, with JFK being one of the busiest international airports in the area. Hell, one of the busiest in the country. A few murmured thank you as they walked by, but he ignored them, his focus directed at his dog instead. Chris had no clue how long they sat like that, with him cradling the crate to his body, his hands inside and trying like hell to communicate to DA all was okay, that he was safe and could come out. His back screamed, his legs were restless, and a kink developed in his neck.

"Mister?"

Chris sat up at the call, the voice closer than he liked, and turned his head. Behind, to the right, stood a little girl no older than seven or eight. She wore black leggings, a pink hoodie sweatshirt, and black UGG boots. His brother, Matt, used to refer to those UGG boots as uglies, and the thought caused him to smirk.

The little girl's blonde hair fell around her face in complete disarray with large bouncing curls. She had the strap of a backpack over her shoulder and her eyes on him. Chris searched for her parents and frowned when he didn't see anyone.

"Kid, you shouldn't wander around without your parents. This place isn't nice."

She shrugged and pointed to the closest carousel. "My mom is getting our bags. She knows I'm here."

Chris twisted his body further and looked in the direction she pointed. Sure enough, a woman stood amongst other travelers, clear as day with almost a cloning resemblance to the little girl standing in front of him. Just about twenty years older.

"You should go back to your mom, kid."

"What are you doing?" she asked, instead of listening.

He sighed. "Talking to my dog."

Her cobalt eyes lit up, dancing with renewed interest. She looked over his shoulder, not that she could see inside the crate, seeing as he blocked anything from getting in or out with his torso.

"Can I pet him?"

He shook his head. "Sorry, kid, he's not a dog

you can pet."

She glanced at the side of the crate, narrowed her eyes, then turned back to him. "What's a military working dog?"

"That's my dog."

"Yeah, but what is it?"

Chris drew his brows down, never asked that question before. Sure, everyone he'd been around for the past sixteen years knew exactly what an MWD was. "A military working dog is a dog trained to work with the military. Have you ever seen a dog with police?"

She nodded, eyes wide.

"Well, that's what he is. Sort of like a police dog, only he's a military one."

"I've pet police dogs before. Can I pet yours?"

He shook his head and fought a chuckle. Cute kid, even if she annoyed the hell out of him. "He's not a petting type of dog. He's trained to attack. Do you understand?"

She took a step closer and Chris about bugged his eyes out. Who the hell would walk closer after a statement like that? "He's sad," she said, scarily perceptive.

"He's hurt."

Her face fell. "Oh! What's wrong with him?"

"He got shot."

She ducked her head, bending as if she'd be able to see past him. As he answered, she'd moved closer and stood only a foot or so away. "Why is he sad then?"

"What makes you think he's sad?"

"He's crying," she answered. And suddenly, his dog's soft whines pierced his ears. He whipped around, facing DA again, and looked inside. Sure as shit, his eyes were full of pleading emotions.

"Come on, buddy. You can do this. I'm so sorry."

A little hand landed on his shoulder and he about jumped out of his skin. Dropping his head, he laid it on the front of the crate, feeling not the weight of that hand, but more like the world on his shoulders.

"Mister," the little girl called. "Sometimes when I'm sad, my mom tells me it's okay to cry. She says you need a good cry in order to feel better."

He kept his head on the crate. A little voice came from the side of DA's crate now, and he knew she spoke through the holes on the side.

"Feel better, puppy."

"Susie!" a lady shouted. "Leave that man alone."

"Coming, Mommy! Bye, mister!"

Footsteps sounded behind him to his left and Chris looked up as a young man in a nondescript light-blue uniform walked toward him. "Sergeant Gonzalez?"

What now? Chris nodded. "Yeah?"

"I'm Mark with the rental agency. We got a call from Sergeant Fusko a few hours ago telling us your flight was running late. He said you might need some help getting things sorted and wanted us to bring the car to you."

Part of the weight on his shoulders lifted and Chris nodded again, his throat tight. Thank fuck for Sergeant Fusko. "If you don't mind, I'll take care of the dog, if you can get the bags?"

The guy took one look at the crate, read the warning sign with his eyes wide, and turned back to Chris. "Deal."

Chapter Five

Samantha knifed up in her bed, fear pumping a sporadic rhythm in her chest. The pounding vibrated through her apartment walls again and sent her skittering, plastering her back to the headboard as she tried to get her bearings, tried to remember she wasn't stuck in the past, and had moved miles away from her asshole of an ex. She was perfectly safe in her little apartment above the vet center.

She looked at the clock, which read two in the morning. The walls shook again, and she dragged in a shaky breath, the taste of fear and the need for flight left a fine sheen on her skin, a sour taste in her mouth. Sam slid off the bed and pushed aside a curtain, attempting to see who was at her front door downstairs, but the overhang in front of the entrance prevented her view. Whoever it was, they weren't going away, and from the sound of it, they were eager to get her attention.

After falling into a fitful sleep just two hours ago, her brain felt foggy, her body laden, and her skin hot. Battling against her nightmares, against being woken to a scene she'd lived in the past when she'd locked Manuel out of the house, had her on edge. Jumpy. Freaked the hell out. Looking for a weapon, anything she could use, and making a mental reminder to check out local gun permits for future reference, she spied a hammer sitting on the small kitchen table by the window and grabbed it.

In short pink boxers and a white tank, she crept down the stairs, almost jumping out of her skin as the banging started again.

"Doctor Eagen, open up!" a loud voice shouted through the walls.

Well, at least the use of her new name gave her somewhat of a measure of relief. She released the air from her lungs and swallowed hard. Thoughts of this being an emergency with someone's pet had her picking up her step until she rounded the corner into her lobby. Across the front of the building sat a half-wall of glass, so the sight of a tall man wearing military fatigues was so out of the norm she blinked, halting in her steps. He returned her blink with dark eyes—she couldn't see the exact color from where she stood, but they were dark—then did a leisure scan down her body and back up. He brought his eyebrows together in a sharp V, displeasure written clear as day—which it was not, it was night—across his face. She frowned.

Well, then… Hello to you, too, mister two-o'clock-in-the-morning visitor.

Reaching beneath the front counter, she grabbed the keys to the door but didn't unlock it.

"Can I help you?" she asked through the window.

Tall, dark, and—*yes, let's get cliché*—handsome blinked at her again. She resisted the urge to roll her eyes then mentally questioned opening the door at all. Her trust identified as a blind, mutinous crowd chanting in the back of her mind, reminding her of how quickly she'd been subdued before. She calculated how far she was from her phone and tightened her grip on the hammer.

Sergeant Chris Gonzalez had been a no-show that afternoon. No call either. No email. She suspected this may be him, but she'd learned in the past that assumptions could very well have dangerous consequences.

Mister who-she-hoped-was-Gonzalez, also known as TD&H, shook his head and snapped it back as if he were shaking something out of his mind.

"Samantha?" he asked, his eyes taking another leisurely scan. She tried not to fidget.

"I expected you hours ago, Mr. Gonzalez." Maybe talking to him through the glass made her a bitch, but with her history, she wasn't taking chances. All she wanted was an explanation. She'd gauge it then decide from there.

"Yeah, I'm sorry, but our plane got delayed. Wind hit us coming in, had to stop up north to refuel. It's been a bitch of a flight." He sighed, and she felt his exhaustion in that one sound. "Look, it's late. I'm sorry for getting here at this hour, but can you open the door? I've got Delta Alpha in the truck. He isn't looking so good, and we're both wiped."

She glanced over his shoulder at the mention of a vehicle, and sure enough, a black Ford Explorer sat parallel to the front of her building, lights on. A quick glance around showed no other vehicles, just the solitaire lamppost across the street giving off a soft yellow glow.

She let out a small sigh and unlocked the door.

Chris pulled it open, holding it with his foot, looming in the entranceway. Now with no obstacle between them, she got her fill. And oh my God, what a fill it was. Tall, a good foot above her five-foot-six. He also had about a hundred pounds on her. With her build, she was curvy, and she'd never really felt she had to worry about too much, other than her infinite love of chocolate and what it did to her hips. But she was happy with herself, somewhat confident in what she looked like.

Standing next to Chris, on the other hand, made her feel small, vulnerable, and womanly. Something she had never felt before. He was huge. Wide shoulders, big arms, and hands that looked like they could crush her with just a thump on her head. His short, dark-brown hair screamed military, and his eyes were so, so dark. With just the overhead light on the entrance, she couldn't make out the exact color. He had thick scruff on his face that spoke of the time he'd been on the plane. With his size and brooding features, he looked menacing with a hint of sexy.

The bad boy thing had always done it for her. What made this guy any different?

"Do you have someplace Delta Alpha can relieve himself?" Chris asked, snapping her out of her perusal.

"Uh—out back. Has he had the chance to go yet?"

He shook his head. "He had the chance but was too freaked at the airport and didn't go. I'll get him from the car, let him out back, and see if he'll do business. Do you want me to bring it all in?"

Bring it all in? Taken aback at that out-of-the-ordinary question, she asked, "What's it all?"

He jerked his head to the side. "His Kong, meds, food, crate." Each item ticked off with what she figured was a military precision to her question, but it still came out too sharp for her liking. *Geesh.*

"Um, sure. How about you bring him in and I'll take him out back while you get the rest of the stuff? That way it'll give me a chance to look him over."

He stared at her for a few minutes, assessing. "Are you being serious? You feel comfortable handling an MWD with no briefing? After all the push-back you gave me on the phone?"

She bristled, not liking his condescending tone. "Is he going to bite me?"

He rubbed his eyes and slapped a hand to his side. "Woman, I have no idea *who* this dog is right now, so I don't think I can answer that question."

Before she could ask what that meant, he went

on. "How about I bring him in, we'll both take him out back, and I'll explain to you what I mean."

She pressed her lips together, her gaze jumping to the dark car, questioning what she was getting into. She had no experience with MWDs, but she knew animals, and for his handler to say he didn't know the dog, something was really wrong. "Okay," she answered reluctantly then moved to hold the door open as he stepped away.

He walked to the back of the SUV and popped the latch. His torso disappeared for a minute and reappeared with a huge multi-colored German Shepherd in his arms. The dog had a muzzle around his snout, and his eyes rolled around almost listlessly but still took everything in. Chris moved inside and through her lobby. She directed him down a hall, grabbed her sweater, and stepped behind him as he pushed out the back door.

The town of Nyack was filled with different lots and income levels. Up the hill, big mansions sprawled across acres of land. The lower on the mountain and the closer to the center of town, those homes turned into regular colonials and ranchers. The two main roads of the village were Broadway and Main, which housed various businesses, and to the back of those were more residential areas. When she moved into her shop, she had a landscaper come in to pull out the concrete and lay sod so her animals could have a chance to get up and move around. A doggy exercise course sat off in the corner. It wasn't much, but just starting out, it would do.

Chris set Delta Alpha on the ground and under the soft light of her backdoor, she saw the dog's four limbs shake. His tail curled between his legs and his ears laid flat against his head.

Traumatized.

Her heart broke. Moving slowly, she knelt next to

Chris as he murmured in his dog's ear. She couldn't decipher what he said, but the tone said it all. And what it communicated was love.

"For the most part," Chris started, speaking softly, "MWDs are pretty easy-going dogs. They may be trained to attack, but with a good handler, they can read a scene and know when to just be. Delta Alpha, who we also call Dumb Ass," he said with a wry glance at her, "has always been laidback. He's served for four years. I've never seen him act like this. Actually, the team gave him the nickname Dumb Ass because he's always goofing off when we're on down time."

The side of her mouth tipped up in a smile and she slowly lifted a hand in the direction of Delta Alpha. "This began after he got shot?"

He nodded and stroked Delta Alpha's head as the dog jerked his gaze to her and her reaching hand. "Easy, bub. This here is Doc. She's going to help you get better. Go ahead and take a whiff."

Samantha turned the back of her hand toward Delta Alpha, who leaned in and took a sniff. His eyes, though, they held hers, assessing, as his handler had done moments earlier. Fear and intelligence shone from his black orbs. His tongue gave a hesitant lick through the muzzle and she smiled, moving her hand to stroke the top of his head. After a few minutes, his body seemed to ease the shakes, but his tail still stayed between his legs. Chris rose, and she followed.

"Go on," Chris said, and the dog turned and walked off to the grass, sniffing around.

"I'd like to take his muzzle off before I leave tonight, but I'd rather do that if you're okay with it. And I'd rather do it knowing he won't be around others. I don't think he'll bite anyone, but again, this isn't the same dog I've served with. You get me?"

Watching Delta Alpha find a spot and complete his business, she nodded. "I do. I have a place he can rest and I'll make sure my staff knows he's off-limits to anyone other than myself." She said *staff* as if she had anyone other than her and the temp who started tomorrow. She really needed to get someone hired fulltime and gave herself a subtle reminder to add that to her list this week.

"He has a lot of commands he understands, but the basic ones you'll need are Sit, Stay, Down, and Out."

"Out?" she asked at the odd command.

"It can be used to get him out of his crate, or to drop something he's biting."

She snorted. "Hopefully not people, right?" she asked.

He turned and gave a grin. "Hopefully." With a jerk of his head, he said, "I'm going to get the rest of his stuff. Are you good here with him?"

"Sure. I'll wait until you're done before we go back inside. That way you can prop the front door open to make it easier."

His dark eyes studied hers for a moment before he gave a lopsided grin. "Thanks, Doc."

Chris turned and grabbed the door. She tilted her head to follow him, taking in the way he moved, like a panther, silent, and even with her knowing how exhausted he must be, full of intent. At the door, he turned back to her.

"Hey, Red," he started, and she arched a brow at the nickname. "I don't have a phone yet, but I'm hoping to get one tomorrow, or rather er, in the morning. Or when the sun is up." He shook his head. "Anyhow, if something pops up and you need me, call the Nyack Police Department and ask for Detective Dwayne Gonzalez. He'll know how to get ahold of me." He gave her a small smile, and his features suddenly changed from a menacing man to a hint of the boy next door.

"I'm sure we'll be fine, but okay." Her cheeks heated at that small smile and the intimate scene, with it being dark, no one but the two of them around. Curiosity got the better of her. "Red?" she asked.

His smile grew, and he pointed to his head. "Your hair." His gaze drifted to the top of her head before he met her eyes again. "It's nice. I can't guess the exact shade of it because of how dark it is tonight, but I can only imagine how pretty it must look under the sun."

With that parting shot, he winked and left. She stood there, staring at the back door, stunned at such a normal thing. Chris was correct in his guess of how her hair looked under the sun. It turned a bright red, drawing a lot of attention, something she'd shied at before. She tried to embrace the color, but after years of abuse, her fledging confidence was slow to build back up. She continued to try to ignore the small things, had taken steps to make her life what she wanted it to be, and yearned to be a powerful woman who could stand on her own two feet. And now, standing in the back of her shop, under the soft white light of her backdoor, she wondered if that confidence could be built with small comments such as the one Chris gave. She hoped, really hoped it would be that easy. She just didn't know how to get the rest of herself to catch up.

****

An hour later, Chris drew the SUV to a stop and stared at his darkened house. Nestled in the woods outside of Nyack's limits, the two-bedroom cabin sat tucked away from populated areas. He preferred it this way. Despite working on a team for the past umpteen years, he liked his solidarity. The peace and quiet. Someplace he wouldn't have to deal with a barrage of activity. When you spent hours, days, weeks, and months at a constant state of alert, looking over your shoulder for the next ripe bullet to take off your head, or watching the ground for any hidden IEDs, your body and mind needed the shutdown. For him, it sometimes took a few weeks before he could adjust.

He shut off the truck and sat listening. The absolute silence was a blessed relief. Tall oaks and pine trees rose from the ground at the back and sides of his property. The front yard contained nothing but gravel and the occasional bush his ma insisted he have. She said it gave the place character. He told her it had enough. But when Mrs. Gonzalez got going, the best thing to do was sit back and let her do her thing.

After all she'd given him, he wouldn't and couldn't stand in her way of happiness. And if doting on a thirty-three-year-old man made her happy, then who was he to get in her way?

Chris got out of the car and crossed the drive to the front porch. Crickets sang their song around him and the soft brush of leaves pushed against branches with the wind. Being surrounded by the wildlife in the middle of a forest again tugged at his memories. He paused on his porch, reaching for the memory despite his exhaustion.

Warmth suffused his chest, the feeling of love and happiness moving through him. He had someone then, a partnership with someone who knew him better than he knew himself. Who was it? He closed his eyes, willing more of the memory to come but a black wall hit his mind, preventing him from remembering anything more.

Frustrated, he opened the front door, clicked on the hall light, tossed his keys on the table by the door, and let out a breath as he took in what he never really considered home.

He paid the mortgage on it, sure. But he'd barely spent any time at the cabin in the past eight years, so to him it seemed like just another place. He walked down the hall, flipping on lights. Ahead of him opened to a kitchen to the left, the living room a straight path from the front door, and to the right, another hall that led to the two bedrooms. He stopped at the mouth and stared at the kitchen counters. Fresh fruit sat in a big terracotta bowl on top of his black counters. Head tilted to the side in curiosity, he opened the cabinets then smiled as he found them full of food. Inside the refrigerator, too. Obviously, his mother had been there.

Again, taking care of him.

He made a point of putting her on the top of his list of whom to call tomorrow.

Leaving the lights on, he turned and went down the hall, heading toward the master bedroom. Dropping his duffle to the side, he kicked off his boots, pulled off his fatigues, and collapsed face-first to the made bed, not even bothering with drawing the comforter. Within minutes, he fell asleep.

Chapter Six

The thing about Afghanistan was that within the untouched beauty of the landscape, hidden dangers lurked beneath. Chris's team had trained for every possible outcome, even the most unbelievable ones, in order to be able to think, plan, and evacuate out of any situation. Doing what they did, infiltrate and take out the enemy, got them into some very hairy situations. And out of all the fuck-ups that this standard op should have been, this situation shouldn't have gone so wrong. Almost as if something—or someone—had planned for it to be one clusterfuck after another. Almost as if they didn't want the team to succeed, or continue to breathe.

Chris looked over at his captain, but instead of hearing any of the anxious, fear-filled words that screamed from his mouth, the roar of the plane's engines overrode the warning. Able to slow it down now, something he didn't quite understand he could do with the threat hovering like a scorpion's stinger on his neck, the motion of Squirrel's lips formed the warning. "Get down, tango at your six. Get down!"

Air punched out of his lungs as if a wrecking ball had slammed into him. Bam! Bam! Boom!

Explosions ricocheted around him. Those little stingers he'd felt eyeing his shoulders now sank deep into his flesh, embedded into hard muscle, and caused ultimate damage as bullets only knew to do.

The warm, furry body atop him jerked, but Chris's mind moved too sluggishly, almost as if he couldn't keep up. As if he were still trying to figure out what his captain had been trying to tell him. His head swam with a fuzziness that told him maybe slamming his head into that rock formation hadn't been the best idea. Not like the choice had been his, anyway.

Adrenaline spiked in his veins. The battle burned like a blaze of fire, still going on around him and his team. He had a job to do, and Dumb Ass had failed to follow his command, something he'd never done before, something he would have a long and drawn-out talk about with his partner.

He didn't care that the dog obviously didn't speak English, or him ... doggy-talk. What the hell ever. But worrying about his partner when bullets flew around fast enough to make anyone flinch wasn't a position he wanted to be put in again.

Yep, as soon as they got back to their compound, they'd have a real long talk.

Chris blinked, thinking this over, all the while staring up at the sky, trying to catch on to the warning blazing like a beacon in the dark that something wasn't right, that this wasn't the time to be taking a breather. The cloudless sky was so blue it almost hurt to look at, but shit, it sure was pretty. Almost as much as the sky back home in Nyack.

Squirrel's face interrupted his view and Chris scowled, about to tell the captain to get out of his way, then frowned at the panicked face of his CO, the dirt and blood on his uniform, the helmet protecting his noggin from taking one of those stingers to the cranium.

"Are you hit?"

The ground shook beneath his body, but the weight on top sat surprisingly still. His hands clenched and released, grabbing soft and warm fur. A familiar, textile sensation, but he couldn't place it. Why was it on top of him? Where the hell was he?

Davis came up next and bent low, his arms outstretched, his face a mask of pity.

What?

His teammate stood, a very familiar fur ball in his arms. Davis's face strained under the weight and he punched out a breath of air. "We got to go ... now. Tangos have us surrounded."

None of that mattered to Chris. He could hardly comprehend how everything happened around him. The sky ... the peace ... the softness in his hands.

Wait. He shifted and pain lanced as he realized with a jolt and a panicked look at lifeless doggy eyes that the conversation he'd have with his partner might never occur.

"Delta Alpha!" he shouted and reached for him, only to pause when the hand in front of him was that of a little kid.

He drew it back, confused. The surrounding landscape changed. No longer was he in Afghanistan, but instead sitting on a revolving floor. The dark, lush greenery spun around him. He blinked, trying to get a grip on reality.

A carousel.

His heart pounded and pounded as if it wanted to be set free. Panic built in his lungs, the scream begging to be released. They were taking him away. Someone needed to stop them!

"Cooper!"

Chris woke to the sensation of falling, still screaming that name, but instead of hearing a little boy's voice, now it was his own. His face smacked into the unforgiving hardwood floor. "Fuck!" He jumped up, senses heightened, the taste of battle and panic sour on his tongue. A sharp twinge in his back protested and his leg howled, but the pain was enough, as was the silence in the room, to bring him out of his nightmare-induced fog.

He wasn't in Afghanistan. He wasn't on that carousel. He'd been sent home on mandatory medical leave, not just in a physical sense, but also to get his head on straight, to get his mind under control, and to make a decision. In his cabin alone with only his guilt and the unrelenting past to keep him company. What the hell was all of that after that scene in Afghanistan, though?

"Shit. Breathe, goddammit."

He forced air into his burning lungs and swiped his face, coming away with a sheen of perspiration across his palm. The nightmares started in Germany, but he'd dismissed them, thinking he needed time. But it seemed as if they were getting worse. And more horrific, yet, the fact that several people—therapists, his CO, his doctor—warned him they'd come, but that it was normal, that it would get better if he just talked with someone.

Like he couldn't handle it. He scoffed.

The carousel part, the screaming for someone named Cooper, was new, though. Hell, he didn't even know anyone named Cooper.

Liar.

The defeat, the reality that it wasn't just some nightmare he could push away with a shrug, slumped his shoulders. He took a step toward the bathroom, wanting to wash away the taste of fear, to rub his skin raw, and grimaced as his leg protested again. A quick glance confirmed the busted stitches to his thigh. While the wound had started to heal, the stitches ripped through the skin, leaving an angry-looking tear and a small trail of oozing red.

He heaved a heavy breath and went into the bathroom to wash and redress his wound. Thirty minutes later, his body still hummed with unspent anxiety. He paced the length of his cabin and scrubbed his hands over his head. The surrounding silence and the past knocking at his subconscious wasn't doing anything to ease the need he had to cause something or someone physical harm. He could feel the anger at how everything had happened churn in his gut like acid, eating him from the inside out.

On the next pass of his kitchen, he lifted his shaking hand to scrub his hair again. "Jesus. I need to get out of here." Riding into town in this mood wasn't the smartest thing to do, and getting behind the wheel when he wanted to rip someone's head off wasn't something he wanted to chance.

Instead, he changed his dressing again, wrapped an extra layer of gauze around his thigh, and swapped his lounge pants for running shorts and a black A-line tank. He slipped on his shoes, shoved his wallet in his pocket, and then hit the road. Each time his foot hit the gravel, his muscles rebelled, but the energy it took to push his body and the pain of his injuries eased his mind into submission. While it was still quiet, the hum of wind through the thick trees and the birds singing their song provided him with enough sensory input to do a light jog on his way down his private drive and to the road that led into town. He took it easy on the jog, taking a break every few minutes so he didn't overtax his body. He wasn't stupid, just messed up in the head.

The sky reflected the very same blue he'd seen weeks ago on the other side of the world, and he had to force his eyes away from the beautiful sight. He didn't want to remember. He wanted to forget everything, if only for a few moments.

He just wanted peace.

Once in town, he stopped and picked up a phone, used a park bench to activate it, and then tossed the package in the trash. He had turned to head back up to the cabin but stopped in his tracks.

His chest tightened and softened all at once. How it was possible, he didn't know. Like weeks before when everything had slowed, the same happened. Only now, he was in Nyack, and the cars on the streets slowed until it seemed as if they weren't moving.

Sounds around him disappeared. Before him, wearing much of the same outfit as his own was his brother, Dwayne, and their childhood pseudo-kid sister, Charlie.

Shock passed over Dwayne's face before a huge grin spread. He didn't take his gaze away from his brother to see Charlie's expression, but in his peripheral, she slowed from a jog to a walk at the same time.

His little brother, adopted or not, had definitely filled out since the last time they'd seen each other. Long gone were the smooth lines of youth, and in their place were the hard edges of age.

"Holy shit, you made it," Dwayne exclaimed, and without hesitation, he wrapped him in a hearty hug. Chris stiffened in an instant. Dwayne felt it, too, with how he froze. Despite the pain, he brought his arms around D and hugged him back hard. One would think two men embracing in public should have been quick and manly, move in and away, but then again, they weren't like most families, had never been. Dwayne's arms tightened around Chris and as sissy as it was, he soaked it in and took it a step further by burying his face into the crook of D's neck to hang on for the ride of emotions.

He didn't know how long they stayed like that, but it must have been a while, and Charlie had never been one for patience, for she snapped, "D, quit hogging the hot guy. I want a piece of him, too."

Dwayne moved back with a quick slap to Chris's back. He grimaced, but ignored D's questioning look and nondescriptly wiped at his suspiciously damp eyes before turning to Charlie.

Black curls were shoved up haphazardly in some

sort of messy ponytail. She wore black shorts and a blue Nyack PD shirt. Her hazel eyes blazed with unnamed emotions. Like D, she tossed herself in his arms and this time he took her face tucked in his neck. *Jesus*, this was what he'd missed being gone. The open affection this town offered, that his family gave without hesitation. The feel of home. He'd never had one until he came here. Foster home after home filled his life until Mr. Gonzalez found him in a dark alley, two steps away from robbing the man of his wallet, the same man who'd given him a chance. Only then did he realize he finally found a home.

Charlie pulled back after a few minutes and wiped beneath her eyes. Chris cupped her jaw and forced her face up to his. "Hey now, what's this?"

She smiled sloppily, and the past—the good part of his childhood, his second life—rushed up. An expression passed, the same damn look she'd given each of the Gonzalez brothers, the ones that told them all without her speaking a word how much they meant to her.

The feeling was mutual.

"When did you get back?" Dwayne asked, taking his attention from Charlie.

Chris scrubbed the back of his head and took a deep breath, the tension in his chest easing, but not dissipating. "Uhh, late last night. Dropped DA off at the vet and drove out to the cabin."

Dwayne lifted a brow. "Ever think of calling to let people know?"

Chris arched a brow back and held up his new phone. "Just picked this up, *Mother*. You were next on the list after calling her, in fact."

Dwayne grinned, a glimmer of wickedness pushing through, reminding him of their childhood, of times right before D would tell Ma something that somehow always ended up with him in trouble. "Oh, you know you're going to have to do better than a phone call with Ma, right?"

Chris grimaced, wanting to see Mrs. Gonzalez like he wanted his next breath, but not ready for the level of scrutiny she'd subject him to. Despite not being his birth mother, she always had a way of seeing what he was involved in, everything he'd been through, and even things he didn't notice. She'd helped raise six boys and managed to provide a home, a life, and more, giving each of them endless amounts of love. It all proved the strength she held in her backbone and spoke of the amazing gift she'd come to be with each of them.

He met Dwayne's gaze again and found his adopted brother smiling at whatever showed on his face. He shook his head, knowing damn well his brother had even picked up on their adoptive mother's sometimes annoying habit of reading people. "I'll drop by soon. I need to make sure everything is settled before heading over."

"Meaning, you have to think up some story. You know Ma isn't going to let that happen, right? Seriously, this coming from the guy who was caught nearly every time he snuck out?"

Chris barked a laugh, internally surprised at the sound he hadn't heard in a while. "And I'm sure it was all on Ma knowing everything, right?" he asked sarcastically. "Nothing to do with a certain nosey little brother who wanted to tag along at every bend?"

Dwayne chuckled. "I've had my fair share, too. Not just you. But seriously, unless you want to make this harder, I'd get over there as soon as possible."

"Did you find everything at the cabin?" Charlie asked, giving him a reprieve.

Chris nodded. "I did. You and Ma?"

"Yes, and D's lady love," she said with an annoying flutter of her lashes at the subject of conversation.

Dwayne tugged playfully on a loose strand of her ponytail. "Brat," he said and turned to Chris. "Brooke helped stock it up."

Chris's smile widened until his cheeks hurt. He didn't remember the last time he'd smiled so much. But then again, there was nothing like home. Nothing like finding his brother had finally gone and done it. "Pulled your head out of your ass, I see?"

Dwayne's grin practically blinded. "Among other things. What can I say? She couldn't resist me."

"Ha!" Charlie laughed. "I'm sure she'd have a different opinion of how things actually went down."

Chris chuckled and rubbed the back of his neck, turning his head toward a certain business shop he hadn't stopped in on yet. The glare of the sun prevented him from seeing past the windows, but his mind pictured exactly what he'd meet once he got the nerve to go. His broken dog, a thousand choices between right and wrong, and one stunningly beautiful veterinarian with smoky, green eyes full of secrets.

He rubbed his chin and realized the laughter had died, the voices faded. He found Dwayne and Charlie watching him and glancing at the same building. His brother had a troubled V between his brows and a frown on his face. Charlie looked contemplative, concerned. Neither said a word, didn't ask a thing.

"I guess I should go check on Delta Alpha."

Dwayne's mouth tightened. "How bad is it?"

Chris let his shoulders drop. With the pressure he felt, one could only hope it'd get to be so strong he'd fall into a pancake on the ground, disappear forever, and finally have the freedom of doing what he wanted, instead of having to handle responsibility after responsibility. Not that he didn't want to take care of DA, didn't want to see him get better. He did. He wanted nothing more. It was the pressure of knowing that if his dog couldn't get better, the decision would be taken out of his hands. Today, a plan needed to be set up, procedures in place in order to get him to heal.

"He's a tough dog."

"But that's not answering the question, is it?" Dwayne asked.

Chris shrugged, not knowing what else to say. "Only time will tell at this point."

"If you need anything…" Charlie started.

"I know where to come." He lifted a hand and moved toward the street. "I'll catch up with you later, okay?"

"Are you sure you don't want us to come, too?" Charlie asked, her face hopeful and full of, damn, he hated it … pity.

He fought not to snap at her. She only did what she'd always done: push her comfort on others. Gave her love openly to any of the Gonzalez kids, ones who'd been just as broken as she. "No, I'll be fine. But later. Maybe when Dumb Ass is up to it, I'll bring you all to meet him."

Dwayne and Charlie nodded but didn't turn away. They watched him until he had to force himself to turn around. He felt their gazes burning into his shoulders all the way to the front door of the vet's office.

Chapter Seven

Samantha stared at her iPad, trying to decipher the medical jargon. Canine PTSD wasn't well known, but the internet held a lot of research and answers. Unfortunately, after Vietnam, there hadn't been much observation with the effects of war on the animal partners, but after Operation Southern Watch and Iraqi Freedom, cases were coming in by the droves. The increasing data stating that dogs were just as affected, if not more than their human counterparts, with post-traumatic stress disorder concerned her.

After reading over Delta Alpha's file last night after Chris left, she'd spent several hours making sure she knew every word inside and out. Wanting to help Delta Alpha wasn't the only reason she'd practically memorized every word, but it was the very real observation that this canine needed help, and he needed it fast. Every noise, no matter how soft or loud, caused him to jump. He hardly ate or drank. And yes, he'd stayed up with her last night despite his eyes rolling with exhaustion. Just as soon as he'd close his little brown eyes, she'd shift her position, and he'd be wide-awake again, hackles raised, looking for the nearest threat. She couldn't seem to leave him alone either, for every time she walked out of the room, he'd whine and whine until her heart threatened to shatter into a thousand pieces.

On a good note, her morning sickness seemed to take a backseat to this newest introduction to her life. She had only upchucked once this morning, and despite praying to the porcelain god, she took it as a good sign, that maybe her body would finally adjust to the extra hormones. Though she really needed to make it official and get in to the doctor's office.

From the information she read, Delta Alpha matched all the symptoms of PTSD in canines. With Chris's explanation, and Sergeant Fusko's—yes, she called him, too—briefing, Delta Alpha's temperament had done a one-eighty. He was not only becoming unusually aggressive, but now he clung to his handler, and her, too, by association.

Treatment was where things got tricky. Samantha bit her lip, considering. The first problem involved communication. Vets and handlers had to make educated guesses about what kind of mood the dog was in while treatment occurred. The important pieces included pushing rest and downtime, which Delta Alpha's retirement would ensure. But they couldn't let up on the obedience training. And that was what worried her. Would they push him too hard, too fast?

And was he too far off to be able to do such a gentle treatment plan, or would they have to move to desensitization training? The thought made her stomach swirl, and she knew it had nothing to do with the pregnancy. Exposing Delta Alpha to sound and sensory details that would put him back in that battle that started all this wasn't something she thought too highly of. To reward him, a dog so obviously traumatized, when he didn't react, and to not give him any reassurance when he cowered, went against everything she had learned in her schooling.

She'd discussed medication with Sergeant Fusko, too, and while some had shown to have positive effects soon after trauma, weaning the dog off the medication often tossed everyone, dog, handler, and vet, back to square one.

Samantha tapped out an erratic rhythm on the counter and tossed the iPad with a loud huff. A low grumbling growl had her freezing to the spot, and each hair on the back of her neck stood on end. Sweat popped along her brow and her breathing grew rapid. She remained frozen but quickly looked around, trying to gauge how quickly she'd make it to the door separating the clinic from the stairway to the apartment, if she'd be able to get the chair between her and a trained-to-kill attacking dog. Why the hell hadn't she locked him away in his crate?

Oh, that was right, she was a total softy and didn't think!

The bell above the front entrance chimed as someone walked in and she met the eyes of none other than Chris. He was in the midst of smiling at her, a lazy, seductive move so out of place from the man of last night that she frowned. The door shut with a soft *whoosh*, cutting off the steady traffic outside. "Hey," he said, and froze in his tracks, his two brows pulled in a frown immediately.

The growling grew louder and Samantha closed her eyes, accepting the inevitable. Mentally, she ticked off the limbs she could do without. Losing her hands would put a damper on things because she had to use both in order to do surgery. But then again, with prosthetics nowadays, who knew how fast she'd be back in action? It'd sort of suck seeing as she didn't have medical insurance just yet. There were so many bills! Unfortunately, she had to prioritize.

If she got out of this, and that was a big *if*, she'd promise to get medical insurance right away. That and a glass wall to separate the rooms from the front lobby.

"Easy, Delta Alpha. Easy," Chris soothed, voice low.

God, he had a nice voice. Irrationally, she wondered how she'd react if she wasn't held hostage by a trained killing dog, and if Chris used that same soothing voice on her. Most likely, she'd do anything he ask, right before she'd melt into a puddle at his feet. Speaking of puddles—*shit!*—now she needed to pee. All that water definitely picked the wrong time to catch up. She bit her lip and clenched a fist which from the louder—*and closer!*—growling was a bad thing to do.

"Shit!" she breathed.

"Red, easy. Don't move, don't talk. Open your eyes."

Oh, that soothing voice was nice. Very nice indeed. But instead of listening to him, his words scared the shit out of her more as Delta Alpha's growls grew louder. She imagined spittle flying out of his mouth, blood, her neck ripped open. Her eyes squeezed tighter.

"Delta Alpha two-niner, easy!" A sharp and distinct command. The dog's growl dropped to a low rumble, but from the pins and needle feeling on the back of her neck, she could tell he was still very close.

"Red, open your eyes. Come on, let me see those pretty greens."

Samantha's eyes snapped open at not only the inappropriateness of the comment coming from him but also at the thought that this man, this unbelievable sexy man found anything about her pretty. She lifted her gaze to his and tried to slow her breathing. Not an easy thing to do when her imagined death images were still fresh in her mind.

"Right on me. It's going to be okay." He glanced over the counter and from the direction of his gaze and where it landed briefly, she concluded that yep, Delta Alpha was *right* behind her. "I want you to blink once for yes, twice for no, okay? No talking. No moving. Do you understand? No talking, no moving whatsoever. Blink, sweetheart, to tell me you understand."

She blinked, one long, hard blink. He called her pretty and sweetheart in just under a minute? Or was he saying all this to keep her calm? If so, it wasn't working. Instead, she could unbelievably feel her breasts grow sensitized. *Well, hello, desire! Long time no see!* God, how could this be possible? How could she be getting turned on with just a few sweet words coming from an albeit very sexy man while being held hostage by an MWD who had recently been diagnosed with PTSD and was unpredictable? And add her previous abusive relationship with Manuel? She literally couldn't make this shit up.

"Okay," Chris continued. "Good girl. Now, has he been like this long?"

She went to shake her head.

"Don't move. Heel, Delta!"

Samantha squeezed her eyes closed and clenched her fists, her entire body pushing toward the counter and bracing for impact. It never came. Breath punched out of her mouth and she may have whimpered slightly, which she abruptly shut off as soon as DA's growl began again.

"Sweetheart, open your eyes. Look at me."

Chris sounded close, and when she opened her eyes, it reaffirmed that he had moved closer and stood on the other side of the counter directly in front of her. "Hi." He smiled.

He. Friggin'. Smiled!

She bugged her eyes and his smile grew wider. If she hadn't been held hostage, and her heart not in her throat, she would have reached for her camera and taken a picture. It was a sight to behold. Little lines bracketed around his eyes, which were framed with thick, dark and curled lashes. Upon closer inspection, she could now see the familiar color, one closer to her favorite whiskey, Jameson. Life really wasn't fair. How a man could be blessed with such perfection? Women paid good money to replicate what he had naturally.

"Let's try this again. Don't move. Just blink once for yes, twice for no. From what I suspect you were doing earlier, I take it he hasn't been like this for long, right?"

She blinked once.

"Is he on any medication?"

She blinked twice.

"Do you know what brought this on?"

She blinked twice.

"All right. I'm going to come around slowly, okay?"

She blinked once.

"It's unlocked, right? The door right there?"

He must mean the latch that separated the office from the public. She blinked once.

The side of his mouth tipped up. "You doing okay?"

She blinked twice.

He frowned. "I'm sorry, Doc. We'll get this sorted in a jiffy. Just stay real still. If he lunges, tuck your head down and put your arms over it, okay."

Her eyes bugged again.

"I don't think he will, but then again, like I said, I'm trying to figure out who he is."

She took a deep breath. He turned to the latch door, paused, and looked at her again. "Oh, and Red?"

She lifted her brows.

"Not for nothing, but you sure are looking pretty today."

With a wink, he pivoted and disappeared from her view. Seriously. Who was this man?

"Delta Alpha, heel."

The click of doggy nails on her tile alerted her he

was no longer behind her. Samantha let her breath out in a whoosh. Her shoulders relaxed and her head fell until her chin rested on her chest. The curtain of her hair slid forward until it shadowed the sunlight streaming in from the front of the shop.

She didn't know how long she stayed like that, trying to control her breathing by concentrating on pulling air in and out of her lungs with measured breaths. The whisper of movement behind her followed the brush of a hard chest against her back and she lifted her head cautiously. She didn't see anything in front of her besides the dark curtain of red hair. In her peripheral, though, two strong arms with very defined muscles were in her view. She drew in a shaky breath. Yup, that was a male behind her, a very broad and wide-chested man if his immovable form said anything.

Manuel used to trap her into tight corners, getting a rush out of watching her squirm. He'd draw out the anticipation of what would come next: a punch to the face, a kick to her back, taking her without her permission. He got his jollies off on making her guess.

And despite being trapped between a counter and a man who was practically a stranger to her, she didn't think any of what Manuel had done to her would come next. No, it was the oddest thing...

Awareness hit her like a punch to the gut. She hadn't known Chris for more than a week, barely met him face-to-face last night, had just been held hostage by his killer dog, and here she was, alone in her shop with both of them. Good God, though, she still felt the simmering sexual attraction to him, which heightened as his deep voice spoke from beside her head.

"Hey, are you okay?"

They were so close, so intimate, in a position she hadn't let herself have for years.

Rather than feeling completely uncomfortable being semi-spooned by him, she shrank closer to the counter and turned her body to answer. She opened her mouth and paused, as he didn't move. Not one single bit. She frowned, but pushed to ignore it, and instead gave him a hint by raising her brows as she tried to turn completely to face him.

The side of his mouth quirked, but he still didn't move. His eyes never lost their seriousness, their concern. But his mouth said he received her message and understood but refused to follow orders. Some military man he was...

"What ... what was that?" she asked, and much to both her delight and despair, managed to turn completely around to face him, only to have her knees brush against the tops of his thighs. Her face flushed with heat, and she tried to pull back from the intimate position, but the counter dug into her back.

Chris dropped his head between his shoulders and turned toward the room where Delta Alpha must be for his crate was empty. "I was hoping you might be able to tell me. Something must have spooked him." He turned back to her and glanced up beneath dark, thick lashes. "Like I've said, Red, I have no clue who that dog is right now. What happened?"

She frowned furiously, mulling over the few minutes before she heard the growling. "I was researching PTSD in dogs and treatment options. I got fed up with the suggestions, as it seemed that no matter which option we took, it'd either set him back a step or cause undue emotional harm. I tossed the iPad on the counter, and ... maybe," she said and sighed as realization set in, "actually that could have been it. The iPad probably sounded loud to him. It was quiet in here this morning. Oh, poor DA." All of the fear of the past few minutes rushed out and, in its place, sadness and guilt overtook her. She'd done something so stupid after he'd been through so much.

Samantha shifted to toss a leg over the stool, intent on going to check on Delta Alpha and apologize to him. Chris stopped her by stepping forward and laying a hand on her hip. She froze, the intimate position they'd been in minutes earlier completely PG compared to what they were in now. His hips were between her legs, his hand resting in the crease of where her hip met her thigh, and the setting entirely something it shouldn't be between what amounted to as two practical strangers.

"What are you doing?" she asked, her voice breathy. She winced at the sound and cleared her throat.

"I was about to ask you the same thing, although from that look on your face I can guess. You need to give him a few minutes, Doc. Let him calm down."

She darted a glance to the room and back. "Alone? Do you really think that's best right now? After everything he's been through?"

Chris's eyes softened, and he reached up to brush her hair behind her ear. Her skin tingled where his hand met and she shivered, resisted the urge to rub at the same spot. "He'll be fine. We'll give him a few minutes, then I'll go in first, and when I give the okay, you can come in, too. I want to make sure he understands who's in charge here, even when I'm gone. I hate to think of what would have happened had it not been me who walked through that door."

She scoffed and tried to ignore where he stood by leaning back a little bit. The counter once again dug into her back and she winced in pain, knowing full well there'd be a bruise there later. Chris's expression said he saw it all and got a thrill out of making her squirm.

Once again, the thrill he seemed to get was

nothing like the thrill Manuel would get. She didn't know Chris and had no idea what he was capable of, so she had no idea why she knew he'd never hurt her. It didn't make sense.

She glared at him. *Move back.*

He smiled. *No.*

She scoffed. "No one else is exactly busting down my doors for business just yet. I'm not even due to open for a few more days seeing as I got put behind."

"My point exactly."

"Do you mind?" she asked as he leaned in more.

His grin grew. "Not at all, Doc."

"You're not moving, Mr. Gonzalez."

He turned, looked over his shoulder, then turned back to her and came in closer, his face only a foot apart from hers.

"I thought my pop was here, you calling me Mr. Gonzalez."

"Maybe he should be here to teach you some manners."

He chuckled. "Manners? Like?"

"Like getting in people's personal space and touching them," she huffed and threw a pointed glance at his hand still on her hip.

He threw his head back and laughed. Samantha sat frozen, mesmerized by his throat muscles working fluidly and the beautiful sound coming out of his chest. He recovered quickly, removing his hand and replacing it and the other one until he caged her between him and the countertop. His face hovered inches away, and unable to do anything else, she stared at his mouth. Her knees cradled his hips. Despite everything, a heavy ache started between her thighs. *Geesus.*

"Who do you think taught me everything I know, sweetheart?"

"Chris," she breathed. "What are you doing?"

"Don't deny it, Samantha. There's something here, like an ache that needs to be rubbed. An itch that needs scratched. Something. I don't know what it is, but it's been a long time since I've felt this, much less been around a woman, any woman, especially one who looks like you."

"Eeep."

He lifted the side of his mouth in that same sexy, lopsided grin again.

"Oh, shit."

His chest shook. "What's wrong?"

"I said that out loud, huh?"

He chuckled. "Sure did."

She groaned. "So it's true? What they say about military men being away from women for so long?" Why, why did she ask that?

He looked as if he were trying to figure out the answer to the universe with how deep in concentration his face was. Twin brows settled in a deep V and his gaze settled on her mouth.

"I think you're referring to sailors being out to sea for so long," he said, taking a step closer.

"And?" she asked with a hitch in her breath.

"I've been around women, just not women like you. There's something…"

There's something…what? She desperately wanted him to finish that last sentence but instead, he cradled her face gently in his palms, the move so light and careful that it went against everything he looked to be. Big, bad, military guy with those dark, troubled eyes. She sat captivated.

"What are you doing now?"

"I'm going to kiss you, Red. That all right with you?"

What? Seriously? Who was this guy? "I ... I think this is highly ... inap—"

****

Damn straight, Chris kissed her. He dipped his head, cradled her jaw, and fused his mouth to hers, both to stop her denial as well as finally get an answer to what she'd taste like. Samantha, with her dark-red curls, bright, hazel eyes, and pouty, plump lips. A woman begging to be kissed. Sort of like how some people were made with a permanent scowl, a resting bitch face as he liked to call it. They usually looked as if they searched for a fight, constantly scowling, their expressions as if they wanted to scream at the world. Those people looked for trouble.

Samantha, however, looked like she begged to be kissed.

He was all too willing to answer. Something that kind of surprised him. He didn't accost women like this, but since the moment he spoke to her over the phone last week, he'd been unable to get the vision of him kissing her out of his mind. She could punch him for all he cared, because after this he would damn well deserve it, but he had to have a taste.

She went stiff against him for a beat but then reacted. They both inhaled air together, their chests rising and pressing against one another. He inched forward, gentled his mouth, and brushed his nose against the crescent of her cheek. Her breath whispered shakily over his mouth.

Adjusting his grip to tunnel his hands in her hair, he gave a slight pull, angling her face more for the position he wanted. Her mouth trembled, not in fear, which he could tell by the way her hands gripped his shoulders, how her body curved into his, and how her lips parted in anticipation. Oh, she wanted this as much as he did.

The tension built between them, and his blood heated.

He dipped his head again and nibbled a path across her lips before plunging his tongue inside and twining it with hers.

His actions shocked him a little. He didn't take what wasn't freely offered. But something about Samantha Eagen put him in a position he couldn't deny. If it earned him a stinging cheek, so be it. He would apologize profusely and offer himself up to Dumb Ass as a chew toy.

Samantha moaned against his mouth, signaling the last thing he'd get was a slap for this kiss. He took in a deep breath, breaking away from her mouth for a moment to adjust before he'd dive back in.

A muted, agonized whine pierced the air behind him. He immediately recognized it as DA from the other room.

Samantha went stiff, her fingers tightening on his shirt, her mouth freezing against his.

Chris pulled back and sighed before dropping his forehead to hers. They both breathed as if they'd run a marathon, but he was anything but tired. He wanted to take her up the stairs and find out what color her panties were … before he took her to bed.

He wanted to blame this attraction—this lust—on the fact that he'd been away from civilization and women for months, but a little voice in the back of his head argued that wasn't the case. He wasn't a saint. He had friends who he met up with when he was home, who wanted the same thing he did—no-strings sex. Just raw, and, the-dirtier-the-better, sex.

The whine continued, steadily getting louder.

The sound tore at his gut and he pushed away

from the counter and out of the arms of Doctor Eagen. He did an about-face and headed for his dog.

Several minutes later, he was down on all fours, talking and giving affection to him when she walked in. He and Delta Alpha glanced up, and he continued scratching behind his dog's ears. His hind leg kicked up and matched the scratches. Chris grinned.

"It's times like this that I believe he can fully recover," he said, hope running through him.

She sighed but said nothing.

He wanted to kick himself. Of course, she'd know exactly what the military planned to do, and what Chris or Dumb Ass couldn't do. Meaning, be partners again out on missions. There was no passing go on that little idea.

"Look," he started, wanting someone else rooting for DA. "I know he won't ever go back to the team. I get that." He scratched his dog beneath his chin. DA's tongue lolled out of his mouth and Chris swore he saw the hint of a doggy smile. "I know he'll never go back to the military, but that still won't stop me from wanting him to have a full recovery. To be healthy and happy, not a shell of who he used to be."

"You can't blame yourself," she responded, her voice firm but soothing. "Delta Alpha broke his orders, and he did it for a reason. Call it fate, call it acting on his gut, whatever it is, he saved your life. I'm sure he'd do it again. You can't continue to blame yourself for what happened."

Chris didn't look at her, but curiosity won out. "Fusko tell you that?"

"Yes," she whispered. "But even if he didn't, I would have been able to figure it out all by myself from reading his file and injury report." She pushed away from the wall, ambled into the room, approached his dog, and held out her hand. He was a little amazed that she'd risk interacting with DA so soon after almost being bitten. Her attention stayed on the dog, but she kept her body language nonaggressive, an act that spoke of being open and taking the next step in their doctor-patient relationship.

DA gave a quick whiff, then, as if apologizing, licked the side of her hand. She chuckled and sat on the opposite side from them, cross-legged on the floor. "I sure hope he wasn't getting a sample of what he'll bite later."

Chris chuckled. "Nah, this guy will be fine, right, buddy?"

"His dressings need changed. Can you get him to sit still?" she asked, and at his nod, grabbed more gauze and a small pair of silver scissors.

She began to cut away the old bandages, some spotting with blood, but the sight of it was nothing compared to all the crimson fluid they had to soak up on the plane ride back from the mission. How a dog held so much blood in his body was amazing. He'd always been told they could carry six or seven quarts, but it had seemed like so much more.

"Can I ask you a question?" she asked.

Chris nodded and continued to watch DA move his little doggy eyebrows back and forth in curiosity. He flinched every once in a while, but his ears stayed up and he didn't look frightened or aggressive.

"Why isn't Delta Alpha recovering in a military vet office?"

He hated how this would sound. Hated why he wanted to mince his words. Even though he'd been told several times over on what the outcome with DA would be, he still felt as if he needed to champion for him. Instead of trying to tiptoe around it, he got to the point.

"Military working dogs are tools, not living beings in the military."

"Okay, I get that, but I'm sure they are an important tool."

"That may be. But what happens when a tool stops working and you can't fix it?"

She paused, her gaze snapping up to his. A few beats of frozen silence ticked by. "You're kidding, right?"

He wished he was. "I'm afraid not, Red."

She looked back at Delta Alpha's lower back, paused for a few moments as if trying to get her thoughts in order, and then continued to wrap fresh gauze. "That's horrible."

"Few understand. And before you go biting my head off, I'm not saying that it's right." He scratched at DA's neck as the Shepherd started getting restless. As intended, the touch pulled his attention back to Chris and off Samantha. "There are options, though, one of which I've decided on. I'm adopting Dumb Ass and he'll be medically retired from the military. Means the military will pay for all his medical care until he passes."

"Sort of like a retirement plan, huh? Is that what happens with all the dogs?"

He thinned his lips. While he had the option to choose, some did, or would not. "Not entirely. Those who can't get adopted by their handler get put to sleep."

"But you just said the military will pay for their medical care. Why put down a dog that has faithfully served his country?"

"Sweetheart, what you have to realize is that even though the MWD is a tool, it's still a tool trained to kill, to attack, and are often ran on high stress. They can be unpredictable around children, especially if something were to happen, such as a child pulling on their tail. They can't be around other pets, are extremely dominant creatures, and exclusively work on their own. They don't partner up with anyone other than their handler. That's their sole contact, their best friend and family all rolled into one. The military can't allow these dogs to be adopted out to anyone other than a handler, so that handler can react accordingly to anything that may or may not happen."

Samantha's hands shook as she finished wrapping the gauze. Had he shocked her? "So, the handlers can do as you are, right?" she asked.

"Well," he hedged, "they can. But many don't."

"Why?"

"Because some of these handlers have families, and they know the threat. Other handlers don't want that added responsibility of having a dog that could kill. It's a tough decision."

He wrapped his palm around DA's snout affectionately and kissed the tip of his nose.

"You're such a good guy."

Her words startled him. "What? Why? Because I'm adopting my dog?"

A sweet and slow smile spread across her face, like lava rolling over a meadow. "That's just one reason."

He stared at her, but it seemed like the moment they shared before had splintered. She wouldn't meet his eyes.

Chapter Eight

A few hours later, Chris walked up the steep gravel drive to his cabin. The air grew crisp with the wintery season change moving in, causing his breath to come in little clouds. He shoved his hands in the pockets of his shorts and picked up his pace, looking forward to the very warm shower waiting for him. It'd be nothing like the warmth he'd experienced in Samantha's arms, but he could deal with that. *For now.* This had always been his favorite part of a new relationship, the anticipation involving the sexual dance a couple went through before breaking past the last barrier of attraction and succumbing to the body's needs.

He hadn't expected the punch of lust he felt in her presence. Sure, she had a nice voice, and he was a male. His mind kept telling him their parts would fit together nicely. And normally, he wouldn't hesitate to go after what was sure to be a great time between them.

With her heavy southern drawl, and her throaty rasp almost reminiscent of Patsy Cline, whom his mother listened to nonstop when he was a kid, Sam had a voice that made a man want to beg for her to talk dirty, to explain in detail just what she wanted to do to him, or him to her.

Getting lost in the overly creative fantasy of that conversation—and if he were being honest, looking forward to trying it out—he almost missed the familiar feeling of unease across his nape. The hair back there stood on end and a tightening of his shoulders told him something was wrong. He stopped at the base of his three steps to the porch and froze.

The forest surrounding his property was quiet,

almost too quiet. That was the thing about living out in the wild, he didn't need an alarm when he had nature running his security detail. The birds no longer chirped, and despite the changing weather, there were a few that'd stick around. The *kaaar* of the rough-legged hawk didn't piece the air, nor did he see any sitting in trees close by looking for a treat. The sound of deer and turkey weren't crunching through the layer of fall's leaves blanketing the ground, either. A black bear could be roaming nearby, frightening everything off, but he had a strong feeling the hunter of the forest had already laid down for the upcoming winter hibernation.

No, this silence screamed manmade, and it wasn't him who caused it.

Missing the familiar weight of weapons on his body, he turned three-sixty in a circle, his gaze scanning the tree line. Not a shadow moved, almost as if nature shivered in anticipation for the next move. His shoulders itched as if someone held a scope and aimed it at him, but he refused to give in to backing down.

Chris took a few steps away from his house and looked along at the drive. Sure enough, fresh tire tracks disturbed the gravel, the marks stopping far enough away from his Explorer that it wasn't his rental. He took a deep breath. The heavy scent of diesel sat ripe in the air.

After a few more minutes of looking around, he figured someone must have stopped by to check in on him, but not finding him home, left. He did an about-face and jogged up his steps, then froze again with his hand inches from the doorknob.

The door was cracked open, not enough to let any wildlife in, but enough to tell him someone had been inside. He knew without a doubt he'd locked it before leaving—or had he? He frowned, thinking it over. He'd been in a state when he left, so perhaps with the remnants of the nightmare running through him, he hadn't been as security conscious as he thought.

Mentally cursing himself, he slipped inside and listened for a few beats to the silence surrounding him. He scanned the room, walking through his house carefully, trying to and finding nothing out of place.

Reaching his front door again, he went to throw it shut but stopped. Someone *had* been in here. The locking mechanism was still in place. Below, on the ground, chips of wood scattered along the frame, the evidence stating someone had kicked the door in.

"Dammit!" Who the hell would do this? Why him? Why his house? Nyack didn't have much crime, and even though he lived out in the middle of the woods bordering the town, he'd never had a problem with squatters or home invaders. Hell, half the time he left his door unlocked when he went in town simply because that was the small-town way of life.

His heartbeat, already thundering in his chest, picked up and pounded a rhythm up to his temples. Having his earlier unease confirmed wasn't comforting in the least, but it was enough to have him popping up and making a beeline for his gear in the back. A quick shuffle through his rucksack had him pulling out his gun case, unlocking it, slamming a magazine home, and beginning his search through his house all over again.

Fifteen hair-raising minutes later, he'd found nothing more. Just a few papers scattered in positions he didn't leave them in, and a feeling that left a black mark on any good Samantha's mouth had given him. He dug in his pocket for his phone, grabbed the small green notebook containing numbers to his team, and dialed Sergeant Dean Davis, their squad leader, and one of Chris's best friends.

"Yo, you've got Dean here."

"Sarge."

"Crack? That you, man?"

"Yeah," he answered and set his SIG on the table, taking the chance to rub a palm across his head. The feeling of being watched still hadn't gone away, but being inside and talking to a familiar friend eased the discomfort a little. Sure, a round could pierce through his windows no problem, and on that thought, he moved away from any direct line of sight to the windows. But at the familiar deep voice, the earlier unease started to unfurl. "Listen, I don't know if I'm losing it—"

"I'm going to stop you right there. What's going on?"

Chris sighed and looked around again and spied his gun sitting by its lonesome on the table some five feet away. Close enough should he need it. "I think someone broke into my place."

"Isn't your brother the town detective or something?"

"Yeah, but hell." He huffed. "I didn't want to call him in case I'm just seeing things."

"So, you decided to call me instead? As if I have nothing better to do than talk to your ugly mug?"

Chris snorted. Davis chuckled. Always the jokester. All of them. The humor always helped, and it did now. His shoulders eased. "You get any word from command about that op?"

Silence for a few seconds, then, "Bits and pieces, nothing concrete, just some big internal investigation going down at the Clowns In Action."

Clowns In Action, also known as the Central Intelligence Agency. But the past few years, they'd earned their new nickname. The latest mess-up with his team's mission only added more fuel to the fire.

Chris looked at his front door, frowned, and tried

to get the inkling of unease out of his mind. He'd seen a lot through his years in Spec Ops, things he wished he didn't know. Could this break-in be related? A long shot, but in this day and age, especially with their suspicions that something else had happened to throw their operation off, that his team had been sent in to fail, the conspiracy thought was impossible to miss. Davis, not missing the silence, and no slouch when it came to reading his team, immediately picked up on his thought process.

"Crack, you still with me? What's going on? I know you, man, and I know you won't call for some ridiculous break-in. What are you thinking?"

"I don't know. I have this feeling like I'm being watched. Then I get to my front door and find it kicked in. Also found fresh tracks outside, and while it all could be a coincidence, I can't get it out of my mind that it is. Anyone else check in yet?"

"No," Davis grumbled. "But if your gut is screaming, it's trying to tell you something. I don't want to feed the panic pie, but you're a trained operator, one of the best I know, and with how everything went down, I say trust your gut and be careful. I'll check in with the team and Captain, and if I hear anything, I'll call. You just do us a favor and keep your shit together and be careful, you feel me?"

"Yeah, I feel you." The tightness in Chris's chest eased slightly, knowing at least someone else would be looking into things. He didn't trust anything right now, even his own mind. He was too tired, too confused, and a jumbled mess when it came to thinking straight.

"All right, how's Dumb Ass?"

Chris briefed Davis, caught him up on the action plan he and Samantha had come up with, and laughed off the jesting Davis gave him at having a female vet.

"She sounds like she's got it under control," Davis said. "Are you going to try to see if she's interested in making you feel better, too?"

Chris laughed. "Is it always sex with you?"

"Do I like oxygen? Water? Food?" Davis fired back.

"True. I barely know Doc Eagen, but if it happens, it happens. I won't force it." *Sure. Like you didn't practically force yourself on her earlier.*

Well, okay, but that was beside the point.

"I'll check in with the guys, get Captain to do some searching, then let you know what's shaking. If anything else pops up, don't hesitate, and give me a holler, okay?"

"Got it," Chris answered. "Thanks."

"Anytime. Later."

Chris hung up the phone, surprised to find the sky outside had darkened considerably. He hadn't been on the phone that long, but figuring Davis was a talker, it wasn't unusual.

He tossed his phone down then eyed it, wondering if he should call and check in on his dog. Last he left, Dumb Ass had been falling into a fitful sleep but loving the attention he received under Samantha's eye. He knew exactly how his dog felt. When her attention focused on him, he'd practically preened, too.

Being honest with himself, he really wanted to call and hear her voice again, to see if the connection he felt toward her was just physical.

Giving up on the fight, he dialed her number, frowning when he got her voicemail. He left his number with instructions to call if there were any problems, refraining at the last minute from asking her to dinner. He didn't want to seem too pushy. And he was also trying to heal. Pushing his problems on to her while also trying to make an impression with her didn't seem like the right path to take. Figuring to take his own advice, he promised himself he'd take it day by day. No strings, just the promise of a rekindled friendship, and maybe more.

After making sure everything was locked up, he grabbed his SIG and phone and headed for the bathroom. He waited for the shower to get hot, chucked his clothes, tossed them in the corner, and set his phone and SIG on the counter within reach should he need them. He didn't want to seem as if he were being too cautious, but better safe than dead.

When the small bathroom had steamed up enough to where his reflection disappeared in the mirror, he stepped under the hot spray, palmed the wall in front of him, and let the hot water wash over the back of his neck. The memories of the day ran through his head again and he mused everything over, from Samantha Eagen and the problem with Dumb Ass, to his house being broken into. Whoever had come by hadn't wanted to commit burglary, but searched for something. What? He didn't know. He didn't like it, though.

Thinking on it more and more, the break-in seemed connected to something dealing with what he did. But in a world where the government was supposed to have the back of their military, he didn't want to believe it. Problem was, too much was out of their control. So much they couldn't get their hands on. Files redacted after being read by only the top of the house. People who disappeared into thin air as if they never existed. If there was a way to share information directly with the Special Forces teams who were risking their lives, without all the bureaucratic bullshit, then things would be so much better … safer.

That was what they needed. A specialized intelligence team who supported the units directly and dealt specifically with those assholes at the CIA. That way, there wasn't any loss of information, and the teams on both sides could feel comfortable making a decision that could result in life or death.

For a moment, he considered doing that. Starting this specialized intelligence team, but then dismissed it, knowing it was a battle he'd have to fight, and a war he'd have to win in order to even get a team started. He considered his own team, but knowing how much they loved their military lives, just as he did, he immediately dropped the idea.

Pushing all the problems out of his mind brought Samantha to the front. With her plush, shiny lips. Her long red hair that looked on fire when it caught in the sun's rays. Smoky eyes that spoke more than her words said yet held a million secrets. The feel of her breasts pillowed against his chest. Her thighs clamped around his hips, so strong, yet giving, as if she waited for him to sink inside her body.

She'd fit him, too, of that he had no doubt. And taking refuge in her body would be a sweet, curvy heaven against all the darkness he'd seen. He'd get lost in her for hours.

A tingling between his legs identified the lust raging in his body, an attraction it seemed only she could slake. He leaned a forearm to the wall and looked down at his hardened cock, taking himself in his free hand and giving one long stroke.

His toes curled and breath punched from his mouth. He closed his eyes and imagined his callused hand wasn't the one stroking him, but instead, Samantha's soft, feminine hands. When he couldn't get the stroke right, he grabbed the soap, built the lather, and went back to the task.

Suds gave him the right friction. His back

blocked the water from washing it away. He pumped and stroked, ecstasy heightening with every move. He could imagine her mouth parting as she watched his pleasure. He pictured her nipples, guessing they'd be a darkened rose color matching the shade of her lips, peaked and begging for his mouth. He'd suck one tip in his mouth and she'd grip him tighter, stroke faster, her lust building as much as his.

Her cries would fill the bathroom, shouts of need ringing in his ears. He'd push her back to the wall, spread her legs, and plunge inside with one deep stroke.

The orgasm hit him then. His back arched, her name growling out of his mouth and his seed pumping from his body. His buttocks clenched, his hand wringing the last of the ecstasy from him before he had to let go or fall over.

He blinked to clear his vision, smacked the wall with one hand to steady himself. If it was that good without her, he wondered how it'd be once he got her in his bed.

Chapter Nine

The next day, Samantha struggled to focus on work. The résumés for a vet's assistant blurred from one to another in front of her. She needed someone to help her run the shop, take care of the animals she hoped to be obtaining soon, and deal with the administrative tasks that came with running a business. Sure, she could handle all the accounting and ordering of supplies, but she needed an assistant to give her some leeway when it came to making sure she was a vet, rather than a glorified administrator. The assistant would be a blessing and help tremendously. There were many things that went on behind the scenes of running a veterinarian's office. And unfortunately, the temp wasn't cutting out for the job.

Her lower back also ached from sitting for so long, hunched over reading. She checked her calendar again, knowing she had a few more minutes to check in on Delta Alpha before her first interview showed. Making sure the bell sat on the counter in the event anyone popped in, she grabbed the keys to her desk and a doggy treat, and headed back to the treatment room. With all the space, seeing as DA was her only patient for the time being, she left him in a treatment room by himself. That way, she could leave his kennel open and he'd have a bigger area to explore. The few times she'd check on him, though, he hadn't been out of his crate, and instead sat just inside the opening, dozing off and on for brief periods of time.

It couldn't be good for him, the lack of a deep, long, restful sleep. Nor could the lack of exercise. His wounds seemed to be healing, but his mind struggled to cope. Getting him up and moving around and interacting with others was the first step she wanted to take with his treatment plan.

Making sure Chris got in here to work with him, too, would be a big step in the plan, as well. They needed a set routine, something Delta Alpha could get used to.

Speaking of the man who had invaded her dreams last night and had her waking up in a sweat, all hot and bothered with the tingling remembrance of his kisses, she thought over his voicemail from yesterday. She still hadn't called him back, but she left his number right next to the phone. And if she stored his number in her cell phone, well, that was just to make sure it was handy.

That was her story and she was sticking to it.

Samantha pushed open the door to the room and hovered at the entrance. "Here, boy," she tried.

Delta Alpha didn't move, but his alert gaze snapped up to hers. His ears perked, and she heard the very reassuring single thump of his tail against the crate.

She chewed on the inside of her check and mused over the commands Chris had taught her. "Heel, Delta Alpha," she ordered, strong and firm.

He immediately popped to his feet and came out of the crate. He limped to her and dropped his head low as he reached her side. *Hmmmm.* The show of submission wasn't such a good thing when she thought about a military working dog. But him being up and moving around was.

She brushed her free hand over his head, then clucked her tongue and called, "Come," as she walked toward the back of the shop. The click of his doggy nails on her tile told her he followed.

At the backdoor, she grabbed her light jacket, slid her arms inside, then pushed open the door, and held it for him to pass.

"Ease," she said, and DA picked up his pace and

started sniffing around before relieving himself in a few spots. The soft groan he let out had her smiling. His little doggy brows moved around animatedly. His intelligence that both Sergeant Fusko and Chris spoke of clear as a warm summer day. This dog was smarter than anyone gave him credit for, or at least more than she originally gave him. It wasn't something she'd ever overlook again.

With the treat in her hand, she walked to the center of the yard, took a deep breath, and called for him to come to her.

Once he sat before her, she raised her palm and gave a firm, "Stay."

She swallowed hard, not comfortable with the toughness of the treatment they'd have to get past, but she needed to test each part of his abilities and tolerances before they could move to the next phase. She walked behind him, keeping an eye as she did so. Moving slowly, calmly, cautiously. His ears flicked, but keeping good to his training, he stayed in place.

The bell inside her shop rang, and she cursed beneath her breath for the interruption but used the opportunity to see how much noise DA could handle. "Delta Alpha, you're a good boy," she cooed, then followed with a firm, "Stay," when he went to move. Standing next to his shoulder, she stroked the top of his head once, ordered him to stay again, and then raised her voice to answer the bell inside. "We're just outside. I'll be back in a minute."

Delta Alpha flinched and his frame shook, but he stayed in place, refusing to cower. Pride swelled through her so much that she had to bite back her excited exclamation. Instead, she dropped slowly on her haunches and held out the treat. "Good job, buddy. You're such a good boy."

He sniffed the treat and gently took it from her

hand before flopping on his tummy and biting into the cookie with a simple, yet massively strong, clamp of his jaws.

"You're going to make my dog fat if you keep feeding him treats," a deep, sexy voice called from the doorway.

Samantha jolted and couldn't contain the shiver. If the trademark side smirk said anything, he'd seen her reaction.

She gave DA one last stroke on the top of his head, rewarded with several tail thumps before she stood and faced Chris.

"I wanted to reward him for not cowering."

Chris's brows shot high, and he pushed off the frame, uncrossing his arms. "I take it he did well?" he asked with no small amount of hope.

She grinned. "He did."

"That's great." He dropped to his haunches. "Come here, bub."

Delta Alpha sidled over, his whole body wagging with happiness before he pushed his head under Chris's hands and curled his body into the shelter of his handler.

Chris was gentle, yet enthusiastic in his rubdown, murmuring words of praise under his breath, as well as checking the dog's body thoroughly. The sight melted her into a puddle and had her softening up to the man more. A big step, especially with her history when it came to men. She knew not all were the same, but it was hard to let men—any man—into her circle of trust.

The bell rang inside again, breaking her out of her trance, and she shook off her musings and moved to go inside. Unfortunately, the object of her musing blocked her way and Chris watched as she approached.

Today, he wore a burnt-orange pullover, antique-stained jeans, and tan boots. The sweater bunched to show his forearms covered with just the right amount of hair and tinted with a touch of sun. Dark sunglasses sat on top of his head, and despite the ease in his position, she saw the strain around his eyes, the shakiness of his frame, the way he leaned heavily on the door.

Such a big guy, one supposed to look strong and healthy. She frowned, remembering he'd been injured, too.

"Sergeant Gonzalez," she chided, "are you taking care of yourself?"

His lips thinned, and he straightened, wincing. "I thought we talked about this."

At her blank look, he went on. "You met me as Chris, you can continue to call me as such."

She'd deliberately used his title and last name, a little to do with the fact this his dog was her patient, and a lot to do with the familiarity they seemed to gain. It seemed important to keep him at a distance.

Ignoring him, she moved to sidestep him and DA in the doorway, but stopped as his arm shot out and cut off her path. She took a deep breath and braced to meet his gaze.

"Red," he said, "I've had my tongue in your mouth and my hands on your ass. I've thought about doing a lot more, and will just as soon as I get the chance. Call me by my first name."

Her mouth parted and her breath came out shaky. "Cocky much?"

He grinned wide. "No, sweetheart. Just stating how it will be."

She lifted her chin and squared off. While she hadn't wanted to bring this up again, there was no avoiding it now. But she needed to set the record straight. "Look, Chris—"

"See how easy that is?"

She shook her head and continued. "That kiss was a mistake and highly inappropriate. We were both caught off guard and high on adrenaline. But I'd appreciate it if you'd follow my lead and keep things professional."

His grin grew, much to her bafflement. "I can follow your lead, darling."

She pulled her brows in a frown. "That easy?"

He chuckled and nodded. "Yeah, that easy. You want to wear the pants here, that's fine." He crowded against her until the frame bit into her back. Again, she didn't feel any fear. His face hovered so close. He hadn't shaved in a few days and her hands itched to rub her palm across his stubbled cheeks. How in the hell had she lost control so quickly? "Because, sweetheart, I can tell you I don't mind if you wear the pants for now. If I'm doing anything right—and trust me, I will—you won't have them on for long."

His mouth immediately swallowed her gasp of outrage in a punishing yet very quick kiss. He nipped at her bottom lip, soothed the sting with a quick rasp of his tongue, then pulled away and called for Delta Alpha.

"Doc, you have a customer at the desk," he said as the bell rang again.

She ripped her attention off his very nice ass and met his laughing gaze. *Busted.*

****

Several interviews and hours later, Samantha pushed the second pencil in the messy knot at the back of her head to hold it off her neck. The days changed weather more than she changed the sheets on her bed, even despite the seasons moving into the colder fall. Sweltering humidity had made her hair frizz out and beneath her blue tee, the under-layer tank was soaked. Ugh. After getting an assistant in order, getting medical insurance, and working on the millions of other things she needed to do while watching that black number creep closer to red, she needed to speak to the landlord and attempt to see about going half-sies on another air conditioning unit.

Despite it only being in the upper eighties outside, the humidity made things seem so much hotter. She'd lived in the southeast for years and understood humidity like no one's business, but the northeast air seemed stuffier, somehow denser. Almost like one could take a hand and grab the air itself.

But the day was looking up. She had interviewed three potential employees and settled on one. Just weeks shy of her eighteenth birthday, the young woman with long, beautiful red hair and dark-brown eyes that looked older than her age, had been full of energy and a craving for knowledge. She'd interviewed for a fulltime position but told Samantha that once school started in the fall, she'd need a little flexibility.

Despite needing a fulltime employee, Samantha found that looking into the hopeful eyes of one Hailey Mason and saying "no" wasn't something she could do. Instead, she saw the benefit of having a young woman on staff who wanted to start her career in veterinary medicine, who wanted to learn, and who seemed to be up to the task of taking on a demanding position, and saw herself some fifteen years ago. Had someone taken that chance on her, she wouldn't have been left to the wolves, so to speak.

And even though she was hiring Hailey in a fulltime position for the month before school started, she planned to do everything she could to keep her working the hours she needed in order to receive everything she originally posted for with the job: benefits and a good salary.

The back door opened and the sound of doggie

nails clicked on the hard, tiled floor. Chris and Delta Alpha had been training outside most of the day. She'd stopped to make sure both weren't overtiring themselves, but found the two so engrossed in their work that all she had the heart to do was leave water for both, a bottle for Chris and a bowl for DA. She worried both were pushing too hard, but when she'd scrutinized them earlier, she found they had been so in-tuned to each other they hadn't noticed her standing there.

So, she'd left them to their training.

The door to the front opened. She rotated to the newcomer.

A gorgeous, dark-skinned, and extremely tall man walked in wearing antique-stained jeans, a dark-green shirt that brought out the color of his eyes, and a badge on his belt. His piercing gaze hit her briefly, as did his smile that made him even more beautiful before he turned his attention over her shoulder. Then that smile turned mega-watt, upping his hotness to a whole new level. *Dayum.*

She froze like a mouse caught in a trap as Chris rounded the corner of the counter and clasped hands with Mr. Hottie. The two leaned in and did that man-hug thing where they slapped each other so hard she was surprised neither lost their breath. Leaning into her hand, as she had an elbow on the counter, she rested her head in her palm and took in all the goodness of these two handsome men.

Handsome men were exactly what had drawn her to Manuel in the first place, and it appeared to be a weakness of hers.

If these two could bottle whatever kind of sexiness they exhibited, she could become a very rich woman. Heck, she even considered asking the two of them to come by her shop once a day to do as they were now, just conversing, and simply charge an entrance fee and rack in the dough. Because *ba-a-by*, many a woman would pay a fortune just to lay their eyes on these fine specimens.

"Uh, Red," Chris said, laughter in his voice. She blinked as he waved a hand in front of her face, cutting her off from her musings. She snapped her spine straight and focused on him.

"You okay?" he asked, his head tilted to the side curiously. Delta Alpha had done that to her a few times, too. She wished she had a camera to capture it because she'd combine the two pictures—one of Chris and one of DA—for her eyes only.

"I'm okay," she said with a nod. "Sorry, did you ask me something?"

DA came over and rested his head on her lap, head pushed against her lower stomach. He'd been doing that a lot, and she found it too irresistible to resist, despite protests from Chris. If a dog could cuddle, this pose would be it.

The side of Chris's mouth quirked, which drew her attention to his lush lips. Lips that had done way too much damage to the walls she had built around herself. Walls designed to keep people at a distance. Chris seemed oblivious to all of it. "Are you sure you're okay? Do you need some water or something?"

She shook her head. "Seriously, I'm good. What's up?"

He eyed her like he thought she needed a CAT scan, which, combined with the looks of these two, the day, and heck, the month she'd had, and lack of food, she probably did. "I wanted to introduce you to my brother." Chris hooked a thumb toward Mr. Hottie.

Geesh, the genes in this family were unreal. "Hi!" she said, waving a hand, and internally wincing at how stupid she must look. "I'm Samantha Eagen."

He smiled, his more lazy than sensual like his brother. "I know."

She lifted her brows and lowered them, casting a quick look at Chris. "I take it you're the detective?" she asked.

He nodded, that sensual grin still in place. Like she amused him. Well… Besides the good looks, that was where the two brothers' similarities ended. Their mannerisms seemed similar, but one wouldn't be able to tell they were brothers. "You two don't look like brothers. Anyone ever tell you that?"

Both grinned again and her heart did a little dance in her chest.

Dwayne shook his head. "I'm a lot younger than this guy." He cocked his head toward Chris. "And better looking." He grinned and Chris barked out a laugh.

She smiled. "Okay, then. Nice to meet you."

Dwayne looked at Chris. "She always like this?"

Chris chuckled and shook his head. "No. This is a first. But I think we need to feed her. I haven't seen her eat all day."

They both looked at her and her cheeks heated under their attention. She nodded in agreement with Chris. She hadn't eaten outside of a handful of crackers here and there. She really needed to get a grip on her schedule and take better care, for herself and the baby growing inside.

Two gorgeous, lush mouths grew into a smile. *Dayum.* She'd definitely think about that entrance-fee thing, except now she'd add that smile at the end. A pseudo-kind of happy ending. Because *Oh-Em-Gee.* Gorgeous.

"Darlin'," Chris drawled, "I think you're drooling."

She wiped the back of her hand under her mouth then glared at him. "Am not!"

He laughed.

"Wait," she said and eyed the two yummy men. "I mean it. You two don't look anything alike." And it was true. Their skin colors weren't the same. Chris had more of an olive complexion, whereas Dwayne's coloring was more of a light mocha, all dark and goodness. Their faces weren't the same, either, though their expressions definitely showed similarities. As did the way they held themselves: confident, tall, and proud.

"We're both adopted," Chris said.

She lifted her brows again at this news. "Both?"

Both of the hotties nodded, then Dwayne said, "Our parents adopted six of us. Separately, of course. None of us are related by blood."

"Good Lord, please tell me something is wrong with the other four. I don't think women could hold out against six of you."

Dwayne barked out a laugh and Chris chuckled. She sighed, realizing she said that out loud.

"Adopted or not, you're brothers all the same, right?" she asked, wanting that. A big family, tons of siblings, a house full of love. Instead, she'd been an only child and held at arm's length from her parents who only seemed to have love for one another. Not their lonely child.

"Through the good times and the bad," Chris said, his intent eyes probing her face. He shifted, glancing at his brother. "I'm going to go grab some food. I'll pick you up something. Anything you don't like?"

She shook her head. Her mind tried to play catch up, completely thrown off at the news of their adoptions and wondering what was behind that story. "Whatever you grab is fine. Thanks."

"Sweetheart," Chris said and leaned over the counter to hold her gaze. "I need you to focus here, yeah?"

Focus? Pfft. How the hell did he expect her to focus after all that had happened in the past few minutes? But when he asked her in that soft, kind voice, and called her *sweetheart*, she'd probably do about anything. "I am focusing, Chris. What is it?"

"Christ," he said, his voice only loud enough for her ears, but she had a feeling Dwayne didn't miss much. "If you knew what the sound of my name coming from your lips does to me." He shook his head quickly. "Is there anything you prefer to eat? I'm not picky, baby, and I want to take Dumb Ass for a walk, so I don't care where we need to go."

For a good portion of his talking, she could actually picture herself melting into a puddle at his feet. The low, intimate timbre of his voice made parts of her body respond in a warm, warm way. But at the mention of him taking DA, she snapped her spine straight. "You're not taking DA on a walk with you."

He straightened. "Babe, what did I just say?"

"He's not ready."

A muscle in his jaw jumped. "He'll be fine. I'm putting on his vest, which identifies what he is, and his muzzle. He's not going to hurt anyone."

She shook her head, rising out of her chair. Ready to intervene, to hold DA inside … something. "*He's* not ready."

Chris's face grew soft, and he stared at her. Something she couldn't read worked behind his eyes. The two of them faced off. She didn't know how she'd win this, whatever it was, but she worried he pushed Delta Alpha too soon into going outside in public. DA barely stood calm in her presence and she was the one feeding him right now. Everyone knew the fastest way to a dog's heart: food.

If she could barely get under his skin and be around him after giving him two square meals a day, how did Chris expect him to do well outside with crowds of people around him?

"Sweetheart," he said, his voice ultra-soft. Her tummy flipped then curled with warmth. "I love that you are championing for Dumb Ass. I love that he has that. What I don't think you realize is I'm right there with you. He means the world to me and I'm not going to do anything right now that will push him too far."

"He's not ready. And do you really need to call him that?" She understood the reasoning behind it, that this team had used laughter to get through their tough jobs, but she had a difficult time getting past the nickname. She needed to find a stronger leg to stand on, but for the life of her, the matter in her brain refused to work to come up with a stronger objection.

"He's ready."

They stared at each other for a few seconds, then she huffed. "Fine. But at the first sign…"

He flashed a grin. "Yes, ma'am. I'll bring him back."

Samantha looked over at Dwayne. He held a huge grin on his face, his gaze darting between Chris and her. *What was that all about?* "Can I trust you to keep him to his word?"

Dwayne's grin spread. "Yeah, I got your back, Doc. I'll make sure to kick Chris's ass if he pushes his dog too hard."

"But Chris is hurt, too, so don't kick his ass too hard. I'd hate to have to start practicing on humans, too. They make horrible patients."

Chris snorted and rounded the counter again, this

time with Delta Alpha. "Shit, sweetheart, you *do* realize I'm a trained Special Forces operator, right? You're bad for a man's ego."

She just stared at him. Of course, she knew. She also knew the man could move his body in such a sensual way even when he wasn't aware of it.

Chris shook his head. "Jesus. Sam, what do you want to eat, babe?" He said this like he couldn't deal with her any longer, but there was a bit of humor behind his words.

"Fine. I'll take a panini from that place down the street, next to the library. Just cheese and tomatoes. And tell them not to skimp on the salad."

Chris's lips twitched. "That it?"

She nodded, trying and failing to ignore what that lip twitch did to her stomach.

He lifted his chin toward the door, then at Dwayne. "Let's go."

Chapter Ten

A little over an hour later, Chris leaned back in the stool next to the main counter and pushed his delicious food away. One thing he missed while being overseas was the convenience of fast food. Despite having to stop at two different places, the café down the street for Samantha, and a burger place for him and Dwayne, they'd made the food run quick and without incident with DA.

His dog had done great. Stayed by his side, didn't flinch at the late afternoon crowds and traffic in town, and had only cowered twice. Those two times couldn't be helped, each a result of the backfire of a vehicle that moved much too slowly down the street.

Outside the one niggling feeling of being watched, and that damn feeling itching across his shoulders, the entire run had gone off without a hitch.

They'd returned to Claws and Paws to Samantha hanging up the phone, a huge smile on her face, and at their entry, she lifted her hands in the air and shouted, "She accepted!" Obviously, she found an assistant. He hadn't seen any of them come in that morning, so involved in working with DA, but he was happy that she seemed pleased. That obvious pleasure dimmed when her eyes landed on DA.

The damn mutt must have already figured out Samantha's soft spots because she immediately tossed him a stink-eye, the effect not doing much to him because little did she know, her version of the stink-eye just made her that much cuter.

"Sergeant Gonzalez," she chided, "just look at him. Poor baby." She relieved Chris of the leash, whipped off DA's muzzle, and then ran her hands over the dog's flank, her eyes assessing, her touch visibly comforting. It happened right before his eyes. DA's tail thumped again the side of the counter wall, and his little doggie head fell back, his snout in the air, his eyes turning to Chris in what had to be doggie heaven.

"He's fine," Chris said, narrowing his eyes at his dog. "Did great, actually."

She turned to him, her brows drawn with displeasure. "I bet he'll be better with a treat." She turned back to DA and her voice rose two octaves with, "You want a treat, big guy? Who wants a treat?"

And so was the end to DA's big, badass military persona. His dog, *his damn dog* followed Samantha to the back, his attention glued to her as if she were handing him the world.

That had been twenty minutes ago. They'd all sat at the counter that separated the office, Samantha having pulled out barstools from thin air, and ate their meals, chatted freely, and the time passed as if there weren't any worries of what tomorrow, or hell, even the next ten minutes would bring.

The lowering sun cast a yellow hue to the room, drawing out the vibrant red of her hair, where glints of copper and gold layered until he couldn't figure out which color he liked more. She seemed more relaxed this afternoon, and he wanted to figure out what it was so he could be sure to give her the same day in and day out.

A loud smack sounded through the room, startling Chris out of his musings. Dwayne had his hand over a manila folder, drawing the file toward him, his narrowed eyes on Samantha. What the hell was this?

"D," he said, "what the fuck?"

Dwayne ignored him and addressed Samantha. "Mind telling me what you think you're doing?"

Her wide-eyed gaze didn't move off his brother. The second time he'd seen that look in her face, a look he didn't want to see again—the first being when DA had stood snarling and dripping with spittle right behind her shoulder. One could visibly see her hackles rising and a fear wash across her face. She looked ready to bolt.

"Detective," she said and cleared her throat when her voice cracked. "I have no idea what you're referring to."

"How about you start with telling me why Hailey's name is on your folder?"

She swallowed and her shoulders went down a bit. Surprisingly, she didn't slide right out of her chair. "How about first you tell me why you're asking?"

Chris's eyebrows went up. She had balls, he'd give her that. The intensity coming off Dwayne even gave him pause.

"Why is her name on your folder? Answer me."

Samantha took a deep breath and glanced at Chris so quickly he didn't think she realized it. The breath seemed to give her a little courage for she met D's eyes head-on, then leaned across the counter and grabbed the edge of the folder. Dwayne matched her lean with one of his own. "Detective Gonzalez, please, let go."

Chris didn't like the aggression or Samantha's response to it. Could this be one of her secrets? "D," he said, "I suggest you take a step back."

"Why is Hailey's name on your goddamn folder?" Dwayne bit out.

"You're kidding me," she said, her grip tightening on the folder so much her hand turned white, as did her face. Samantha curled her free hand over her stomach, her little fist matching the color as her face. She darted a quick glance at Chris. "Tell me he's kidding me right now."

"Woman, you do not want to mess with me," D snapped off.

"Christ," Chris said. "Chill the hell out, bro." He turned to Samantha, more than unnerved by everything that had happened. "Sweetheart, just tell him what Hailey's name is doing on there. In fact, I'd like to know myself, seeing as she's my niece."

Breath rushed out of her in a rush, her shoulders falling, her ass hitting the stool she'd been on before. "Oh my God. Jesus." She took a deep breath and waved a hand over her face. "She's my assistant. I just hired her."

Chris relaxed minutely, leaning back in his stool. The intensity coming off Dwayne lessened, but not completely. He watched as his brother took a considerable amount of time releasing his grip on the folder one second at a time. He understood D's protective instincts when it came to Hails. But he didn't understand the cowering woman Samantha had turned into, nor why she seemed to curl into a protective ball. Her reaction seemed very outside of who he'd grown to know these past couple of weeks.

"Doctor Eagen," Dwayne said, "I apologize. I'm very ... protective of Hailey. She went through something not too long ago and it's not something I want to experience again. Nor something I want *her* to experience again."

Samantha snatched the folder off the counter, placing it out of reach. "I'm a vet, Detective. What do you expect me to do to Hailey?"

Dwayne's lips tightened. "You're a stranger to me, Doc. I have no clue *what* you'd do."

"Now wait a second," Chris interjected.

"No," Samantha interrupted, her face no less pale than it'd been two minutes ago. "That's fine, and it's true. He doesn't know me, you don't know me, and I don't know either of you. Perhaps it'd be better to leave it that way."

"The fuck I will," Chris said.

Dwayne sighed and stood, the chair legs screeching across the laminate floor. "Look," he said, "I'm sorry. I overreacted. Had I known Hailey was applying to work with you, I probably wouldn't have had that reaction. As it is, I think I need to have a chat with her about communication. In any event, I'm glad she took the chance, and I'm glad you're giving her one. Please don't let my actions affect the relationship you and her will have. She's a wonderful young woman, she loves animals, and she would be a great worker given the chance."

Samantha thinned her lips. "I know all of that about Hailey. Those are exactly the reasons why I hired her. Your actions here today aren't going to affect that."

Dwayne gathered up his trash, nodding his head. "Thank you. Thank you for understanding and thank you again for taking a chance with her. She's special. One of the most special young women you'll ever meet." He tossed his trash in the can, then turned and held his hand out. "Please, accept my apology. I was wrong to react the way I did."

She cautiously slid her hand in Dwayne's, her eyes catching every movement D made as if she expected him to attack. She held her body back from him as if she were afraid to get too close. The history with his niece was a precarious slope, one none of them wanted to find themselves in ever again. But something else was behind D's reaction today. And there was an alarming reaction that Samantha had to him that he wanted to get to the bottom of. His brother had always been the levelheaded one, the calm one. Chris had never seen him react to anything the way he had today. In addition to Dwayne talking to Hailey, it seemed like it was time for Chris to have a little chat with his younger brother. Then he needed to get whatever secret Samantha seemed to be hiding out of her, too. He gathered up his trash as well, tossing it in the same can as Dwayne had, then turned to her.

"I'm going to head out with D. Same time tomorrow?"

She nodded, her attention distracted. Almost as if lost in her mind. The past few minutes had been intense. He could understand that. He didn't like the distance in her expression, though.

She rounded the counter, walking them both to the front door. Her eyes wouldn't meet his no matter how many times he tried to catch her gaze. It irritated the hell out of him, even though he knew it shouldn't. He wanted to demand her attention, wanted to push her up against the wall and kiss her until all she could think about was him and nothing else. But something held him back. A haunted look in her gaze, one he needed to figure out before he got any more involved.

He didn't want to leave with this cloud hanging between them though, because no matter that the escalated situation hadn't been between them specifically, there was definitely a wall going up now.

At the entrance to Claws and Paws, he turned to her, waiting until her startled gaze jumped up to his. Dark rings under her eyes spoke of her exhaustion. Perhaps she wasn't sleeping, or maybe she just had a long day. But beneath the darkness lay a heavy sadness, so heavy it shocked him he hadn't noticed it before.

"Red," he said, brushing his knuckles across her cheekbone, "don't sweat what just happened."

She crossed her arms, her hands clenched against her body. "I'm fine."

"No, you're not. You're running yourself ragged."

"Chris—" she said, but he cut her off.

"No, no excuses. Just take it easy, gorgeous. There's not much to life if you really aren't living it. And there's only so much you can do to keep others pushed away."

She tightened her lips and turned from him, walking back into her shop alone. He didn't like it one bit and vowed that he'd figure out what she was hiding and how to make her smile more.

****

Over the next few weeks, Samantha expected Chris's daily visits. Not that he shouldn't be coming around to assist with Delta Alpha, anyway. He was, after all, the one DA was closest to, and his trainer. More so, the visits seemed to not only center around helping to get the military working dog functional in an everyday kind of life, a retirement of sorts for this courageous animal. But with each stop in, she gravitated closer and closer to Chris. He seemed to break down every one of the walls she'd constructed around her heart, though she fought it every step of the way.

After the way things had ended with her and Manuel, she wasn't so sure she'd ever be able to let anyone, male or female, into her life again. At least not at a level of comfort which would open the door for friendship.

And it wasn't like she hadn't paid attention to all the warning signs with her ex. Sure, she noticed when his behavior changed from cajoling to controlling. When they'd dated, he acted the perfect gentleman. Opening doors for her, holding her hand as they crossed the street, calling her as soon as he walked in the door following their date to tell her how much he already missed her.

Their relationship had been a whirlwind of a romance, from flower deliveries, sweet messages left on her phone, and soft, sexy talks late at night. None of it caused any alarms until a week after he'd proposed. By then, she'd moved to the south with him, alienated from everyone she'd ever known. Her family, her friends, her old life.

That was when things started changing. He'd gone from Mr. Perfect to Mr. Temperamental. The accusations, the arguments, and the questions seemed endless. Almost as if he expected her to step out on him, cheat on him with some stranger in the grocery store, all because of a polite smile. And it hadn't stopped there.

Those accusations had grown physical, becoming a slap across the face, a push down the stairs, and finally, her head being bashed against the wall before she'd realized that no matter how much she wished things could go back to how they were before, no matter how much she thought she could soothe him with sweet words, nothing would be good enough until she escaped.

And escape she had. She'd ran first to her cousin, who owned a private investigation company, and he'd helped her get to a safe place, helped her get the restraining order, and helped her disconnect her life from the only person she'd ever been close to. Andrew had wanted to do so much more after seeing the bruises on her face and body, but she'd begged to just let things lie, to help her disappear, and after much reluctance, he finally agreed.

So, after nine hundred miles, several weeks, and a name change under sealed court records, she'd settled in Nyack, New York. She was trying to rebuild her life, trying to poke her head outside of the shadows and stand in the sun instead of cowering at every sound. Establishing her own business helped. She'd been hesitant about that too, knowing the business would leave a paper trail, but with her new name and hiding behind the purchase with the use of a lawyer, she'd decided she'd be able to do what she'd always dreamed of: live a happy life doing what she loved, which was working with animals.

Manuel could find her here, she had no doubt. But she hoped she'd made it clear that she wanted nothing to do with him any longer. She hoped the restraining order would keep him away.

She hadn't thought she'd let anyone under her skin again, not after the nightmare of her engagement, but reluctantly, she found both Delta Alpha and Chris doing just that. There hadn't been any more stolen kisses, no touching, or outrageous flirting since all those weeks ago, but she could still see the heat in his eyes when he looked at her. Could still see him holding back just a bit. Whether that was for her comfort or his, she didn't know.

It made her profoundly curious.

She was finishing up with Ms. Robinson's feline friend, Fluffy, who matched the name with every bit as the word described, when the bell over her entrance jangled. *Right on time.*

She snapped off her gloves, washed her hands, and explained to Ms. Robinson that Fluffy didn't need three cans of Fancy Feast a day. After finishing with that very lengthy conversation, she opened the door to the exam room and ushered her customers out to Hailey to pay their bill.

Chris wasn't in the front reception, so she detoured and headed back toward the grassy knell, wanting to watch DA's and his handler's interaction for a bit. Who was she kidding? She wanted to observe Chris for a while when he wasn't watching her, and if she had a chance to gauge DA's training then that was a plus.

She opened the back door as quietly as she could, getting the reminder with the squeak that still occurred, that she needed to put some WD40 on the hinges. The cooler but humid air pushed against her in a rush, bringing the scents of fall: drying leaves, the river, and of man and dog.

Chris squatted before DA, his face close to the Shepherd's snout. Both the man and dog's eyes held an intensity and trust only years of partnership could achieve.

"All right, Dumb Ass," Chris said, his voice full of encouragement, "you can do this. Keep your head in the game, your focus on your task, and let's prove all of them wrong."

Samantha leaned against the wall, amused and a bit curious. If she wasn't mistaken, DA visibly pulled his head higher and gave a little doggy nod.

"Good, boy. Now, ready?" Chris stood, snapped his shoulders back, and threw out an arm, indicating the yard before him full of boxes, bags, and piles of leaves. She hadn't seen him bring any of that in. "Seek!" he commanded, and DA shot off like a rocket.

Doggy nose to the ground, DA moved past different items, dismissing them with barely a flick of his head, his path clear only based on the extreme sense of his nose. So in tune to watching DA, she let out a little yelp when a loud hissing noise sounded from Chris's hand. He held a big red can out to his side. She bit her lips, about to admonish him, but stopped just in time.

Training. He knew DA would find whatever he'd hidden, but he wanted him to focus on his task, not be interrupted by whatever went on around him, including loud sounds. A perfect training aspect she hadn't thought of. She'd been more about working on the dog's mind and physical injuries, not in keeping his training regimen on what he'd known.

She turned back to DA as Chris let out another stream of air, the sound abrasive even to her own ears, to see DA's ears flicker, his entire body buck, but not giving up on his task of finding whatever Chris had hidden. The sound kept up in sporadic intervals until DA sniffed twice more then sat directly in front of a large black bag. His little doggy eyes turned to Chris as one more hiss escaped. Then the yard was quiet for one, two, three seconds...

"Good boy!" Chris shouted, his voice a few octaves higher than she was used to hearing from him. He darted toward DA and whipped a red Kong up in the air. DA broke from his holding position and raced after his toy. Chris grabbed the bag, opened it, and pulled out a blue box that had *TRAINING* written in big black letters across its width.

DA came back with his Kong and Chris took it, throwing it in the air for his dog to chase again.

"Wow," she said as Chris walked up to her, a big smile on his face, his straight white teeth stark against his olive skin tone, his eyes shining bright.

"He's kind of great, isn't he?" Chris asked.

"Kind of?"

His smile turned lopsided as he dropped the training box next to the back door. "Okay, he is great. Sorry for dropping in like this, but Hails said you were with someone and I wanted to see how Dumb Ass would do before I headed over to Ma's."

There was a lot to address in those two sentences, so she picked what she wanted to address first. "It's not a problem. You know his recovery is based on you and I working together, so anytime you want to stop in and train with him, you're more than welcome to. Honestly, I think he might be ready to head home with you soon if you think you'll both be up for it."

He lifted a brow, turning to lean against the wall with her, but facing her slightly. "What about if I just want to stop in and see you and him being here gives me a reason to do just that?"

Heat rose over her face and she pushed away from the wall to get a chance at the cool breeze. "I didn't realize your mother lived in town, too," she said, rather than responding to his question.

He shot her a look that said he knew exactly what she'd done. "Yeah, Ma and Pop still live down off Cedar Hill by the river. It's been a while since I've been home, and I've put off this visit for too long."

"You haven't seen them since you got back?"

He shook his head.

"Chris," she admonished. "Your mother must be worried sick, especially with why you're home."

He had the grace to look embarrassed then shook his head. "She doesn't know all of it, but yeah, that's my bad for not seeing her sooner. Ma," he said, then hesitated before he continued, "has a way about seeing more than you want her to. She knows things before even you do, and I just didn't … I don't know if I'm ready to deal with that yet, but I know I need to go see her and Pop."

"How long have you been home now? Three, four weeks?"

He lifted a shoulder. "Yeah, I know that makes me a horrible son." He grabbed a lock of her ponytail and gave it a tug. "I'm going over today to fix that. But don't think I didn't miss that you never answered my question."

"Chris," she said, trying to figure out a way to let him down, give a reason why, without hurting this comradery they'd seemed to gain. "I don't know if I'm open to anything other than what we have. I have a lot going on right now."

He scooted an inch closer, both of them facing each other by the back wall. "Why do we have to put any kind of title on it? What if I just enjoy hanging out with you?"

She stared into his deep, whiskey-colored eyes and tried to see through the question. Was he playing some kind of game? Did he want to just get in her pants, or was it something more? Something less? Nothing she'd learned about Chris over the past few weeks told her he was anything like her ex, but she'd been down that road before, and it became a nightmare. One she never wanted to experience again. Sure, call her gun shy, but she'd barely escaped that scene with her life, and now that she had the freedom, and her dream of running her own business, it wouldn't be so easy to get up and go again. This time, it might just break her completely. And she wasn't so sure that heartbreak would be because of what she had going here with her new life.

And she couldn't forget the fact that she wasn't a single deal anymore. What would happen if, and when, Chris found out she was pregnant? Would he look at her with disgust? Like damaged goods?

Chris stared right back and seemed to come to a conclusion before she did, for he straightened and took a step closer. "Look, Red, I get we have a past, and I see something else haunting you. It sits behind your eyes." He held up a hand when she opened her mouth. "No, hear me out. I see it sitting behind your eyes, and as much as I want to know what or who did that to you, I'm not going to ask now. I get with our history and the fact that we barely know each other now I don't have that right to ask yet. But I'm also a straight shooter kind of guy, so I will say this…"

He leaned in and cupped the side of her neck, tilting her face to him so she had to stare into his eyes. "I want to get that chance to be able to ask. Not only that, I want to earn your trust to take care of those shadows. We can put the past behind us. We all have something we're fighting against, some dark secret or demon we have to deal with on our own. Some of those demons, though, are too big to conquer on our own, so sometimes we need friends to help us get through it. I'm learning that now, and sweetheart, I want you to learn that, too. Let me be that friend to help you work on whatever you need to get through, and maybe we both could get through this dark period together."

When did he become so sage? His offer was so very tempting. His heartfelt words sounded as if he truly wanted to be there for her. "You want to be friends?" she asked, her voice a little breathless.

His gaze darted to her mouth and back up, heat igniting within his eyes. "Hell no," he said, his words rough, "but until I get you to trust me, I'm willing to work on us being friends before I work toward us being something more."

Oh, boy. She grabbed his wrist of the hand attached to her neck. "Chris…"

He took a deep breath, letting it out slowly before stepping back from her and releasing his hold. Whistling, he patted his leg. "I need to get to Ma's before I do something that shows you just how much I want that more between us to happen."

She bit her bottom lip, kind of curious what that something would be.

"Red," he warned, his heated gaze on her mouth. "That look on your face is telling me to move in now, but I want to show you I can be someone you trust. So, I'm going to say this: all you need to do is give me a word.

But you need to make that conscious decision and let me know you're ready for more. Until then, we're friends."

Still biting her lip, she nodded. DA joined Chris at his side.

"Christ, that look on your face," he bit out and yanked open the door. "I'm going before I go back on my word. I'll be back later to check in. If you need me, you have my number."

She released her lip and nodded, following them in. Chris got DA settled, and she disappeared to an exam room, chastising herself as soon as the door closed. There was no reason to get involved with another type-A personality man like her ex. But something about Chris called to her, and she worried she wouldn't be able to hold off for much longer.

Chapter Eleven

Chris headed down Broadway in his truck, listening for any rattling or weird noises. The Bronco had been sitting in his brother's garage for the better part of him being gone, and despite assurance that Matt had been keeping it running every few months, sixteen years was a long time with no tender loving care for a car, so he wanted to be diligent and jump on top of any issues before they became a problem.

Despite the cooler fall weather, he'd removed the doors, deciding he wanted to feel the bite of the air against his body before the winter-cool air moved in. After that visit with Sam, and the hungry look that'd come over her face and what had passed through his mind on how he wanted to answer that look, he was grateful he'd thought ahead on the matter.

He didn't understand his deep connection to her. He'd never felt something like that before. Sure, it could be because she was his lifeline when it came to DA, or even because she'd been the one he'd first relied on coming home, but he hoped it—and this was a first—was more than that. He'd never been one to form close attachments outside of his world in the military. Even though he had five other adoptive brothers, and they were technically considered his family, he'd never been able to connect with them on an intimate level. His brothers in the military were different. They all had a common thing that bonded them. The same goal they worked toward.

And even then, that connection had taken years to form and bind.

With Sam, the invisible thread that linked her and

him together seemed to be almost instantaneous.

For the first time in a long time, he pictured himself settling. Building roots. Starting a family. And it wasn't some nameless woman he saw at his side, but instead a red-headed, curvy woman with eyes the color of grass in the spring. And her scent ... her scent was sweet, reminding him of the aroma of a freshly sliced peach. He'd never much cared for sweet things until he met Samantha. And now he craved her with an abundance that shocked him.

He slowed as the light ahead turned red and stopped, turning his attention to the shops along the street. The library that seemed always to be under construction, the old gas station that hadn't changed in all the years he'd been away, and the café where Sam preferred her food.

A male with dark hair and thick black sunglasses came out of the library.

Chris stilled, everything coming to a stop around him.

No way...

He narrowed his eyes, wishing he was closer, wishing that man would remove his glasses so he could get another look at his face. The guy turned right, giving Chris his back, and walked away.

He tightened his hands on the steering wheel, wishing for quick parking, something nonexistent in this small village, so he could pursue on foot. Instead, he was forced to wait out the light.

Tayseer.

He would never forget that face. Had studied him for weeks prior to their mission, had seen his picture hundreds of times. Hell, he knew Tayseer's face better than he knew his own!

What the hell was Tayseer doing in Nyack, New

York? His hometown?

Why was he here?

The light changed and Chris urged the drivers to move faster than the twenty-five mile-per-hour limit. There'd been a video he watched not too long ago that explained traffic and how one car waited for another before moving itself. This was the cause of why things moved so slow. The video went on to explain that if all cars moved at the same time, traffic would be extinguished. A silly thought, seeing as shit often happened on roads, accidents and whatnot, but at that moment, and seeing Tayseer's head disappear around the corner, he wished people would adhere to that thought process.

What felt like hours, but was most likely a minute later, Chris sped up to the corner he'd seen Tayseer disappear around and turned onto the residential street. Houses and tall trees thick with colorful leaves lined the stretch before him. The river sat directly at the end. What was missing was the man he'd sworn as his biggest enemy.

He slowed the truck to a crawl, eyeing each of the houses as he went by, looking for anything to give him a clue. A rental sign, a car with out-of-state tags, something saying someone was in the area who hadn't been there before.

He drove up and down the street three times, but nothing. On his final pass, he pulled to the end and stared at the river, wondering if he'd been mistaken.

Sure, Tayseer wasn't in the US government's custody anymore, he'd somehow escaped, which was a whole other clusterfuck for how that had happened. But there was no reason to believe one of the world's most wanted terrorists ran around in his backyard, in a tiny town outside of New York City.

He could only deduce he had been seeing things, something the doctors in Germany had warned him of. They cautioned jumping to conclusions, told him to speak to a professional while he was home, and to take it easy, but he hadn't thought any of that would affect him. He knew his mind, understood what his body could take. He'd pushed both to the brink of collapse many times.

But maybe it was time to take a breather for a few days and get some rest. He could have half-scared someone out of their mind rushing up on them, with him thinking they were Tayseer.

Shaking off the lingering feelings of unease, he turned his truck around and headed through the back roads to his parents' house. The further he moved away from the place he thought Tayseer to be, the more his shoulders loosened and the throb behind his eyes slowed.

The white and black colonial rose before him as if a beacon was telling him where home lay. Kind of compared to a lighthouse giving ships a place of comfort. The twin beams flanked the front door and were wrapped in orange and gold garland, bringing the black trim of the house out in stark relief.

His mother had always been a stickler for decorating during the holidays, giving each of her boys something to look forward to, even though he had always thought she enjoyed it just as much. Each holiday, decorating had turned into a day-long event where it was all hands-on deck, each of them given a task to get the house up to par. They'd often ended the day with a home-cooked meal and s'mores by the firepit out back.

Some of the best memories he'd always cherish. Time spent with his adoptive family, one he'd always be grateful to no matter if they weren't the same blood.

Karen and Daniel Gonzalez had done the unthinkable and adopted six different boys, all from different backgrounds, after coming upon them. Karen had worked for social services and when she found out she couldn't have children of her own, she refused to let that get her down and worked on resolving the matter in her own way.

She'd taken him in at a young age and given him the life he'd always longed for. One filled with warmth and discipline, love and understanding. His adoptive parents had shown him it didn't matter where he came from, and instead, the only thing to focus on was where he was going.

He'd never looked back.

And he couldn't be more grateful to the two wonderful human beings inside that house.

He hopped out of his truck and crossed the yard, running up the steps two at a time like he had done as a kid, before rapping on the door twice and entering.

Even though the door was unlocked as if expecting company, it was an empty nest and he didn't necessarily want to walk in on anything that would cause him to wash his eyes out with bleach. His parents were known for sneaking kisses in the most awkward places, making any one of the boys finding them in the pantry, the coat closet, or the downstairs half-bath groan and wish they had hot pokers for their eyes.

As a grown man, he could appreciate them having that romance after being married all these years, but as their son, there were some things one did not wish to see.

He walked into the foyer and unlaced his boots, tossing them to the side with his pop's, before walking down the hall. A black-and-white photo above the mud-mat caught his attention. The six of them, the Gonzalez troop of his brothers and he, had their arms linked over each other's shoulders, each smiling into the camera and tilting their heads toward one another. His ma had taken that photo just after he'd signed up to join the military. Seemed like eons ago.

"Ma? Pop?" he called.

"In here," Pop responded, sounding as if he stood in the family room. Spices and meat scented the air, making Chris's stomach grumble appreciatively. Roasted pork. Awesome.

Chris stepped into the hall where the family room and the kitchen opened up into each other, something his brothers and his pop had helped with when Ma asked for an open floor plan between the rooms. She explained she wanted to still spend time with the men in her life when she cooked her big family meals and asked Pop to get a contractor on it. It'd taken a month, but the space worked for all involved. Them—the boys—in getting to pop in and out of the kitchen, taking snacks and samples of what she cooked as they went, and for Ma, so she could still interact with the men in her life as they watched the games.

To the right sat the family room, a wide space that held two leather couches and two recliners, all facing one another in a blocked-off pattern, the focus before them being a large brick fireplace and above it, a large flat-screen TV. Pictures of their lives and the memories they had created littered the walls until practically none of the burnt-orange paint from behind shone through.

Windows lined full length along the back wall of the house, showcasing the river that ran behind and the large expanse of a green yard.

To the left was the kitchen with white cabinets and a large, dark-gray island in the middle. A small kitchen table sat off to the side adjacent to the windows. Another larger table was in the dining room, the one they used for holiday meals and bigger crowds.

He took a step toward his pop when he stepped

into the opening, seeing him in the family room watching something on TV. Daniel had risen, a look of wonder on his face as his gaze rested on Chris.

But Chris stopped in his tracks as his gaze went through the kitchen and landed on his mother who had tears in her eyes and a tan kitchen towel clasped between her two hands. She wrenched the towel in her fists, twisting and turning the cloth. Her face grew redder as he stared at her until he started to grow alarmed.

He turned and took two steps toward her, sending her a questioning, "Ma?"

"Christopher Daniel Gonzalez," she snapped, her voice booming through the room. He stopped in his tracks and winced.

"Ma—" he tried again, only to be cut off.

"Four weeks, my boy couldn't come down to check in with his mother."

He sighed. Behind him, he heard Pop call her name softly.

"Sixteen years you've been gone and yet you take another four weeks before finally stopping in to make sure we can see with our own eyes you are okay."

"Ma," he said again, stepping closer. "Listen to me."

"I will not!" she snapped. "I don't care if you came home for holidays and we would see you only a week or two here and there. When you hear that your baby boy has been shot and rushed to Germany for better medical care, then is forced to come home to get better, you do not wait four weeks to come see your mother!"

She burst out crying. Chris rushed across the room to her and took her much shorter body into his arms, pulling her to his chest and holding her as sobs wracked over her frame. He got it.

He was such an ass.

"I'm sorry," he murmured, his mouth at the top of her hair. She still smelled of autumn spices, something he'd always associated with her. Her hair also had more gray in it than he'd seen last year when he'd been home for Christmas, but under all of that, she was still just his mom.

Her little fists smacked at him every so often, followed by a soothing mother's touch. If his heart didn't feel as if it was crumbling to the ground with each cry she wrenched out, he might have laughed.

Instead, he felt like absolute shit for doing this to her. And he had no excuse. He should have been here the day after he'd come home. He'd been too wrapped up in his own world, had grown too independent on himself, to realize that he had others who wanted him to rely on them.

His mother included.

Karen pulled back in his arms and took his face between her hands, her eyes watery, tears tracking along her cheeks. "Ma," he said again. "Stop crying. I'm fine. I'm here. I'm alive."

"Don't do that again, Christopher Daniel," she admonished. "You've just bought yourself yard duty with that stunt. And pool cleaning for the next month. I expect to see you over here more."

He wouldn't remind her he was in his mid-thirties, that she really couldn't hold that kind of punishment over his head, but they'd both know he would be lying. He'd be over more per her wish and do his punishment because it was the right thing to do.

"Come give your old man a hug, too," Pop said from behind, and Chris turned to do as bid. His pop gave a hearty slap on his back that caused him to wince before pulling away. Not fast enough though, if Pop's face was any indication. "Sorry, son, are you okay?"

Chris nodded. "It's healing up fine."

"Sit," Ma said and motioned toward the stools at the island. "I'll get you some food and you can tell us all about what's going on with you."

Knowing this was the real reason he'd come home today, he did as told and went through it all, from the mission—leaving out the confidential stuff and his suspicions about the leak, to his injuries and DA's, and the recovery needed for both. His partner's retirement, and the town's new veterinarian.

The roasted pork was as good as it smelled, spices exploding on his tongue and the meat soft enough to make a man beg for more.

He pushed his bowl across the table with a questioning look to his mother, for which she grinned and scooped up another serving.

"So, what are your plans with Delta Alpha?" Pop asked.

He lifted a shoulder and dug in for more roast, chewing and swallowing before responding. "I have no say in him coming out of retirement. That's a done deal. There's a lot that goes behind keeping an MWD's certifications up and there's no way I can safely say he's not going to relapse at the most inopportune time. So, I'm adopting him. I plan to give him a good life … for what he has left. It's the least I can do."

"I think that's a good plan," his pop responded. "What about you? This Barber guy brings up a good point. You only have four more years before retirement, then you'll be set with a paycheck that comes in every month for life. Four years doesn't seem that long in the whole scheme of things."

It didn't, that was true. But he wasn't sure that was what he wanted to do. He shrugged. "I'm not sure. Still thinking that through."

Daniel lifted a brow. "Wanna share what you're thinking?"

Chris finished his second helping of roast then pushed the bowl away, his stomach full to bursting. "There are … some things I can't say yet, but I'm not real certain I'm up for another four years." He lifted a hand when his mother opened her mouth. "It's a lot of stress on the body and mind. While I think I could get through that, I'm uncertain I want to. I was thinking of starting my own contracting firm to do some security missions. Ones I will have control over. There's a lot that goes on behind the scenes with these missions. And I'm wondering if, or how, I could build a team that would, or could, make that process better."

"I'm not going to pretend I understand any of what you just said, son, but I know you'll make the right decision," Pop answered with a conviction that made Chris sit a little taller.

He nodded. What more could be said? Nothing he wanted to put on their shoulders. They were all things he needed to work out, stuff he needed to communicate with his team. The compromise of their mission was looking more and more like they'd been set up. But why? And by whom?

"Anyhow," he said and wiped his mouth with a napkin, "how are my brothers doing? Have you all heard from them? I saw D in town a few days ago, and Matt gave me the code to his garage to get my truck, but outside of some short texts, I haven't been able to keep in touch or up-to-date with any of what they are doing."

His mother laughed, the sound so much better than her heartbreaking cries from earlier. He shot her a grin. "Oh, *mijo*, you boys are all so much alike. It's a wonder you came from different places."

His father winked at her before turning to Chris.

"Mike is still working with the Secret Service. He's down in Washington right now on the SWAT Team. Met some pretty young lady he's been seeing for a few months now. Your mother keeps asking him to bring her up, but you know how Mike can be."

He nodded. Mike looked at meeting the parents as the equivalent to promising marriage. He'd only bring a woman home when she was the one. He also spent so much time in the gym doing CrossFit that it was any wonder he had any kind of social life at all.

"Matt is still doing his thing with the DEA. He's off on some assignment and calls only slightly more than you do," his mother said with an admonishing frown. "Last I heard he was somewhere in South America, but a few weeks before he'd been in Texas. So who knows where he is now."

"Jake," his father inserted, "is still in New York and was recently promoted to detective. He's coming home this next weekend, so maybe you might want to stop by then."

"Sounds like a plan. Be good to catch up with Jakey Snakey."

His mother laughed again. "I'm still curious how he got that nickname."

Chris shook his head. "There are some things a son cannot tell his mother. Sorry."

His pop chuckled, then said, "And Luke just graduated from the US Marshal Academy, so he's getting geared up for what he's going to do. So far it's been serving in some court cases."

"Okay," he said, "that's great and all, but I need the dirty. Give me the juice, something that I might be able to either wow them with knowing when I see or talk to them next, or something that they might not want their big brother knowing."

"You mean the big brother that teases them mercilessly?" Ma asked with a smirk.

"Um, is that not a reason to live?" he asked back.

His pop's bark of laughter was short and loud. "All right, son. Grab a beer from the fridge and let's settle in. This might take a while."

And he did. This … *this* was why he came home.

Chapter Twelve

Late the next night, Samantha fell into bed with a sigh. Thunder rumbled over her apartment, sounding loud upstairs. It had been a humid day, so her normally tame hair seemed to grow a mind of its own and poof in every which way. She'd ended up setting the mass in a messy bun atop her head and set in to get the day's tasks completed.

It'd been a full day of appointments and well-care visits. The town seemed receptive to having a new vet, and some horror stories she heard about the surrounding town veterinarians had made the hairs on her arms stick up. From broken bones failing to set, to the wrong medications being administered, she'd made a vow to the town's folks, and their furry friends, that she'd do everything in her power to be there for them all, to care for them all, and to provide the best medical support she could.

As a result of the busy day, she'd been late getting to the other tasks she had and by the time she and Hailey had managed to get all the rooms clean, she'd been a walking zombie. This would be an adjustment. That was what she kept telling herself, from the weather to the people, to the culture, her ever-growing worry regarding her pregnancy, and the new business pains. She couldn't be happier that things were going so well, but she needed to think about getting another assistant. One that could hold down the fort when she went out on maternity leave.

She winced. She still needed to get in to see a doctor.

Good business practice would be to wait a few

months to settle in before she decided to bring in an assistant, but she had a very real need for one, and would need someone who knew the ins and outs of her business before she went on leave. The thought of waiting even one or two more months before getting the additional support she needed now made her bones ache even more.

She closed her eyes on that last thought, only to have them jar open again what seemed to be minutes later. A loud boom shook the apartment, followed by a flash of light outside, then another boom.

The storm…

Wind howled outside her window and downstairs DA whined. She took a moment to glance at the clock, which was dark. *Ugh.* "Power must be out. Dang it."

She had an emergency generator that would power certain pieces of necessary equipment and the alarm to the main clinic, but that generator didn't extend to the upstairs. From the low whirring of an engine she heard between the rain and thunder, she knew it was on.

She needed to check on DA and the clinic. He normally came upstairs, as he'd graduated to sleeping upstairs, but he wasn't in his usual spot. When she'd gone to sleep, he'd been beside her bed deep in doggy dreamland.

Slipping out of bed, she grabbed for her pants. Because of the darkness in her apartment and the storm outside, it was difficult to find her way out of the studio and to the stairs that led to the clinic below. Only the deep glow of blue lights—set to charge constantly in the electrical outlets when the power was on—sporadically placed along the clinic's walls helped kept her from tumbling down the stairs.

At the bottom, she slid under the hutch separating the front reception from the clinic. "Delta boy," she called.

A low, growling noise responded, sounding to the rear of the room near the back door. Memories of a few weeks back when DA had first cornered her at the desk flipped through her mind, but she pushed it away. He wasn't the same dog, and she wasn't the same vet as she'd been then. She understood now how she'd need to interact with him should he have a setback. Sure, fear still coursed through her veins. He was a trained animal, designed to bite and kill on command, but over the course of the past few weeks, she liked to think their bond had grown to where he wouldn't hurt her.

"Delta Alpha," she called again, moving toward the back door.

His low grumble and whine responded to her almost immediately. A light-blue light next to the back door illuminated him standing there, shaking and cowering.

"Damn it," she said under her breath, witnessing a setback happen before her eyes. It must be the thunder. Even she had to admit it was loud and scary.

DA pawed at the door and rather than holding him in from doing any business he may need to do, she turned the alarm off to the clinic and opened the door.

He shot out like a cannon. With the door open, the storm was even louder. Rain came down in a wave, and with each gust of wind, it sent the liquid smacking against her. Lightning spun one rod after another, followed by the clash and bang of thunder.

DA's whines and growls filled the air, his entire body shaking with the force of his fear. He completed his business quickly but rather than coming back inside, he went to a corner and curled into a ball, his lips curled back from his teeth, and growled viciously. She could hear him over the storm, but the image was clear as if it was day.

She couldn't leave him outside like that, nor did she know how to get him inside. She tried a few commands, but he didn't respond.

With nothing left to do, she grabbed DA's leash and headed outside. Rain soaked her to the skin immediately, hitting her like needles with its force. Wind pushed her body sideways as she tried to make it to DA's side. With each step closer to him, his growls became louder to her ears.

"Delta Alpha," she tried in her most stern voice, "come!"

He let out a snarling sound in response. Definitely a setback. And with the thunder sounding even louder by the second, she knew she was in over her head. She needed Chris. As much as she hated to have to call him so late, as much as she regretted having gotten herself in this situation—again—and as much as she wished she didn't have to ask him to drive in this storm, there was no one else available that could get DA calmed down and inside the facility but him.

She went to turn and a loud snarl froze her in her tracks. *Shit. Not this again.*

Rain pushed her hair over her head, drawing the strands over her face and eyes. She didn't dare move. Not with the sounds coming out of DA's mouth.

The snarling came closer and closer until she shook with the need to run. That would be the worst thing she could do with a dog. The growling sounded as if it were right on top of her and she jumped slightly as DA brushed against her leg then stood sentry in front of her. She didn't dare move. Didn't dare look down, but she had a suspicious feeling he stood guard for her. Why else wasn't he attacking her?

She risked a peek and sure enough, DA faced forward in front of her, growling into the shadows off to the corner of her yard in a spot she couldn't see without light. That spot caused some concern as it had a walkway that led out to the front of the building.

"Delta Alpha, heel!" came a familiar voice.

Relief rushed through her body like a drug, almost taking her knees out from under her. DA sprinted away, causing her skin to practically jump from her body. She turned to the back door, pushed the hair from her face, and looked at Chris.

DA stood at his side, his doggy body quivering under the sounds of the storm, his face buried in Chris's hands. "You look like a drowned rat," he said as a greeting.

She laughed, the sound somewhat hysterical. "How did you get in?"

He gave her a look. "Your front door was unlocked. And it was a good damn thing considering what I just walked in on."

Hmmm, he didn't sound happy, but still... "The front door was locked."

He lifted a brow. "Uh, sweetheart, I'm here, aren't I? It wasn't."

She frowned. "It had to be locked. I remember..." Did she? Did she lock the front door?

"Red, the front door was unlocked. Think we can move past that now. How about you get inside? It's raining."

She shot him a look in return. One that told him he was Captain Obvious as she moved to the back door. Once inside, she grabbed towels from the spare rack and tossed him a couple to dry off DA. He did so with quick hands, his movements somewhat aggravated.

Once complete, he tossed the towels in the standing white hamper next to the rack then turned his attention to her. His mouth thinned. "Now, you wanna tell me why this is the second time I've walked in on DA about to rip your head off?"

She settled her hands on her hips, not liking his tone. "Um, first off"—he winced, as he should seeing as when a woman started her response with a list, you knew she was pissed. "Chris, why don't you take a moment to listen to the storm? The thunder scared him. Second, he wasn't about to rip my head off, he was growling at something in the yard. If you paused and paid attention to where he was, he had been standing in front of me, guarding"—she pointed to her chest—"me."

He tossed his hands out. "Why do you think I'm here? I had a feeling something like that would happen. What I want to know is what the hell do you think you were doing engaging with him when he was like that?"

She tossed a wet towel in the hamper and grabbed another, wrapping her hair with it. "It's my job."

"He's a military working dog," he snapped, his tone beyond pissed off.

Well, fine, she could get just as pissed. "I seem to recall that, Christopher."

He sucked in a breath. "By God, woman, if I didn't have the sense to know I needed to take care of DA right now, I'd put you over my knee."

The area between her legs convulsed at the image that shot to mind, but her anger was so much more. An anger she relished in, because despite the fact that she was going back and forth with Chris in what was clearly a heated argument, despite him being visibly angry, she didn't fear him. With Manuel, she would have cowered and waited for the beating to begin. A newfound confidence rolled through her. "How dare you?" she yelled.

DA barked a low warning, bringing her back into focus. It seemed to snap Chris out of it, too, for he immediately hunched down to speak in low tones to his dog. She spun on her heel, done with the conversation and done with Chris. Soaked to the bone, she wanted to get out of her clothes.

Without explaining herself, she left the clinic and dashed up the stairs to change. She ripped off the soggy clothing, right on down to her underwear, then slipped on a pair of black, fleece-lined track pants, ignoring how the waistline felt a little snug, a bra, and a long-sleeved white t-shirt. On her way back out of the apartment, she grabbed the matching jacket to the pants and slipped it on as well. Her feet were still cold, seeing as she'd gone outside without shoes on, but the pants were long enough to cover the tops of her feet, and the rest of this conversation with Chris wouldn't take long.

He could take his brooding, bad attitude and go back to sleep. Maybe tomorrow, he'd wake up and rethink his approach toward her.

Yeah, he'd riled her up, and she wasn't thinking straight about how to handle him.

She hit the bottom of the stairs, rounded the hutch again, and came to a stop as Chris walked out from where she kept DA's kennel with his dog following at his side. At the sight of the muzzle now strapped to DA, she saw red.

"Seriously?" she snapped.

"What part of him being a military working dog do you not get?"

"But he's better now."

Lightning and thunder struck on the heels of that statement, causing DA to cower close to Chris's side. Chris raised a brow, and despite the darkness of the room, she saw his expression clearly.

"Chris," she said on a sigh. "I don't like muzzling him. It can't be comfortable, and once the storm passes, he'll be better."

He matched her sigh. "Look, I don't like it any more than you do, but I don't want to take a chance that he will bite you. You wouldn't believe the fear I felt when I walked outside, how…" He clenched his hands at his sides and looked away.

And she got it. All at once, her anger rushed out and, in its place rose a more tender emotion. All this time, she'd been trying to keep him at arm's length, when he'd been trying to open the line of friendship. And without her even realizing it, he'd burrowed right in, just like DA had done. That Chris had to experience something being out of his control, a man who thrived on controlling everything around him from his dog, to his mission, to how he trained his own body, must feel like he was completely losing it, seeing he couldn't really control anything.

That was just life.

She took a step toward him, hunched down, and reached for DA. "Come here, boy."

"Red," Chris started, but she raised a hand.

"Delta Alpha, come," she said again, voice gentle but holding a command.

DA dropped his head and lumbered over, kicking his head under her hand once he reached her. His tiny doggy tongue came out in the small space and licked her palm. "I know you're sorry for being scared, big guy. But the three of us will get through this together. You have to learn to trust me. And stop growling."

She leaned down to whisper in his ear. "And we both know you'd do nothing to hurt me. I thank you for protecting us from whatever was outside." Something *was* out there, and as much as Chris wanted to dismiss it, she was sure of it.

DA's tail thumped behind him as she gave him a

rubdown, taking care to not go near his still-recovering injuries. Once she had DA rolling over to his belly, she finished petting him before she stood and faced his handler.

"The same goes for you."

He crossed his arms over his chest, causing the material of his long-sleeve white shirt to stretch.

"You need to trust me," she said. "And stop growling, too. The three of us will get through this together."

He stepped closer and kicked up the side of his mouth. "Are you going to give me a rubdown, too?"

She laughed, the sound startled out of her, then asked, "You want your belly rubbed, big guy?"

He waggled his brows. This man was entirely too handsome for his own good. Especially since he'd started letting his facial hair grow in. The soft covering made him look more rustic, as if he belonged in the great outdoors with his dog at his side. "Maybe not my belly, but I got something else in mind."

She laughed again, and his smile grew.

He cupped her cheek, stopping only inches away. There, he dropped his face until he hovered even closer. "All jokes aside, Red. I don't know what I'd do if something happened to you."

With the mood twisting suddenly to something serious, she took a moment to catch up. They'd known each other for a few weeks, but somehow, she knew she wouldn't be able to dismiss his words with a joke. The set of his jaw and what he also communicated with his eyes told her he'd never been more serious in his life. "I'll take care next time when dealing with him," she promised.

He moved closer, bringing his other hand up to thread through the hair at her nape. "I'm not just talking about with DA. I see that hand you've been holding out, keeping me at a distance, Red, and I meant it when I said I want to be here for you. I know you have secrets. We all do. When I tell you I'd do everything in my power to keep you happy and safe, I mean that."

She couldn't help it. She leaned forward until her body met his, chest to chest. He supported most of her, seeing as she'd given him her weight. And she had to admit, it felt good. Better than good. It'd been a long time since she'd felt so warm, so comfortable this close to a man. "I believe you," she said, and she did. That much she was sure of.

His gaze dropped to her mouth before lifting again to meet her eyes. "You going to drop that hand?"

She bit the inside of her bottom lip. With everything that had happened before, with her history, with the baby, and even how busy she was now, this request surprised her, both coming from him as well as the fact that she considered it. "Can you be patient?"

He made a low sound, almost a growl. "Baby, I'm one of the most patient men you'll ever meet. In everything I do."

That caused a shiver. He felt it, too, for his eyes, so close, heated with hunger.

His gaze dropped to her mouth again. "I'm going to kiss you, Red."

Her stomach clenched. She wanted that, too. "O-okay."

"You get what I'm saying?"

Huh? Did she…? "You're going to kiss me."

"Yeah." This time, he growled.

"Okay, then do it."

"I will."

"I'm waiting."

"Now who is impatient?"

"Chris—" she said, but he cut her off and covered her mouth with his. His lips brushed against hers once, twice, before his tongue came out and traced the seam, requesting entry. She parted her lips, thinking he wanted inside, but he moved so painstakingly slow, tracing along the edges before moving in and sucking her top, then bottom lip into his mouth.

Her stomach flipped, and the area between her legs tingled. Good Lord in heaven, this man could kiss. And he'd been right. He was so patient. He hadn't even put his tongue inside her mouth yet!

His hands tightened in her hair, drawing her closer as one left her face and wrapped in a band around her waist, lining their bodies up from crotch to chest. He pulled her up, plastering her along the length of him, tilted her head back more, and then plunged inside.

And goodness, all she could do was hold on for the ride of her life.

He thrust deep, encouraging her participation by wrapping his tongue around hers, then sucking hers into his mouth. She whimpered and pulled at his shoulders, wanting to be closer, as if it were possible.

Instead, he ravaged her mouth, drew out her pleasure, and surrounded her in every way.

And even though it was only a kiss, it felt so much more intimate than anything she'd ever done. She could grow addicted to his touch, his taste, could see herself acting like a junkie just for a hit of him.

That last thought should scare her, but all she could think was she never wanted the kiss to end. Hell, she kind of wanted more. Like a between-the-sheets, whispers-in-the-night, moaning more. The problem was she still had yet to tell him about the baby.

Chapter Thirteen

Chris's heart thundered in his chest so hard it was a wonder she couldn't feel it against hers. And the poor organ was definitely getting its share of adrenaline today, with the scene he'd walked in on between Samantha and DA earlier, and now this kiss.

But could it really be described just as *a kiss*?

It felt like so much more. She tasted of so much more. Of warmth and sunshine, of attitude and laughter, of caring and vulnerability. Hidden sensuality all wrapped into one curvy package called Samantha.

Her breasts pillowed against his chest and despite the layers of clothing, her nipples poked against him, demanding attention.

Her body was plastered along the length of his until every divot, every curve, and angle of hers became his own. His cock pulsed between his legs and against her stomach, begging for more, wanting to get inside the sweet space between her thighs. She clutched and pulled at his shoulders, so he tensed and prepared to catch her as she hopped up and wrapped her legs around his waist.

Then it was go, go, go. He kept kissing her, walking toward the stairs, breaking off from her mouth only to give DA a command to stay. He half-walked, half-stumbled his way up the stairs with her in his arms. She nipped and sucked at his neck. Around him, she felt like a soft, satin pillow he wanted to bury inside of. His hunger for her became wild and consuming.

His hunger. Hers. He didn't know which was which anymore.

They fell to the bed, yanking at each other's clothing. He licked and bit exposed skin, the slope of her neck, her collarbone, where the curve of her waist met her hip. He couldn't get enough, and from the sounds she made, low groaning and soft gasps, neither could she.

"Chris," she breathed.

"Right here, Red."

"There's something … oh, my God, that feels so good."

He practically ripped off her simple, white laced bra, making a note to apologize later before he fell on her tits like a starving male. Full, big enough to overfill his palms, her breasts rose in the air like a man's biggest temptation. And they were. Soft and perfectly shaped, they were what many men would write sonnets about. Become poets just to capture their beauty with words.

He was no poet, though. He was very much a breast man, however.

In between the lightning strikes, rose-colored nipples no larger than a quarter made his mouth water. Answering the demand Samantha gave with her hands in his hair and his own body's hunger, he dipped and took a tempting bud into his mouth.

Beneath him, she cried out, tossing her head back and arching her spine while tightening her fingers against his scalp. She smelled of woman and comfort, but more than anything, her essence gave him every feeling of contentment. Something he'd never had before.

Needing more contact, he palmed her other breast and tweaked the ignored nipple before he pushed up on his knees, drawing and spreading her legs with him, and began to replicate what he wanted to do without clothes.

His cock pulsed painfully within the confines of his pants and boxers. The heat between her legs saturated through their pants. He wanted more, needed more, craved every bit she would give. But he didn't want to rush this. Not this first time with her.

"Chris," she moaned, and Christ, the sound of his name from her mouth caused his cock to weep. "I need to tell you something. We need to slow down for a second … oh my, do that again."

She ran her nails along his back, and he switched attention, covering her other breast with his mouth and sucking deep. Her hands fisted at the back of his pants. She wanted his pants off. He was all too happy to help.

Ripping his mouth away, he leaned up and pushed his pants down while she scooted back to do the same. She hesitated and damn if his heart didn't stop on a dime. Her indecisive eyes looked up at him.

"What is it?" he asked and squeezed the base of his cock to try to calm down. He was ready to blow, and he hadn't even been inside her yet.

She took a quick, wide-eyed glance at what his hand did, and yeah, it made him shallow, but his chest puffed out a bit at her look. His dick jumped again and damn, but he really needed to be inside her before he embarrassed himself.

"There's something I need to tell you."

He wanted to groan, his need driving through his veins. But whatever she wanted to say must be important as her facial expression turned serious. He tried to calm his rapidly beating heart. He leaned back, ass to the back of his calves under him and focused on her face, showing her she had his entire attention, not that she didn't have it before.

"What, Red?"

"I-I…" She bit her lip, which had the unfortunate effect—for him—of making her look sexier. Her kiss-swollen lips, hair mused from his hands, and being half-naked called to him like nothing had before.

She moved surprisingly quickly with a shake of her head, then whipped off her pants and panties, tossing them across the room before lying back on the bed, spread eagle.

Christ!

He fumbled with his pants, trying to kick off his shoes and getting tangled.

"Chris, please," she whispered, a hand between her legs, watching him from beneath heavily hooded eyes.

"Hold on, sweetheart. My pants are caught on my shoes." He flipped over, pushing at one shoe.

"It's coming. Please, Chris." Her body bowed up, the hand between her legs moving quicker. Eyes closed, she looked like a sexual goddess put on the planet to tempt any man.

"Samantha," he said, arrested by the sight.

She opened her eyes and focused dazedly on his face. "It's been too long. Please," she urged.

He cursed, forgot about his pants, grabbed his wallet, slipped on a condom in record time, and then, with no finesse or another way to describe it, fell between her thighs.

Her limbs wrapped around him, the hand between her legs coming up to clutch in his hair, and he sank deep between her thighs with one powerful thrust.

They both moaned at the feeling. She wrapped around his cock with such a silken heat his eyes crossed. His toes curled. She was a vise around him, her walls holding him tight, almost too tight.

"Red," he said on a breath, stilling, "I don't want to hurt you, sweetheart. Let's slow down."

In response, she wrapped her legs around his, rotated her hips up, and kissed him, urging against his mouth, "Move."

Unable to hold back after that demand, but keeping in mind about the possibility of hurting her, he did. He set a rhythm that punished them both for waiting so long. She met him thrust for thrust, her hands clutching at any part of him she could get ahold of. He wanted to spread his legs and change his stance to get closer, but his pants were still locked around the bottom half of him.

Instead, he wrapped one arm around the top of her head, the other around the slat in her headboard, and gave her everything she asked for.

She stared up at him, her eyes full of hungry desire, her face a mask of decadent delight. Her nails bit into his ass cheeks, urging him to give more. So, he did. He fucked her until it felt like he'd burrow deep inside and never come out.

Her walls tightened around him, telling him she was close.

"Give it to me," he demanded, and her eyes grew hazy.

He dipped his head, touched his tongue behind her ear, and then told her again, "Come for me, Red."

She did. Her walls gripped him with such strength he wouldn't have been able to hold back even if he tried, which he did not. One thrust, two, and he shouted out his release, hearing her call out at the same time.

In the back of his mind, he wondered at the beauty of coming with his partner, something he'd never experienced before. He also wondered at the glorious mark of a woman who could come with just his cock.

He pushed in and stayed rooted inside, his cock twitching in its release before he lifted his head and kissed her. She matched his mouth, kiss for kiss. This one differed from before, slow, lazy, almost as if in gratitude for what they'd just experienced.

And he was thankful, at least. Thankful that she'd finally given him a piece of her, though her gift had been more than he'd ever hoped for.

****

After dealing with the condom, Chris rejoined Samantha in bed, taking her within his arms. He liked that she hadn't hesitated to curl right into him, and it wasn't because of the chill in the air. Sure, despite them knowing each other, and meeting each other under an extremely stressful situation, there was something about her that made him want to hold on and never let go.

A surprising discovery, since he'd never been one to want such a commitment. He had married teammates, or those in long-term, but what he did, what they all did, would never be used as a poster-board for how to make relationships last. They were deployed too much, gone for weeks at a time without any contact with home. The stress of knowing someone was waiting on you, questioning your every move, couldn't be risked based on the areas they went to and the level of classification they dealt with.

He'd heard horror stories regarding broken relationships, the trust questioned, and the families who all suffered. It hadn't given him hope or even a wish to move into the same boat. The extra stress wasn't worth it.

But then he'd come home, and he'd see his parents and their relationship, and even more recent was Charlie and that FBI agent, Rossi. Those relationships gave him pause and caused him to wonder if he could actually do it. If he could make something worth it work.

With Samantha in his arms, he found the opportunity of something to work for. She was definitely worth it. The question was, would she see him as someone to take that kind of chance with?

While he'd been thinking, she hadn't said a word. He curled her tighter to him. "What's got you so quiet?"

he asked.

She trailed her fingers along his back, a soft caress. "I could ask the same of you."

"I asked you first," he said on a smile.

She chuckled. "Is it always a competition with you?"

"Sweetheart," he said and gave a quick squeeze of his arms, "when you grow up in a house with five brothers, then join the military at seventeen only to get an even bigger family who all compete against each other, there's really no other way to be."

Her chest shook again his with silent laughter, and he had to push the feel of her breasts against his chest out of his mind, otherwise, they'd get no sleep.

"Your poor mother."

He grinned, staring out the window across the room. Below sat a dark dresser, bare on top as if she hadn't had a chance to move in. He could sympathize. His house barely looked as if he lived there, and he had owned it for over ten years. "Daniel and Karen Gonzalez aren't of blood, but they are the best part of my life. Always will be."

Samantha pulled back and laid her head next to his, staring into his eyes. "I have so many questions, I don't even know where to begin."

"Ask your questions. Start wherever."

Her eyes widened, showing the whites more as if surprised. "How old were you when you were adopted?"

"Nine. Old enough to know my past, but too young to understand it."

"What do you mean by that?"

"Well," he said, kicking a leg under hers and pulling one long thigh over his hip. Not to try anything, but more because he wanted her closer. "Both of my birth-parents were arrested for some drug offenses around the time we were taken from the only place we called home. Had it not been the third time, and had the charges not been what they were, which was felony possession with an intent to sell, things might have been different. I definitely wouldn't be where I am today, not even close."

He paused for a moment, but when she said nothing, he went on, getting lost in the memories. "Karen hadn't been the social worker assigned at first, but she was the third. By the time she found me, I had ended up getting kicked out of multiple foster homes because of fighting and disrupting the peace." He kept talking over her gasp. In his chest, something clenched at the thought of those times and something or someone he had lost. He tried to hold on to the thought, but it slipped away.

He sighed. "Turns out both of my grandparents had wanted nothing to do with me … us?" he asked in question. Why did it feel as if there had been someone else? Samantha adjusted her leg, bringing him back to the present, and he shook his head. "Anyhow, they had wiped their hands of their own children years ago when both robbed them blind. But all I could remember back then was feeling nothing but a blinding anger at everyone I came into contact with. They say it came from a lot of the neglect I … we … shit, *I* experienced from years of being forgotten about. Heck, even after my parents were arrested that final time, it took the principal calling to report my absence for so many days in a row to even get someone to realize I'd been left behind."

"Why do you keep changing it, as if you're talking in the plural sense?"

He shook his head again, trying to think. "I don't really know. It's almost like I'm forgetting about someone who had been with me then."

She lifted a brow, but he didn't have an answer.

He didn't understand it either.

"Chris, I'm so sorry."

He shrugged, having worked through the past. He still felt the pain, but now he could manage it. "It is what it is. Had none of that happened, I wouldn't be where I am today."

"That's one way to look at it, but it still isn't right. No child should have to experience that."

He nodded once. "You're right. But with people like Karen and Daniel Gonzalez, at least there's hope at the end of that dark tunnel."

He pulled her against him again, loving the feel of her skin on his.

"You're amazing, you know that?" she said, her voice soft.

He pulled her in tighter. "Not amazing. I'm just driven to be the best I can be with the cards I've been dealt. There are a lot of things that could have been done differently, but I knew my path from the moment my pop, Daniel, took me to a football game at West Point. It wasn't the big football players, or the field, the pomp and circumstance of the event, it was what I saw outside of that. Those standing guard to the base, the soldiers standing around and helping others. I wanted to give back and get to a place where I could do that. So, I decided then I would join the military."

"And you did."

"Yeah," he said with a short laugh. "And you should have seen Ma's face when I came home with the enlistment papers at seventeen, just after 9/11. I had to get their permission, of course, but after a few days of pushing my case and the reasoning behind it, they finally relented. Though I don't think I'll ever get the sight of Ma's face out of my mind the day I left for boot camp."

"She loves you. Are you the oldest?"

He nodded, but still said, "Yeah. I was the first they adopted. But by then, we had a full house. Still, she said it was like seeing her most troubled heart leave."

"She still wants to look out for you. I bet it was hard to let you go after everything you all had been through."

"It was, for both of us, but it was for the best."

They were both quiet for a few minutes, the sound of the rain from outside growing softer. The storm was passing. "I'm glad you have that," she said.

He pulled back to look at her. She wouldn't meet his eyes for long periods of time, only glanced at him every so often. Her fingers played with the hair at his chest as if she were distracted. "You ready to tell me what happened?" he asked, hoping, really hoping she said yes. He wanted to remove those shadows from her eyes.

She bit her lip, glanced at him again, but shook her head, and his hopes plummeted. He tried to not let the disappointment show.

"Not the full story yet, Chris. I need time."

He got it. But still, it stung. To cover that up, he pulled her close again, pushing his leg up higher between hers. She shivered and moved closer, the fingers that had been on his back moving over the curve of his ass. Perhaps she wanted to distract him, or maybe the position of their bodies, but it seemed like she was up for another round. He was only all too happy to comply.

Hooking his hand under her knee, he pushed his leg higher until the warmth between her legs rested against his thigh. His cock lengthened between them, coming to rest against her belly. If he pushed his hips up, as he was tempted to do, he knew the tip of his dick would slide between her plump breasts.

Her mouth opened over the base of his throat, her

tongue coming out to swirl and lick against his skin. She moved against him in a lazy grind, using his thigh to work her pleasure higher. He loved how responsive she'd been earlier, how she went after her pleasure and took it. If that was what it had been like for their first time, he could only imagine what more trust and time would bring.

They'd be explosive.

Her breath stuttered across his collarbone as her hips rotated faster against his thigh. He pressed her ass against him, encouraging the movement as he pushed his hips forward, working his length against the softness of her belly.

With each thrust, the tip of his dick touched the underside of her breasts, beckoning.

"Chris, yes," she whispered against his neck, her head tilting back. He took the offering and dipped his head, tangling his tongue with hers for a deep kiss.

She panted in his mouth and rolled her hips faster, taking her pleasure. "Don't stop," she begged."

"Baby, I don't have any plans on stopping anything." He rolled his thigh higher, spreading her wider, when her breath hitched and she cried out. Her hips rocked against his leg wantonly, her eyes losing focus, face awash in pleasure. He'd never seen anything so beautiful.

"Fuck, Red, you're fucking gorgeous when you come."

She smiled a little lazily then wrapped her hand around his throbbing shaft. "Let's take care of you now, shall we?"

He grinned lopsidedly but stilled her hand. "Lie on your back."

She did, her brows coming up in question. He removed her hand from him, bringing both of hers to the sides of her breasts and pushed them together, plumping her tits high. She glanced to the side, and he suspected she gave a pretty blush, but she looked magnificent, holding her tits for him.

"Stay right there," he ordered then reached to the side and grabbed the bottle of lotion on her nightstand. He put some in his palm, coated his cock with it, then climbed over Samantha, a knee on each side of her arms. Shifting, he brought his cock to her chest, watching as her eyes grew hungry before she pushed her breasts closer, and he slid inside the haven she'd created.

His head rolled back on his neck at the feel of such softness, yet tightness, surrounding his pulsing shaft. He pumped forward, using her chest to work him higher, loving the fire in her eyes. She was enjoying this, too.

Each thrust pushed him higher and higher up her chest, his excitement causing his length to grow. Samantha tilted her head and opened her mouth, allowing each swipe to slide inside the wet haven. Just the tip. *Christ!*

He wanted to ask her to stretch her neck to take more of him, but his hips were losing their rhythm, the sight and feel of her almost too much to take. He grunted, a tightness at the base of his spine building, ready to explode.

"Sam," he said, voice rough. "I'm about to come."

She looked up and met his eyes, then as if reading his mind, stretched her neck and took more of him with each swipe. The coil at the base of his spine sprang open and exploded. Samantha held his gaze as she took all he offered, sucking him dry, drawing out his pleasure with a little flick of her tongue.

He stilled, grabbing the slats of her bedframe

before gently removing himself from her mouth. He dropped down, wrapping her in his arms and kissing her softly. "Jesus. Jesus," he said, speechless.

She smiled and spread her legs, letting him fall between. "Ready again?"

"Jesus," he said again, and she laughed.

A low growling noise came from downstairs, causing the hairs on the back of his neck to stand. They both froze.

He must really be out of his element, not in the field anymore, as Samantha shot out of bed before he had a chance to react, scrambling from beneath him like the covers were on fire.

"Red," he said, rolling over the side and coming to his feet. She hopped into her pants and grabbed a sweater.

"He has a muzzle on," she said, running from the room.

He grabbed his boxers on the move, really missing his piece, which sat in the gun safe back at his cabin. DA didn't sound too happy. His snarls reached up the stairs at a deafening sound, getting louder and more aggravated by the second. "Dammit, Red, wait!" His request was useless as she'd already disappeared from his sight.

He took the stairs two at a time, coming to a stop behind her, DA flanking her side. The Shepherd's hackles quivered, standing at attention, pressed tight to Samantha's side as both woman and dog looked out the front window.

Good news was at least DA focused on whatever had caught his attention outdoors, and not on her situated at his side. Bad news, she was still too damn close to his dog, especially one growling. But the weird thing was that it seemed as if DA were protecting her.

She turned to him, wide-eyed, but didn't move from DA's side. "He must really have some territorial instincts."

Chris looked to the other side of the wet glass and tried to focus past the shining glow of the yellow streetlight outside, but he didn't see anything or anyone. "Why do you say that?" He purposely stepped between her and DA. His partner ceased growling and gave a little whine, looking up at Chris then back outside.

With a quick snap, he released the muzzle and tossed it aside.

"Some guy was walking down the street. Why would Delta Alpha react like that?"

Chris shook his head, craning his neck to see past the shadows along the sidewalk. Nothing. "He's never acted like that before. You get a look at the guy?"

"No, only saw the back of him. He looked like he was limping pretty bad though."

Chris's heart, which had been coming back down from yet another rush of adrenaline, suddenly spiked in its pulse, slamming against his chest like a sledgehammer. He turned to Samantha. "A limp?"

She nodded. "Yeah, maybe he was hovering too close to the window or something. Can't say as I blame him with the rain and all."

Dread sank in his gut like a block of old butter. The coincidences over the past few days added up to something that had to be impossible. Surely his mind and the different situations were just playing games on him. But after the feelings of being watched, the break-in at his house, the sighting of someone looking like Tayseer, and now this? Something was going on. That much he was sure of. He needed to find out what, once and for all.

Chapter Fourteen

A week and a half passed with no sign of Tayseer in the area. Despite all being calm on that front, Chris was anything but convinced. The events leading up to that rainy night with the mysterious figure were too coincidental for him to dismiss. None of it felt right. And he'd learned on more than one occasion out in the field to trust his gut. If it was telling you to run, you better run—fast.

So, despite being home, on US soil in Nyack, New York, he still looked to the oily feeling in his gut with the only thing it told him: something was about to go FUBAR—fucked up beyond recognition—soon.

Chris grabbed his phone on the heels of that thought, knowing another conversation needed to happen, and dialed Barber's number.

Barber's gruff voice came a second later. "Crack."

"Sir," he said in response.

"Please tell me that while you've been home you haven't been gorging on all that fast food bullshit, letting it weigh you down so I have to worry about carrying your ass across the field in a training exercise and breaking my back from the weight you've put on."

Chris snorted. "Since you've asked so nicely, I won't tell you I've been living and breathing Five Guys," he said, referring to the local, delicious hamburger joint. They weren't so much local as they were national, but that didn't stop the chain from making some of the best burgers he'd ever tasted.

Choked laughter sounded over the line. "Five Guys? You want to tell me something, son?"

Chris squinted out across his yard, trying to make sense of what Barber asked. "That I like hamburgers?" he said, though it came out as a question.

"Wait … is that what the joint is called?"

"Yeah." He paused. "Wait, what did you think I was talking about?"

Barber hooted with laugher and Chris scrunched his face up more. "I don't know anything about what this Five Guys is. You call me saying you've been living and breathing five guys, what am I supposed to think?"

Chris dropped his feet from the railing to the floor with a surprising thud. "Are you shitting me right now?"

Barber's laughter came down through the line again, and yeah, his commander sounded like he was really enjoying himself. The ass.

"Christ," Chris said.

Barber's laughter took a few more minutes to settle. "So, got a bad news/good news situation for you. The rest of the team has been briefed, but I wanted to wait until you called me to tell you."

He hated the sick feeling in his stomach. Being left out of something the team had been told. But it was a feeling he'd have to get used to soon. "Hit me."

"Well, let's just say it's been real busy around here the past few weeks. Had some panties get twisted up at headquarters after everything on the mission went to shit. A lot of people who hadn't asked questions before started asking questions, and one thing led to another before an in-de-pen-dent"—he broke up the word, enunciating each syllable carefully—"contracting investigation agency was brought in to review with our own guys and the CIA. Turns out this contracting agency isn't just good at investigating embezzlements and Joes slipping out on Marthas for a good night with Tina, but they are fucking great at finding shit that wasn't supposed to be found."

Chris scratched his head, trying to keep up with everything. Joe? Tina? "Who is looking at what?"

"Some big-time black op investigators, and when I say black, I mean the blackest of black. Even I didn't know they existed. And I know plenty of super-secret shit, but this group is well above my security clearance."

"Sounds pretty secret," he said lamely, still trying to figure out what was happening. "So, I take it since you said they are fucking great at finding shit, they found something?"

Silence, then, "In case you failed to see through the phone just now, that was me nodding."

Chris's heart slammed against his chest, the impact making his breath catch. He knew it. Knew it! "What did they find?" He took a deep breath.

"A mole."

"Where?"

"In the CI-fucking-A."

"Christ!" Chris sat back in his chair, stunned. That whole mission had been a big headache, one clusterfuck after another. To think there had been a mole the entire time, that they sent his team in under those conditions … he shuddered. It could have been so much worse.

"The mission," Barber went on, "was designed to fail. Pisses me right off knowing what I know now. Would have never sent you guys in had we known even half of this information we do now. And now, with Tayseer in the wind, a whole lot of people high up in the government have some pretty puckered holes."

"That sounds like an understatement," Chris said, leaning forward to catch his head in his free hand. DA's whole career went out the window because of some stupid mole setting them up. Years of hard work gone in an instant. The back of his neck heated under the sun and with renewing anger.

"Needless to say, just about every alphabet-soup agency is searching for that boy. They want him something bad and they are spending tons on inside and outside agencies to achieve that goal."

Chris hesitated to say anything because what if he was wrong? But with the very real threat Tayseer presented, should something have already made it to the US, not saying anything would be wrong. "Actually, I'm not sure if this is anything, but…"

"Spit it out, Crack."

He took a deep breath. "A lot of weird shit has been happening around here. I've had this feeling like I'm being watched, like I have eyes on me all the time."

"Could be just because of all you've been through."

Chris nodded. "True, and I thought the same thing, but I don't think that's quite it. Then, last week I swore I saw Tayseer himself walk out of the library and down the street."

"You check that out?"

"Unfortunately, not. I was in my truck and by the time I tracked that guy down, I couldn't find him. He disappeared."

"Have you gone to talk with anyone yet?"

"Ah, hell," Chris said. "Don't start on that shit with me."

"Look, I don't like it any more than you do, but orders are orders, and maybe with you thinking you are seeing the person who is the cause of where you are right now, maybe that's a sign you need to talk to someone."

"My house was broken into, too," he inserted, wanting to change the subject. He didn't want to see a shrink. Barber remained quiet, so he went on. "Then, last week there was this big night storm and Dumb Ass started growling at this limping figure walking down the street."

"Hell… You get a good look?"

"No, but Samantha did. I heard DA growling and I've never really heard that sound come out of him before. He was pissed."

"Samantha?" Barber asked.

"DA's doc. She's the local vet here."

"Hmmm, Samantha. Night storm. Huh. Since when did one of the most military men I've ever met call someone in a professional capacity by their first name? Not Doctor so-and-so, but Sam-an-tha. I see…"

Chris snorted again and shook his head. "All I'm saying," he went on, pushing that line of conversation away … again, "is all of that adds up to too much. Something is telling me everything isn't as kosher as it should be in Nyack."

"Hmmm," Barber said, and that word weighed on Chris's shoulders like a two-ton bag of concrete. Silence passed by with shuddering ticks and the sound of a branch rubbing against the side of his house. "You're pretty sure about all of this?"

"What aren't you telling me?" he asked, more than convinced there was something. Barber never beat around the bush, and unless he had gone completely off his game, something was up. Chris wouldn't have been able to explain the feeling, but there was one thing: he wasn't being told the entire story.

Barber sighed, the sound coming out as if he carried the weight of an elephant on his back. "All right, it could be nothing, or it could be something, but there's been some chatter going on amongst intel groups, something about numbers passing via encrypted messages between known associates of Tayseer and some unknown email addresses. What's weird is that each time there's an email to this unknown address, no other communication is used on that email. It's the damnedest thing, and something no one has seen before."

Chris screwed up his face, not following. "What kind of numbers?"

"That's the thing, just numbers. A few spooks think it's some kind of code, but no one knows exactly how to break it. There are no patterns to it, nothing that makes any sense based on previous communication. It's up in the air."

"Okay, so what's the big deal about it? What are you seeing that I'm not?" And he wasn't seeing anything. Using numbers to communicate? What were they supposed to do, become computers in order to understand a mathematical language? That Tayseer's group was communicating in this way wasn't surprising. The guy was super-smart. He had developed that insane chemical weapon, after all.

"The IPs have been traced, and while they bounce all over the friggin' globe, one common city keeps popping up."

"Don't say it," he groaned.

"Not Nyack. But close. Just up thirty minutes across the river from you in White Plains."

Chris popped out of his chair, and his back let out a sharp, piercing warning at the sudden movement. "You didn't think to mention this until now?" he asked, his teeth clenched through the pain.

"None of it makes any more sense than I've said. But combined with what you've mentioned, I figured more information couldn't hurt."

He rubbed at his back, trying to massage the muscle into submission. The skin was still tender and raw from where the bullet had shred through him. With the muscles around the wound still tightening in reflexive response, he had learned to move much slower until he healed. "What else? No more holding back."

"There's nothing more, but as soon as something pops up, I will let you know first." He paused while Chris let everything sink in, then, "I think you need a rendezvous."

Again, Chris's face screwed up like he had been sucking on a lemon. "Did shit just get weird between us?"

Barber barked out a laugh. "You wish, but I was thinking more of sending your team out to you, have them look around a bit, ask some questions. What could it hurt? Besides, I think everyone would feel better if they saw you in person and that you were okay."

He rubbed his face, hating that he felt both elated at seeing his team again, yet apprehensive. He'd been thinking long and hard about his decision to stay in the military and had finally settled. To have his team here would make it all so much worse. The guilt would eat at him. Letting them down was the last thing he wanted to do. Sighing, he dropped his hands, knowing the time had come.

"What is it?" Barber asked.

Leave it to his commander to have his finger on each of his men. To be able to read them even through the phone. "I'm not coming back."

Silence.

"Look," he continued, "it's not that I don't appreciate everything you've done for me, for the team, I just think it's time. This last mission and everything that happened, everything that's happening, has set it in stone for me."

"Would you be surprised if I told you I'm not shocked?"

Chris lifted his brows. "Kinda, yeah. When did you figure it out?"

"Before you left Ramstein. I saw it in your eyes." Barber blew out a blustery breath. "I'm still sending the team your way. You have more leave until you're out for good, and I'd rather spend that time doing as we've discussed: letting the team see you're okay and handling this matter with Tayseer, if he's in the area, that is. This shit isn't going to happen the way I think it is on my watch."

He smirked, one side of his mouth kicking up. His commander didn't take anything from anyone. It was a great asset to have—*he* was a great asset to have.

"I'm on board with that plan."

"So, what are you going to do after?" Barber asked.

Chris leaned against the railing that ran the length of his porch and looked out over the yard. Fall was showing, dropping hints of colors in the trees lining the back of his yard. Red, yellow, and orange sparked through the foliage of green, heightening the serene scene he'd always loved. The browning grass could use some TLC, but mostly, it was like a picture out of some fancy calendar. He loved this season, the colors, the cooler weather, the beer, football... "I've been putting some thought into an investigation or hostage rescue agency. Even before you mentioned such a thing existed."

"Huh," Barber grunted. "You don't say."

Chris narrowed his eyes, focused on what his commander wasn't saying. "Why do I hear the smile in your voice and know you're up to something with a few short words?"

"Maybe because you're not stupid, son. Whelp," he said, and a loud smack sounded through the line, as if he slapped his desk, "I have a few calls to make. Team will be in contact. You let me know when you start your thing and I might just have some help I can push your way.'

"Wait, are you serious?"

"As a heart attack. I'll talk to you later."

And with that, Barber hung up. Chris looked at his phone and the ended call, then brought his brows down in a V, wondering how in the hell he'd get over just how much he would miss his team.

****

Later that night, after he'd worked some of his pent-up energy out on the yard, raking the yard of fallen leaves, dead grass, and weeds, Chris sat back on the same chair he'd sat in earlier in the day while on the phone with Barber and popped the top off his beer. He set his feet up on the banister and looked out across his dark yard.

At night, being so far from town but not too far from civilization, the sky reflected against distant city lights and shone a dark azure. His porch wrapped around more than half the house, and he planned to eventually set up a backyard barbeque area. Somewhere family could come, hang out, and connect. When he bought the house, he had decided on the property because of how far it had been from any other house. But now, and especially after his mom's reaction, he realized how important family was, how much he missed them, and how much he wanted to be closer to his brothers.

Each of the Gonzalez troupe, as they were referred to, were spread out around the world. And that didn't quite sit well with him anymore. He'd spent time doing his own thing, but now he felt as if he were doing a one-eighty, wanting to establish a foundation in order to build a home and a life, a family.

A car rumbled up the drive as that last thought left his head, sending a pair of headlights slicing through the darkness.

He took his feet off the banister and brought them down on his porch, causing the lantern sitting on the wood to shudder. He stood as the undercover Crown Victoria rumbled to a stop. Dwayne stepped out and eyed him over the top of the vehicle.

"You talk to Doctor Eagen?" he called out.

Chris cocked his head, digging in his back pocket for his phone. He shook his head in answer to Dwayne but tightened his lips and lit up the screen. "Two missed calls," he said once Dwayne stepped up on the porch. Without waiting for D to explain, he hit the screen and brought his phone up to his ear.

"Paws and Claws, this is Hailey."

Chris popped a brow and met the gaze of Hailey's stepfather. "Hails, what are you still doing there?"

"Uncle Chris," she said with what sounded like a relieved sigh. "Doctor Eagen has been trying to get ahold of you."

"I hear that. Everything okay?"

Some rustling sounded through the phone. "Yeah, everything is fine now. Something spooked Doc E earlier and after D stopped by, he said he was going to make a trip up to your house but would be back to get me on his way down again."

The hairs on his arms stood at attention. He'd been with Samantha the other night when that mysterious figure had been outside and she'd been cool, calm, and collected then. That situation had freaked him the hell out. For something to "spook her," as Hailey said, it must mean that his danger-radar would have been going off the hook. "How about you grab Doc E for me, Hails, and we'll catch up in a bit?"

Dwayne shifted beside him, leaning against the wooden rail and catching his gaze. D's lips were in a flat line and his eyes alert.

What the hell happened?

More rustling. "I'll get the door." This from Hailey.

"Sergeant Gonzalez?" Samantha asked, slightly out of breath.

He couldn't help it, he smiled. The sound of her voice washed over him like a soft summer breeze along the lake. Refreshing, alive, so different from his dark life. "We're back to Sergeant Gonzalez again?" he asked.

She huffed and dropped her voice low when she replied, "Your niece is here."

"And?"

"How professional is it going to look if she hears me calling one of my clients by their first name?"

He screwed his face up and couldn't help the laugh that escaped. "One, it's Hailey, she's a lot more perceptive than you're giving her credit for. Sweetheart, if she hears you call me Sergeant Gonzalez, she will think something is up.

"Two," he said over her loud sigh, "you're in Nyack, New York now. And one of the things about Nyack is we are all about that small-town feel. The place has *village* after its name for a reason."

"You have an answer for just about everything, don't you?"

Man, she sounded feisty. He grinned, liking it. "Now you're catching on."

She snorted, and while the sound was anything but cute, it did something to his insides. Gave him a warm feeling that had long been missing from his life. For her to feel comfortable enough to be who she was without all the other games normally played between a man and a woman, he looked to what grew between them as something more. He and Samantha were building something here, no matter how much she kept her arms raised between them.

Dwayne shifted again, which brought Chris back to the matter at hand. He grew serious and focused on the tree line edging his property, trying to picture her little shop down the hill. "All right, Red, tell me what happened earlier that has you so spooked."

"Okay," she said, her voice a little lower than it had been before, "some guy was here earlier, asking questions about Delta Alpha. Really strange questions, too, and normally I wouldn't pay attention to this sort of thing because let's face it, I'm a vet, and people are always curious. Not only about my job, but about the animals I treat, and who can really blame them, some of these animals are really friggin' cute, DA included, of course. I mean, he's cute in a military working dog, I-can-bite-your-head-off kind of way, not in an aw, look-at-the-cute-puppy kind of way."

Chris blinked, trying to catch up. But it seemed as though Samantha had developed a case of verbal diarrhea and her sentences ran one right after another. A clear sign that whatever had happened had gotten her either super-excited or super-scared. He counted on the latter.

"Red—"

"Anyhow," she said, right over him, "the reason it got weird was because I had walked in the door with DA and not two minutes later, this guy came in right after me. You see, we'd gone to the park, and I felt bad because it's been such a dreary week and today was so pretty. Not like I'm going to lay out in a bikini in the backyard, no way. I mean, it is only forty degrees outside, and while I tried the Polar Plunge once when I was twenty-two, I really don't think I could handle that now. It is just too dang cold up here to even consider something like that, you know? And a bikini only covers so much skin. I should have tried a one-piece instead. But I really don't think it would be much better. They call it the Polar Plunge for a reason."

Chris's eyes crossed at just the simple, damn thought of Samantha in a bikini, and he did an about-face immediately, walking a few steps away from D so his brother couldn't overhear what he said next.

"Jesus, sweetheart, focus here. There's only so much I can take, and from the way you're talking, I know that whatever has you spooked is big. But when you start mentioning you wearing a bikini and diving into cold water, my mind kind of loses focus and I wonder just how cold your nipples were. Do you get me?" He let out a deep breath. "Focus, baby. What happened?"

Silence, then, "I get you."

He lifted his head and stared out across his darkening lawn. Bright spots started twinkling in the sky, the night life waking up. She got him. That was huge.

"Okay, okay," Samantha said, her voice dropping lower as if she were trying to keep their conversation from carrying. "This guy asking questions kind of struck me as odd. He wanted to know what was going on with DA, who his handler was, and the whole time he talked, his eyes kept skipping to the front of the shop as if he were keeping an eye out for someone, something, I don't know. The questions were starting to weird me out, and I could hear Delta Alpha in the back room growling his head off. He sounded just like that night … at my place, you know."

The line went silent, so he figured her last was a question. "I know what night, baby," he answered, trying to soothe her with his voice. She sounded panicky as hell. Not good. "What else?"

"Well, when I asked the guy his name, he gave me this really creepy smile and said he was a friend of yours. That got me thinking and had the hairs standing up on the back of my neck. I mean, if he were a friend, wouldn't he already know DA and who DA's handler was?"

Chris sucked in a breath, not liking where this conversation headed.

"Then," she said, her voice breathless. "When he turned to leave, he was limping. Limping, Chris. Like that night."

His heart slammed against his chest, begging to be set free. He closed his eyes as a dozen scenarios rushed through his mind. The surrounding sounds amplified until it was as if he could hear the wind through the trees, the night creatures scampering through the forest, the sound of a far-off vehicle on I-287. The earth's scent filled his lungs and every sense he had sharpened. He knew what was happening. His body did this every time he headed into a mission. Battle-ready.

The different coincidences kept adding up until he was almost one hundred percent certain Tayseer had found him here. In his hometown. What the fuck?

"All right, Red, I want you to come up and stay the night here. Bring DA with you."

"I can't," she said, exasperation in her tone. "I have early appointments. I don't think it's that big of a deal. The guy freaked me out. I have a superb alarm system here, and plus, DA won't let me come to any harm."

Superb. Jesus, she was a hoot. Warmth spread through his chest hearing his girl talk with such confidence in his partner. Especially when not but a few weeks ago, she'd been frozen in fear of getting bit by the same dog.

"Fine. But I'm coming down to stay with you then. I will not argue about this, so it'd be better if you just accept this is how it will go."

She huffed. "Bossy much?" But she went on without waiting for him to answer. "Fine, you can stay the night." Like he asked. She was cute. "I'll see you in a bit."

"Sweetheart, you're lucky you're so gorgeous or you'd be an extreme pain in my ass."

"As if!" she snapped.

He grinned. "Have you had anything to eat yet?"

"Thank you, Hailey," she said, voice muffled, then, "not yet. I planned on ordering something in a bit."

"I'll bring some food down. Should be there in about a half-hour."

"Okay. Hold on a minute." A few seconds later, her voice came over the line, low and husky. "Chris?"

"Still here, baby."

Her breath skipped. Now he really listened, wanting to know what she was about to say.

"My nipples were really hard." Then she hung up. *Christ!*

Chapter Fifteen

Hours later, Chris opened his eyes. Something had woken him from his sleep and he took a moment to survey his surroundings.

He lay on his side, Samantha pressed along the length of him, face tucked in his neck. Her soft curves pressed into him from her breasts pillowed against his chest, to her leg hitched over his hip. They were both naked, and despite the cooler weather outside, beneath the blankets, he was nice and warm.

He'd never been one for cuddling, and he didn't want to think too much into it now. Somehow, in the short time since he'd entered into her life, Samantha had burrowed her way into his mind just as she did to his body physically now.

At the foot of the bed, Delta Alpha let out a warning woof. Not a full-out bark, but just beneath his breath as if he were trying to stay quiet. Chris lifted his head and looked at the door. They'd closed it earlier, wanting to keep the heat inside the apartment. It must be really late or very early as the room was still black, and outside her window the sky was still dark.

DA growled.

"What is it, boy?" he asked, his voice pitched low.

Another woof, this one louder, accompanied by a snarl. Samantha tensed in his arms as Chris sat up and threw his legs over the side of the bed. DA whined and barked again, this time louder. He grabbed his pants. Amazingly enough, his partner also backed up on the bed until he stood as an over-watch for Samantha.

"What's going on?" she asked.

He grabbed his shirt and shucked it on, then palmed his M9, keeping his eyes on the door and his ears strained, listening for whatever DA heard. "Something has Dumb Ass spooked. I want you to stay here while we check it out."

"Chris," she said, and nothing more.

He looked over and found her clutching the comforter to her chest, eyes wide in the darkness. "It'll be okay. If you feel more comfortable, get dressed. But stay in this room. Can you do that for me?"

She hesitated but nodded quickly. DA jumped off the bed and barked at the door, jumping against it as if he were trying to knock it down.

He double-checked the chamber of his weapon, making sure one was ready before moving to the door and inserting a knee in front of DA. "Heel." Then, he opened the door, taking care to do so in case the hinges creaked. They didn't.

"Heel," he commanded then began to move down the stairs, DA flush at his side. The cool air caused his breath to pump in front of his face in white circles. Way colder than it was when they went to sleep.

A low rumbling sounded from the clinic, and he tried to identify why it sounded familiar. At the bottom of the stairs, he crept around the corner, popping out once then coming back to make sure it was clear.

"Shit!" He ran out into the hallway. DA started barking like a crazy person was at his heels, hackles raised, but Chris only had eyes for the very small, but dangerous fire spreading across the clinic. He rushed to the phone, kept his M9 raised, and scanned the room with his eyes, but hit 9-1-1 on the phone, giving instructions to the operator who picked up half a ring later.

Seeing he was the only person in the room, he

pushed his gun in the back of his waistband and called for Samantha. "Red!" he yelled. "I need you down here, now!"

He turned and searched beneath the counter, looking for an extinguisher, something to stop this fire from spreading. If he didn't find one quick, he'd have to drag her out the front door, and she'd lose her entire clinic.

"Oh, my God," she exclaimed. "Chris!"

"Here," he said. "Where is your fire extinguisher?"

No sooner than he asked did the overhead sprinklers kick on, drenching them all in under five seconds. Sirens sounded from outside, the wail of them louder due to the wall of broken glass.

Samantha grabbed a fire extinguisher from the wall hidden behind a large cabinet. He took it from her and began to douse the already depleting fire. The loud wail of a siren stopped directly in front of the store and he stopped the extinguisher. "Red, take DA upstairs."

She turned to him with wide eyes, her expression stricken. Shit.

He cupped the side of her face. "Sweetheart," he said and dropped his face to hers. "Take Delta Alpha upstairs, yeah? He's going to get pretty freaked with everyone coming in pretty shortly. He needs you to take care of him."

That snapped her out of it. She blinked and turned to DA, calling him to her side and leading him upstairs.

Moving to the front door, he unlocked it as the first firefighter walked up. A Crown Vic pulled up next to the trucks and Dwayne stepped out, his eyes on Chris. He walked up as several more firemen stepped inside, bodies decked out in full gear. The water overhead stopped seconds later, and he looked over to see the fire extinguished. They were lucky the fire had been small and centered on one side of the clinic. But it was doubtful Samantha would be able to open for a few days. This situation would break her heart. His fist tightened at his side.

Dwayne stopped at the entry of the shop and looked at Chris. "I've been patient enough, but I think it's about time we have a chat."

Chris thinned his lips and nodded. "Not here. Not now. Let me get Red and DA situated first. My cabin, an hour, two?"

Dwayne nodded but didn't leave. He simply turned and stood like a sentry, his arms crossed over his chest, eyes scanning the street. His backup.

Chris couldn't have been more grateful.

****

Ninety minutes later, Chris opened the door to Charlie, Brooke, Hailey, and Dwayne. The three women looked as if they'd been dragged out of bed, each wearing the same uniform of black track pants and white t-shirts, hair piled on top of their heads in that messy-do women usually perfected without trying, no makeup, eyes red and tired.

The side of his mouth kicked up at the sight, but before he could tell them all to go back to bed, Charlie raised a hand. "Don't start. I heard everything over the radio, and since Trent is out of town, I couldn't sleep. I inserted myself into this little pow-wow, and these two"—she pointed at Hails and Brooke—"never listen to a single thing D says, and I don't fight them on it because it's amusing to watch him get riled. Now…" She clapped her hands and looked around, acting nosey as ever, not that he'd ever known her as anything else. "Where's the coffee?"

Chris smiled indulgently and motioned toward

the kitchen. He turned amused eyes to Brooke and Hailey, leaning down to accept a kiss from each before tilting his head toward the back porch with Dwayne.

"*Preciosa*," Dwayne said to Brooke. "I'm going to go out back with Chris. How about you and Hails check in on Doc?"

Both women nodded and walked off toward the back of the house, gaits moving in sync as if they were twins. Chris shook his head at the wonderment then led D out back. The air nipped at his exposed skin and he shivered, casting a quick glance at Charlie as she stepped out back, the coffee mug sending off waves of steam in her hands.

"So," he said and rubbed his hands together, giving a quick blow of warm air to his fingers, "there's a lot I can't tell you, and it's classified so don't push on that, please, but it seems as if we have a problem."

Dwayne leaned against the side of the house and leveled his gaze on Chris, then took a deep breath and nodded. "Hit me."

Chris laid out what he could. From a mission gone wrong, forgoing any details on exactly why they were there to take Tayseer, or even the subject's name. As much as he hated it, all of it was classified information that if he told them, it could cause some serious harm to all. He went through what had happened, when DA bit Tayseer, the following fire fight, his feelings and observations since he'd been home, and his suspicions of just where the subject of his mission currently was. By the time he'd finished, both Dwayne's and Charlie's eyes and bodies were as alert. He used to have the same look right before a mission.

"Are you sure?" Charlie asked, holding her mug by its handle, the contents long gone. Her dark gaze also looked more alert, any signs of sleep long gone.

Chris nodded. "I'd bet my life on it."

"Christ, Chris," Dwayne said.

"Sorry, bro, but it's the truth. There's not a single doubt in my mind that he's here. Why? I'm not certain. But any way you look at it, it's bad news. If he's managed to track me specifically back here, then it's even worse news than we thought. Who knows what that mole had his or her hands on."

Dwayne rubbed a hand down his face, grabbing at his chin before he refocused. "So, what now? Anyone have any plans or next steps?"

"My team should arrive in the next day or so. Once they get here, we should know more of what we need to do. Until then, I just need to keep alert and try to keep everyone I can safe." He shoved his hands in his pockets, his fingers long-gone numb, but shrugged his shoulders, at a loss for what else to do. There really wasn't anyone to call as he didn't know who outside of his team and his brothers he could trust. Seeing as there had been a mole in one of the most highly classified operations had his trust in others at a complete minimum.

"We'll all work to keep everyone safe here, C-man," Charlie said, resorting back to his childhood nickname. "You're not alone in this anymore. You are allowed to lean on us for assistance, you know."

The side of his mouth kicked up in a grin and he wrapped an arm around her shoulders, bringing her in close and resting his chin atop her head. She smelled as she always had, like sunshine and determination. Tonight was no different. And she was right. He did have others to depend on now. Working toward allowing them to help would take some work. "I gotcha, kid. I'm trying."

She mock-punched him in the kidney and leaned her upper body back to look at him. "Try harder."

He cupped the side of her face, feeling the old

and very familiar love for someone he'd always considered a kid sister, no matter blood or not. She'd always been there, and he had no doubt she always would be. "I've missed you. You know that, right?"

She blinked a few times and cleared her throat, then wrapped her arms back around him again.

"Oh, God," Dwayne said next to him. "This shit is getting way too mushy. I'm about to throw up in my mouth. Matter of fact, I think I just did. *Urp*."

Charlie twisted her face to Dwayne, still resting against his chest. "I don't want any lip from you!"

D grinned at her and rubbed the top of her head. She punched Dwayne in the stomach, this punch not so mockingly. Chris grinned at both of them then turned to the sliding glass doors and met the beautiful and worried gaze of Samantha. A crease had set up residence between her brows, and lines of wrinkles from her scrunched face had formed on her forehead. She turned from him before he could lift a hand or acknowledge her presence.

He tilted his head, wondering what that was about.

"All right, I'm going to head back down and get these girls in bed," D said.

"Women! We're women, you asshat!"

Dwayne lifted a brow. "With a mouth like that, of course you are."

Apparently, Charlie didn't appreciate the sarcasm for she took a swipe at D that he dodged, laughing.

They tumbled into the house, Chris following with laughter in his chest. Such a foreign feeling and sound, he couldn't remember the last time he'd laughed with such ease. He'd been away from home for way too long.

Fifteen minutes later, he pushed his front door shut and locked the deadbolt. Running on a few hours of sleep, his back protested all the standing he had done that day, or the previous day, seeing as it was three in the morning. His head pounded out a fierce beat, too. He stopped by the bathroom and opened the cabinet for the Advil. Samantha had already unpacked a few items, her toothbrush and toothpaste, and what looked like facial cleaner. He liked the look of her stuff in his space. Warmth settled in his stomach at seeing it there. Yet another unfamiliar feeling moving through him.

He tossed back a few Advil then took some water in his cupped hand to help the pills down. He went to shut the cabinet then stopped, his eyes arrested on his bottle of Oxy. Had he taken so many of those since he'd been home? The bottle was half-full, but for the life of him, he swore he'd only taken one or two.

He scratched the back of his head, making a note to pay more attention to how many pills he popped in the next few days, then went in search of Samantha.

He found her in his room. There was really no other place for her to be, seeing as this room was the only one with a set-up bed. She sat half-underneath the dark-blue quilt his mother had made for him over fifteen years ago. She'd pulled her hair on top of her head like it'd been with Brooke, Charlie, and Hailey. She wore a white camisole with small pink flowers dotted haphazardly.

She looked up, her hands rubbing lotion on her arms. "I'll be out of your hair in a sec, Chris. I was just taking a breather."

"Not in my way, sweetheart," he said then walked over to his dresser to grab his pajama bottoms. Typically, he slept in boxers, but this situation was kind of weird, and he had the naughty feeling like he'd snuck his girlfriend into his parents' house. He'd never invited a woman up to his cabin, and while he was a grown adult now, everything about this was new to him.

He spied DA in the corner and bent to give him a good rubdown.

"Do you have an extra blanket and pillow?"

Chris looked over his shoulder. Her shorts were bright pink, and standing in front of the soft, yellow glow of the lamp, he had to take a moment to swallow before he responded. "Are you cold?"

She shook her head. "Not entirely. I was going to go sleep on the couch. It's a little chillier out there."

He frowned, standing and turning toward her. "Why are you sleeping on the couch?"

She bit her lip and turned her face away. "I want to sleep on the couch."

"Sam," he called. When she didn't answer, he took a step toward her. "Red, look at me."

She did.

"Why do you want to sleep on the couch, especially when not just a few hours ago we were both sleeping in the same bed?"

She sighed. "I don't want to play any games right now. I'm too tired."

He took another step, then another, until he stood not a foot away from her. "Are you going to explain what you mean by that?"

"Stop it," she said, her voice a harsh whisper.

"What the fuck, Red? Stop what? Are you going to explain yourself?"

She crossed her arms, wrapping her palms around her upper biceps. The move pushed her unbound breasts up, daring his eyes to take a peek. He forced his gaze to hold hers.

"Please get me a blanket."

"No. Seriously, what is this?"

"Fine," she said and turned to leave. He grabbed her wrist and pulled her back, stepping into her and pushing her against the wall. She let out a yelp, her eyes wide, and lifted a hand in front of her face.

As if he was going to hit her…

What the fuck?

He immediately let go and stepped back until there was so much space between them, he didn't think he'd ever reach her. Why had she cowered as if he would hit her? What in the hell was going on?

She trembled, pressed against the wall, looking over at him. Her arm slowly lowered and still, she didn't say anything. A million thoughts ran through his head, all of them making no sense. Many of them making him want to find whoever had put that fear in her, so he could beat the hell out of them.

He took a deep breath, then another. When his pulse had slowed enough to where he could speak, he tried to use a calm, low tone. "What was that?"

She straightened her shoulders, still pressed against the wall. Acting as if she didn't want to be vulnerable and give him her back. Like he'd attack her. Fuck.

"I overreacted. You just took me by surprise."

He took a step toward her and held out his hands, palms facing her. "That wasn't an overreaction. That was instinct. Did somebody"—he swallowed—"did somebody hurt you, Sam?"

She didn't move. Confirmation enough.

"I would never, ever hurt you, you have to believe that. I've never raised my hand toward a woman, nor do I ever plan to."

She still said nothing. But she also didn't bolt from the room, as he suspected she'd wanted to a few minutes earlier. He tried again and took another step toward her. "I'm not him, Red. I will never be him. You're safe with me. You're safe here."

"Am I, though?" she asked so quietly he almost didn't hear her.

"Yes."

She shook her head, tears welling in her eyes. "I don't think I am. Not after tonight."

He hadn't realized he moved until he scooped her in his arms and blessed mercy, her body plastered along the length of his. "I wouldn't hurt you. I'm sorry I scared you, Red."

Her face shook back and forth, tucked against his neck. "I don't think I'm safe here anymore. I hoped we would be safe, but I don't think we are."

We?

"What isn't making you safe?"

"The fire..." She hiccupped, her body silently wracked with sobs. "He had to have found us. I don't think there's anyone who would be cruel enough to break the glass window and set a fire. It has to be him. He won't let me escape."

Pieces of the puzzle started falling into place. The secrets she'd kept were specific to her safety. He got it. While he'd never dealt with domestic violence, he knew enough, had read enough, to understand the very real fear of being in such a relationship.

"I don't think he found you," he started and looked down at her as she pulled back to meet his gaze. "I think whatever happened to your clinic tonight has more to do with me. Not you. You're safe here, Red. Dwayne, Charlie, and I will make sure of it. You have nothing to fear."

"Charlie?" she asked.

He nodded. "Yeah, you saw her earlier out on the deck with D and I."

She froze and pushed aggressively away, her face shutting down, yet again. This time, he wasn't having it.

He crowded into her until he backed her against the wall. He didn't touch her. Only set his arms next to her head.

"I think it's time you explain yourself. What happened? Did someone say something to you?"

She looked up at him, her big green eyes pleading. What the hell was this?

"Please, Chris."

"Woman. Tell me."

"Let me go, please."

"Tell me!" he snapped.

"I saw you!" she yelled.

Delta Alpha let out a warning bark.

He froze. Her tone and the look crumpling her face caused some serious palpitations in his chest, as if his heart had suddenly taken up the idea of playing on a trampoline.

"Sweetheart, what exactly did you see?"

She took in a shaky breath and looked over his shoulder. "I saw you holding her. You two were so familiar with each other. Your face was soft, so much softer than I've ever seen before, and I realize what we have is new, casual even. We should stop this now before it gets any worse."

He took a minute to gather himself. What woman did she refer to? And casual? Other women? Had she not been paying attention at all?

"I need you to focus on me for a minute or two, Red. And pay close attention because we have a lot to go over here. Look at me."

She took longer than he liked but finally lifted her bright gaze to his.

"When did you see me holding another woman?"

"Outside," she said. "Just a while ago."

He blinked and the outburst from when he entered the room made sense with a slap across his senses. A silly misperception, but he was the idiot who hadn't explained who anyone was. Charlie and Samantha hadn't met, and seeing things through her eyes, he could picture how the entire scene would have looked to an outsider.

"That's Charlie Lopez."

She bit her bottom lip, turning the normally bright pink skin white. He cupped her face and pulled gently at her lip before swiping his hand over the abused skin.

"She's Dwayne's partner. Has been for as long as I can remember."

"She's very pretty."

He smiled.

"Chris…"

"She's also like a sister to all of us. She's practically a Gonzalez, sweetheart. I've never looked at her with anything resembling a sexual attraction."

She blinked her big green eyes, and her mouth parted slightly. Christ, her face, what she did to him. He didn't think she realized how much she had already burrowed under his skin. He inched closer, the slight brush of her breasts against his chest a sensual delight.

"Now there are a few other things we need to cover." He trailed his hand he had at her cheek over her shoulder, watching the progress. Reaching the strap of her camisole, he hooked a finger beneath the cloth and moved it over her shoulder, sliding down her arm. "There are no other women in my life."

The tank had pulled so low that one breast popped out. Her dusty pink nipple, the same shade as her lips, tightened under his gaze. Chris shifted, turning his attention to the other strap on the opposite shoulder. "And what's going on between us, Red, is anything but casual."

He pulled the other strap down, and her other

breast came free. Sucking in a breath, he looked at her bared to him. She took his breath away. Her body was damn near perfect. A collarbone jutted out with each breath she took, but her breasts, they were perfect for his hands, and even more beautiful under the soft glow of the lamp.

"Chris," she said on a shaky breath.

"I want this," he said, tracing around one of her nipples with the tip of his finger. "And I want this." He placed his free hand over her heart, directly above her breasts. He looked into her eyes. "And I'm going to spend as much time as I need proving that to you."

She stared up at him, her bright green eyes full of a vulnerability he would have never guessed she'd have. Samantha, a woman who seemed to have such a strong stance in the world, one who had reduced even his very aggressive partner into a pile of mush when it came to her. Who would have thought she had a chink in her confidence, had such violent secrets of her past, would have questioned anything going on between them?

Her breasts shook with each shaky inhale, tempting his gaze. Her lips quivered under his attention. And she called to him as a woman called to a man. He was all too ready to answer.

He leaned down slowly, holding her gaze. His hands tightened on her arms, feeling the sculpted muscle beneath telling him she worked daily at her job and didn't sit around. She tilted her face up to meet him. Their lips stopped a breath apart.

She sighed, fanning his mouth with her desire. Her hands clutched at his shoulders.

Someone pounded at the front door, and the rumbling sound echoed throughout the house.

"Christ," he said, squeezing his eyes shut. "Who now?"

Pulling away from a very warm and tempting Samantha was about the hardest thing he had to do. He stomped down the hall and flung the front door open ready to light into whoever had interrupted what was looking to be a very nice night.

"Holy shit," he said under his breath.

"Crack!" Squirrel yelled then took one, two steps before jumping into Chris's arms. Captain's legs wrapped around his waist and he took two steps back, tightening his hold on him lest he drop him on his ass. As it was, he was still active duty and despite Captain Ford acting very unbecoming for an officer—not that he had ever really acted one before, Squirrel would always have enough of Chris's respect that he'd never let him down.

His arms shook under the bulky weight of the captain, but rather than toss him off, Chris set him down and gave a good-natured shove. "Thanks, Squirrel. My friggin' back will be screaming for the next week."

"Here he goes again," said Sergeant Dean Davis, stepping across the threshold, "always complaining about not getting hurt. You would think this guy wanted to go back to Security Forces, rather than hang with the adults in Special Forces." Davis grinned, his white teeth a stark contrast against his dark-as-night skin.

Chris laughed and shook his head, hooking a finger through his belt loop. "And you're still an asshole."

Davis's grin grew, and he stumbled back a step, a hand to his heart. "You wound me."

Nathaniel McKinney came up behind Davis and rolled his eyes, the team's medic more than used to the jesting among the team. "Watch yourself, Crack, Davis is in one of his moods. The whole way up here he tried to get me to spill on apparently all the doctor-nurse fantasies I've played out." Nate set a duffle bag next to his feet, catching Chris's eye.

He met Doc's bright-blue gaze. "And how many times have you acted that out?"

Nate lifted the side of his mouth in a smirk. "A gentleman never tells."

Chris stared at him, then deadpanned. "So how many times?"

Max Carletto limped in and burst out laughing. "If you're a gentleman, Doc, then I'm the friggin' Easter Bunny."

Davis turned around. "Do you have a thing for fluffy tails in the bedroom, Sig?"

Max groaned. "No. Nope. We're not starting this kinky-what-you-like-to-do-in-the-bedroom conversation again." He faced Chris. "I'm beat, man. Point me to the nearest couch and I'll be out in minutes."

Chris straightened. Plans were his team would be on their way, but the specific date hadn't been clear. He figured he had a few days. Showing up on his doorstep wasn't unwelcome, but they usually all just fell asleep wherever, walked around in their skivvies, and did, well, man things. There had never been any females around during those times so it was all out, not giving a shit. Samantha, however...

"You guys staying here?" Chris asked just as little doggy steps came into the room.

As one, the team turned toward the new sound just over his left shoulder and froze. Like a planned performance, one by one, each turned back to Chris wearing shit-eating grins.

"Oh, yeah," Davis said.

"Totally." This from Max.

"This is going to be fun," Squirrel said with a chuckle.

Nate's cheeks pinkened, and he looked to the

floor, but not before Chris saw him punch his tongue to his cheek, fighting a smile.

He turned and found Samantha.

She leaned against the entry to the living room and kitchen, those same shorts riding low on her hips, a white camisole covered by a white cardigan. Her hair fell in waves around her face and behind her, the soft glow of the room highlighted every beautiful curve. DA stood at her side while she idly pet the top of his head. His dog had his tongue hanging out of his mouth, in heaven with the affection.

Sweet Jesus, she took his breath away.

She captured Chris's gaze with her own, giving him a smile before she turned to his team and lifted a hand. "Hi. I'm Doctor Samantha Eagen, Delta Alpha's veterinarian."

Davis burst out laughing again.

Chapter Sixteen

The next morning, with the sharp aroma of bacon in the air, Samantha at the stove multi-tasking between scrambling eggs and flipping pancakes, Chris took a sip of his coffee, the bitter liquid like nectar to his sleep-deprived body, and tried to focus on what Sig, aka Max, said.

"You're losing me here, bud. Try it again, except this time, how about you explain it to me like I'm in third grade?"

"So not far off from where your mental capacity is now, then?" Davis joked.

He shot his sergeant the bird while Max turned from the laptop to face him.

"Okay, so after Barber started digging around, he mentioned he didn't have a good feeling about anything that had gone down on the mission. Problem was, he couldn't be the one to look into anything as any sort of inquiry he made would be official due to his position."

Chris nodded. "Right."

"But that wouldn't necessarily stop someone else from say…" Max shrugged and tossed his hands out before resettling them on his knees. "Making some unofficial inquiries, right?"

"Right." Seeing as Sig was their resident genius when it came to any sort of investigative skills, he tracked exactly what he was saying. Max, in his hacker-type position, a role he played officially for Uncle Sam, and unofficially in a "dark hat" capacity, had started digging with Barber's not-so-official orders.

"One thing that bothered me was how Tayseer knew we were coming, almost as if someone had given him a heads-up. So, I may or may not have hacked into one of the alphabet agency's email systems."

"Shit. Say you're fucking kidding, man."

Sig looked to Davis. "I'm kidding." He deadpanned, but continued, "However that search didn't turn up much. Only a lot of cryptic emails going to a bunch of outside Gmail addresses." He leaned back and crossed his arms. "Gmail is easy enough to crack in on. Problem with that is each account had somehow received one message before shutting down. That message being from the aforementioned agency account."

Chris brought his brows down in a V. "Doesn't make a lick of sense. Why create an account for just one email?"

Sig held up a finger. "Ah, ah. But it was for two. A received email and a sent one."

Now Chris popped his brows up, but before he could ask, Max went on.

"So, pop into that account, right? Surely there will be more there, right?"

"Right," Squirrel answered from the couch, his feet propped up on the table in front of him.

Max looked over and smiled. "Wrong." He grinned. "Sorry, Cap', I couldn't resist. I have been waiting for-ev-er to say that to you. But in this case, it's true. Same activity on that account, one email in, one out. So, I went to the next, and the next. And so on. You get the drift."

He spun back to the computer. "However, after chasing my dick through a few accounts, I started to notice a pattern. Something I hadn't seen before." He typed something on the laptop and brought up a document that showcased a bunch of different numbers.

Chris pulled his chair closer. "What is this? Looks like a bunch of numbers without any rhyme or reason to them?"

"Didn't you ever play spy as a kid? Captain Midnight? Come up with a secret language?"

Chris turned his head and met Sig's metallic-colored eyes and shook his head. "Dude, my childhood is a long story, but I was more of a dirt-and-mud type of kid than a cops-and-robbers. Catch my drift?"

Max grinned and his eyes danced, his excitement evident. The guy got off on this shit.

"What better way to hide what you're trying to say in plain sight than to create a code? And," he said, typing furiously on the laptop again, bringing up different documents as he spoke, "seeing as the original email came from an agency that employs some of the best spies in the world, it would have to be a code that no one has seen before. Something difficult to breach. So, you'd have to split up the cipher into different messages in order to make sure the receiver could decipher the message. Typically, you see letters and numbers in codes, but this was something I had never seen before, a cipher that really didn't stand out due to the use of numbers only."

Chris rubbed at his temple and took another sip of his brew. "You're losing me again, man."

"No, no, no, I think I'm tracking," Squirrel said. "Go on."

Max nodded and continued clicking through multiple documents. "In order for the cipher to be useful to both parties, there had to be some sort of message prior to them being sent, a method or an algorithm, as many call it, set in place. Otherwise, the receiver wouldn't have an idea how to crack the code. So, a key was set in place. That being said, I went back through some…" He coughed. "Personal phone records from our sender, of course everything total legal."

Chris rolled his eyes. Yeah, right.

"And found a weird text that had been sent to a number that didn't seem to match the rest of the numbers in the history of this guy's calls. Guess what I found?" He drummed a beat on the table.

"The key," Squirrel answered.

"Give the guy a trophy. The key! And this key is a constantly changing one, which makes it even more unique. And with that key, if you put it to use deciphering all the messages sent and received..." In a flurry of movements, his hands moved over the keyboard too fast for Chris to keep up. With a flourish, he hit the last key and lifted his hands.

"Holy shit," Chris breathed.

"Oh, man," Squirrel said from behind, having come off the couch.

Before them on the laptop screen showed a listing of all the messages that had been sent and received, in plain English, the code fully broken. Account numbers and locations, his team's name and arrival time of the mission, their names, movement of money going all around the world, and finally, his parents' home address in Nyack.

Chris stood abruptly, sending his chair toppling over behind him. "We have to go."

"Hold on there, big guy," Max said.

Chris whirled around to him and pointed at the screen. "My parents—"

"Are completely safe," Max cut in. "There's more."

Chris closed his eyes, his mind spinning a million miles an hour. "What more could there possibly be?"

"He's here. In Nyack."

"The fuck you say," Davis barked.

Chris said nothing. Instead, he opened his eyes

and met Max's stare. "Yeah, buddy, your instincts were right on this one. Tayseer is here in Nyack. And you have in fact been seeing him. I think he may have gone to your parents' place, but all the break-ins here, the sightings you said you've seen? That's the one and only."

Chris swiped his hands over his head, trying to gain traction in a world slipping out of control.

"And it gets worse," Max added unhelpfully.

"Tell us," Captain Ford ordered, all business.

Max turned back to the laptop. "The good news is we have the account numbers from the messages and the key that deciphered them. So, being able to trace money wasn't an issue. A little electronic intrusion here and there, and *voila*, you get the full picture about not only where the money came from, which, by the way, pisses me off to say this, but it came from an account reserved for Uncle Sam black hat activities. The blackest of black. But I was also able to track where the money went. And that's where the bad news comes in." He paused.

"Jesus-effin'-Christ, Sig, don't take a breather now," Davis shouted.

"Hold your damn horses, Sarge. I'm getting to it." Max typed a bit more, then another document popped up on the screen. "On one account, the purchases don't look all that bad. A home improvement store purchase here. Some food there. But when you combine all the purchases across multiple accounts, another picture forms."

"And what picture is that?" Chris asked, leaning toward the screen again.

"A picture worth a thousand lives. Millions. It seems," Max answered, his voice much more somber now that all the purchases were there on the screen for them all to read. "It's a picture that paints the full recipe for a cocktail involving one serious chemical agent

Tayseer had planned to bring to the US all along."

"Fuck," Davis said from behind.

"My words exactly," Squirrel said.

Chris couldn't say anything, though. He stared at the nightmare unfolding before them. A nightmare coming to his town. A town that held nearly everyone who meant something to him. A headache that had been hinting at making an appearance again began to throb behind his eye.

He went to the bathroom, wincing at the muted sunlight coming through the window, causing his head to pierce with sharp pain. The earlier throb had turned into a full-fledged migraine that matched the beat of his heart.

He grabbed the pain pills from the cabinet and paused at the weight, still unnerved about how much wasn't in the container. Surely, he hadn't taken so many in the short time he'd been home. With his parents' addictions, he had made a point not to put himself in a situation where he'd want to rely on something other than what his body needed to survive: food, water, the daily cup of Joe. He could only recall taking two the first night after his run, and that was more so to get his body to settle and get some shuteye. But from the looks of it, the bottle was half-empty.

He stared at the empty space, trying to think through the pain in his head. His vision swam, his stomach clenched, and all the while, the ache was a constant reminder that he hadn't fully recovered.

Disturbed at the missing pills, he shook two out of the bottle and tossed them to the back of his throat, swallowing them with a slurp of water from the faucet.

Needing to sleep off the migraine and what the pills would soon do to him, he fell onto his bed, giving a little bounce before settling his head on the pillow with a sigh. He hated how the meds made him feel—out of sorts, woozy, and unable to focus.

Sam came into the room, looking like an angel sent to slay his demons, her long red hair falling around her shoulders. A heavy dose of humidity hung in the air today, and that moisture had caused her wavy hair to turn into big curls. The curve of those curls brushed against her breasts and arms, and if he hadn't been in so much pain, he'd show her exactly how beautiful she was. Instead, he verbally relayed his thoughts.

"You're gorgeous, Red. I don't think I've ever seen a woman as gorgeous as you."

Her cheeks pinkened and she shot him a small smile. "I think you need your head examined. I'm a hot mess." She came and sat on the bed, leaning over him to brush an imaginary hair off his forehead. He knew it imaginary as his hair was cropped short, but he didn't call her out on the action as he liked her touching him, too.

"Are you okay?" she asked. "Breakfast is ready and I have a feeling if you don't get out there soon, those friends of yours are going to eat through everything, maybe even this house." The side of her mouth quirked up in humor.

He matched her grin. "I've got a migraine taking its shot at me. Just need to lie down for a bit." He intertwined their fingers and idly rubbed his thumb across the smoothness of her hand. "While I'm thinking about it, have you used any of my pills?" He shook his head, then added, "It's not a big deal if you did. I'm trying to account for the ones that seem to be missing."

A V formed between her eyebrows. "No, I can't—what kind of pills are we talking about?"

"Oxy."

She whistled low. "That's some serious painkillers. How many are missing?"

He shifted on the bed to get more comfortable. His mind grew a little lazy and warmth started spreading through him. A nap sounded like a great idea. Hopefully, when he woke, his headache would be gone. "I'm not real sure. There's a bit more missing than I remember taking. I'm not too worried about it. Just curious."

She leaned down again and brushed her lips against his. "Why don't you get some sleep? I'm going to head to the clinic. I have someone coming by to look at the damage from the fire, and I'm curious about it, too. It looked huge last night being there, but thinking back on it, I remember it being a smaller one confined to a specific area."

He sat up, his limbs moving as if they drifted through water, his head foggy. "I'll go with you. You shouldn't go alone."

"No," she said and placed her hand on his shoulder, pushing him back to the bed. "Like you said before, I'll be fine in this town. The police department is less than a mile from my clinic. It's daylight. And people will be walking up and down Main Street. Nothing will happen."

He didn't like it. Didn't like the idea of her being out of his reach for more than an hour. But with his current condition and the drugs pumping through him, he was next to worthless. "Maybe one of the guys can go with you. Or I'll call D or Charlie."

Her face tightened at Charlie's name. "Red…"

She shook her head, looking away and standing from the bed. "No, no, I heard you last night. It's just a bit sensitive still. I'll get past it. The guys are looking a bit tired. If something happens, I have my phone and I'll call Detective Gonzalez or you immediately, okay?"

He still didn't like it. But he had a hard time focusing. "Why don't you humor me and take DA?"

He'd noticed how attached DA was becoming to her. If his dog was around and anything happened, she'd at least be given a head start.

She shook her head. "The place is a mess. Glass is everywhere. And a stranger is going to be at the clinic with me. I don't want to risk him getting stressed or cutting his paw. I'll be fine, Chris. Get some sleep."

Her decision sounded final, and he knew better than to push it. He closed his eyes and listened to her moving around the room, peeking a few times to watch her change her shirt, grab a sweater, brush her hair. He liked her in his house and in his life. He could get used to this simple, domestic scene. The pull of sleep started to drag him under with an insistent tug he didn't fight. Each of his limbs felt weighed down, as if they were held with concrete blocks. It wasn't an uncomfortable feeling, just one he wasn't used to, being as he liked full control of his facilities at all times.

That same merry-go-round popped behind his lids, a child's laughter and another's scream. He reached for the memory or vision and tried to see through it, but promptly fell into a deep sleep.

Chapter Seventeen

A few hours later, Samantha swept another pile of broken glass onto a dustpan and dumped it into a contractor bag sitting nearby. She'd met up with the insurance agent, who was a nice, middle-aged man who seemed to be in a hurry. He'd been in her shop for what seemed like the timespan of a minute before handing her a folder filled with forms and instructions on the next steps. Included in that list were approved contractors they'd previously engaged with, and she took the opportunity presented and called three on the list to schedule them to come by to appraise the cost of work.

She'd also rescheduled appointments with her clients, and called the local women's clinic to get on the calendar for prenatal care. Even with the chaos going on around her, she felt mighty good about all she'd gotten completed today.

The fire damage had been limited to one area, which was a relief, and even though the front glass window of the shop had shattered, with everything cleaned up, it didn't look too bad. She'd been open for a few weeks and had driven most of her savings into this place. The last thing she needed was to be out of work when her only source of income was her shop.

She eyed the gaping front window again. That hole definitely needed to be secured, otherwise, there was no telling what could happen. Perhaps she could ask Chris to help her find something to secure it with. He'd have an idea.

Knowing she only had a few more items at his house, and she anticipated staying there a bit longer until they cleared her shop, she went up the stairs to her apartment to pack another bag.

She reached the top step and a sense of dread rolled along her spine. The feeling eerily similar to when Manuel would corner her in a room. Her stomach flipped over, immediately knowing something was wrong. She didn't know what, but her entire being screamed at her to run away … and fast.

The door to her apartment slammed shut. She whipped around.

Six feet and three inches of muscle stood between her and the exit. Manuel never missed a day at the gym, no matter the weather or his health.

"Hello, Samantha," Manuel said, spitting her new name out as if it left a bad taste in his mouth. His brown eyes narrowed, causing her to take a step back.

Her heart pounded against her chest, begging to be set free. Her skin felt as if it were on fire. And inside her head, she screamed.

He looked better than ever. Manuel had always been a handsome man. He had that going for him. But those good looks were only on the surface. Everything inside of him reeked of evil and danger.

"Nothing to say to your fiancé, darling?" he taunted, moving to lock the deadbolt then the knob. Any chance at a quick escape fled.

She watched him like a hawk, expecting the first blow. It was coming, that much she knew. The only thing she didn't know was if she'd survive this time.

"That's okay," he said and stalked toward her. "We have plenty of time."

****

Chris woke groggy, feeling as if he hadn't slept at all. Surprisingly enough, his headache had disappeared, but his body seemed content to stay where he was, in bed. On the other side of his door and down the hall, muted, deep voices carried on in conversation. Lingering smells of spices and bacon filled the air, and from what he could tell with his partially pulled curtains, the sun quickly settled in the sky.

He grabbed his phone and checked the time. Almost six o'clock in the evening. Jesus. He'd been out all day. He had a text from Samantha regarding the insurance agent's visit and the contractor list, but that had been hours ago. Maybe she had returned and was hanging with the guys out in the living room.

With what took far too much effort, he rolled out of bed, used the restroom, and splashed cold water on his face to try to clear the cobwebs from his fuzzy mind.

He padded out of the room and down the hall, finding Davis and Squirrel watching a baseball game on the tube.

"Morning, or rather, evening, Princess," Davis said.

Chris made a point of looking around the corner to the front door. "Where is everyone?"

"Sig and Doc took Dumb Ass for a walk. They've been out for about thirty minutes now," Squirrel said, feet perched on the coffee table, a bowl of what looked to be popcorn in his lap.

Chris cocked his head. "And Sam?"

Both Davis and Squirrel shrugged. "She hasn't returned," his squad leader added.

Chris's heart gave a little jump start. Nothing to get too excited about. So she hadn't come back yet. She'd been gone all day, though. No texts, no calls. And after their conversation this morning, something didn't sit right.

His phone vibrated in his back pocket, and he reached for it. "Has she come back at all today?" he asked Davis.

Davis shook his head.

A quick look at his phone had him freezing to the spot. He answered it, feeling as if his heart was about to jump from his throat.

"D, talk to me," he said.

"Where are you?"

"My cabin. What's up?"

"Listen, no good way to say this, man. But you need to get down to the hospital, and I need you to get here pretty damn quick without breaking any laws. You hear what I'm saying to you?"

A million and one thoughts rushed through his mind at once. "What happened? Is it Ma? Pop?"

"No. Ma and Pop are fine. Get in your truck and get down here. Traffic shouldn't be too bad on the way down the hill."

"What the fuck, D? Why in the hell do you need me at the hospital?"

Davis and Squirrel both stood from the couch, eyes on him, but he barely spared them a glance and turned back toward his room. He needed his shoes. His wallet. Fuck, he needed his mind clear. Good news was, he sure as shit was fully awake.

"I'll tell you when you get here. Drive safe. If you don't think you can, call me and I'll have a unit come get you."

"Goddammit, D. If you don't tell me what in the fuck is going on, you and I are going to have some words..." All of a sudden, he stopped, pieces he didn't want falling into place becoming crystal clear. "Sam..."

His brother let out a broken curse on the other end of the line. "She's hurt, but not too bad. I need you to get down here so we can all get on the same page. There are a few things you don't know about, brother, and with what I've seen of you two, I don't think I should be the one to tell you. She needs to do it. And I need you to get down here so you can see one, that she's okay, a bit knocked up but otherwise fine. And two, I need to hit the town and surrounding areas and start looking for this guy before he gets too far. In order to do that, I need every man I have out on the road. Which means I need someone I can trust on her. Are you feeling me?"

Chris slammed his second foot into his boot, the sound vibrating across the floor. He looked out the window, his eyes not seeing anything in front of him. "What do you mean you're looking for this guy?" Something unpleasant spread across his chest, tightening the muscles there. In his peripheral, he saw Davis waiting at the door, DA at his side. Everyone had returned.

"That's all I'm saying for now. We're in the ER. I'll let the front desk know we're expecting you." With that, D hung up. Chris pulled the phone from his ear and looked at Davis.

"Sam is at the hospital."

"Let's go."

****

Chris rushed into Samantha's room, his heart doing its best impression of pounding out a beat that rivaled a toddler on a sugar high with a new drum set. If he had taken a moment to think on the short drive over, rather than have his mind look for every bad scenario he'd run into, he would have looked inward at this new foreign feeling. Instead, all he could do was let out the deep breath he'd been practically holding the entire ride over at the sight of Sam whole and alive in the small hospital bed.

Dwayne sat in a chair next to the bed, his head bent toward her as she spoke in low tones, his hand holding a pen to a notepad.

Both looked up at his entrance, Dwayne with a

hard look and Sam with something he couldn't interpret. One that almost looked like she was resigned to whatever conversation she was about to impart.

The door closed behind him with a *swoosh*, blocking out the busy sounds of the hospital and phones ringing. An antiseptic smell stung his nose, the scent all too familiar after the weeks he spent in the hospital in Germany. He vaguely noticed his team hadn't entered with him and guessed they stood outside Sam's door. For that, he was grateful. He wasn't acting himself, nor was he thinking on all cylinders.

Dwayne stood and shoved the small notepad in the back pocket of his dark jeans. "All right, if you can think of anything else, you know how to get ahold of me," he said to Sam, then looked at Chris. "The doc should be back shortly. They were running one more test before giving the approval to release. You'll stay by her side, correct?"

Chris nodded, throwing a questioning look at Sam. "I won't leave her unattended."

Dwayne nodded. "You two have some catching up to do. Once I get a better game plan of what's happening, I'll stop by the cabin."

Chris drew his brows together. "Mind telling me what the fuck is going on now?"

D shook his head and moved around the bed, his intention for exiting the room clear. Despite Chris wanting to make him stay, to demand an explanation from his brother, he stepped to the side as Dwayne reached the door. "I think it's best you hear what's going on from Sam. All I'll say is you need to make sure either you or a man you trust is with her at all times. You get me?"

There was a look in his brother's eye, one he wouldn't have expected on any law enforcement officer.

It was an expression Chris had only seen in hardened soldiers forced to do the ultimate worse. A look of resignation in facing a hard task ahead. Knowing his brother had things to do, despite those things being secretive, and wanting to have this conversation with Sam sooner than later, he nodded at D then turned to Sam as his brother left.

"Hi," she said. She wore one of those hospital gowns he'd become all too familiar with. A blanket was draped across her lap and the sheet pulled up over her chest. She looked so achingly vulnerable with a split lip, what he guessed would soon be a black eye if the swollenness of it was any indication, and bandages across her arms, as if she had fended off an attacker who wielded a knife.

He approached the bed, taking the same spot Dwayne had just vacated, and reached for her hand not connected to the IV. "How are you feeling?"

She lifted a shoulder. The move drew attention to how petite she was under that gown. "I've been better."

She wasn't giving him anything. He looked into her eyes, searching for an answer. "What's—what's going on, Sam? What happened?"

She took a deep breath in, letting it out with a controlled exhale, then bit her lip. "Honestly, I don't know where to start. There's a lot you don't know. But what I really want to say first is that I never intended for things to get this involved between us, Chris. If I had, I would have told you sooner. I looked for opportunities, wanted to tell you, but…" she trailed off.

What? What was she struggling to say? He tightened his grip on her hand, wrapped his other around both of them and continued to search for answers in her pretty, green eyes. "Why don't you just start at the beginning?"

She swallowed, the sound audible in the small room. "My real name, or rather the name I was born with, isn't Samantha Eagen."

He stared at her, trying to fight any sort of reaction when inside his chest, his lungs had seized. He forced himself to take in air.

"It's Juliette Graham. I had my name changed about six months ago." She looked away, her grip tightening on his hand as if she were forcing herself to get the words out.

"I had to file for a restraining order from my fiancé, then changed my name and moved five states away to try to protect us."

Us?

At that, his hand spasmed, and she darted her gaze back to him. Now it seemed as if she searched for something on his face. He still forced air in and out of his lungs, trying his damnedest not to get up and pace the room.

"Manuel doesn't like being denied of his plaything. And that's exactly what I was to him. A trophy to be set up on a shelf and admired by all his family and friends. But in the dark of the night, that trophy would turn into a punching bag. And it was steadily getting worse."

The easy breaths he'd been taking in became choppy. Fuzzy memories flashed behind his blinking, dry eyes. He knew exactly what kind of damage a man could inflict on a woman. He'd seen it firsthand. And the thought of anyone laying any kind of violence on Samantha, a woman who'd shown nothing but kindness with animals she'd interacted with, with his niece, his family, caused a different kind of violent feeling to roll through him. He pushed the reaction down. She didn't need to see that right now. She needed his attention and support, despite hiding such a major thing from him. He refused to let the ugliness of it all inside him. He'd deal with that later, when he was alone.

"Go on," he encouraged. "What happened today?"

Her eyes filled with tears, but she didn't let them fall. He scooted closer to the bed and reinforced his grip on her hand. "Manuel was in the apartment." She swallowed. "I've never seen him so angry."

"Did he tell you how he found you?"

She shook her head. The movement caused a tear to fall over her cheek. Before he could move, she swiped it away impatiently. "I fought back this time, though. I fought with everything I had. This time he wasn't going to break me. It's not just me I'm fighting for. And I think that took him by surprise."

"You shouldn't have had to fight him at all. I wish I would have gone with you."

She shook her head again, her pretty red ringlets falling around her shoulders in soft waves. "I managed to get to the alarm panel and hit the panic button. He left once we heard the sirens."

Chris took another calming, deep breath. "You don't have anything to fear anymore. I'll make sure you're protected, Sam. You'll be safe." His words made him feel like a fool, but right now they were all he had to offer. He felt useless fighting a battle he couldn't see.

"That's not all," she said and swiped at another tear rolling down her cheek. They came steadily now, and he couldn't hold out any longer. He dropped her hand and scooted into the bed with her, drawing her carefully into his arms. She held on tight then looked up to meet his gaze.

"I'm pregnant."

Shock stunned him speechless. He didn't move,

didn't even blink. They'd been safe each time they'd been intimate, hadn't they? He scrambled, trying to remember every time. He'd always been safe, had made it a priority to do so, not just to protect himself, but also to prevent situations like this from happening. But if he'd been safe, no way was the baby his. That meant...

"It's not yours, Chris. It's his. The day I changed my name at the court and ran for my life, for our lives, I took a pregnancy test."

That air he'd been working on taking in and out in a steady stream grew ragged. Shit. His hands curled into fists around her back, the rage of it all screaming through his system. He crushed her into his chest, not knowing what to say. He didn't have the words, couldn't think straight. His mind was a jumbled mess, and as if this situation weren't bad enough, hints of visions kept intruding on his memories.

Different times he'd been in the hospital as a child. Fear he didn't understand left a bad taste in his mouth and he tried to push through all he had learned, all of what was spinning in his head. He leaned back on the bed, Sam on his chest, and forced his hand to unclench so he could run a palm down the back of her head. His calluses caught on the soft tendrils, but neither of them seemed to care.

"We'll get through this, Sam. You're safe now. I'll keep you safe."

She tightened her grip on his shirt and let the tears she'd been fighting come. He held her through it all.

Chapter Eighteen

Samantha accepted the cup of steaming tea from Hailey with a smile. "Thank you, sweetheart." She sipped the hot liquid, inhaling the aroma of chamomile and lavender with a satisfied sigh. Her body ached, but the pounding behind her left eye told another story. One that refused to let her push any of what occurred today in the back of her mind.

Not that her body wasn't telling her what a mirror had. The marks left on her face would keep the activity in her head for weeks to come. And the memories would serve as haunting reminders of the very real terror she felt for that hour alone with Manuel.

Then there was the baby. A lifetime reminder she'd never be able to forget. A child created through utter violence, but one she vowed she'd love with everything she was.

Hailey disappeared in the bathroom, coming out a few moments later and sitting on the side of the bed, her shrew gaze far too old for her young years. "Is there anything else I can get for you, Doctor Eagen?"

Sam smiled warmly and shook her head, dropping the smile when it stretched her lips to the point of pain. "You've already done so much. Rearranging the clinic's schedule and calling other vet offices in the area to help the more emergent cases get addressed now. You've done more than I could have asked for, and I appreciate it all."

"Well," Hailey said, and tucked her hands into her lap. "Make sure Uncle Chris spoils you. Don't get up unless you absolutely need to. We want you to be back on your feet quickly."

Sam couldn't help but like the young woman, and even though she had to be at least fifteen years her senior, she accepted the instructions with a firm nod of her head.

"Mom got sick right after she and D got together."

Sam's eyes widened in alarm, about to ask and apologize, as was the normal immediate response whenever someone mentioned a family member "getting sick," but Hailey jumped in before she could.

"Not that it was anything serious. Just the flu. We suspected it had to do with all the stress she had been under." She trailed off for a moment then shook her head and jumped back in. "Anyhow, D wasn't living with us yet and Mom didn't want him to see her like that. When she gets sick, she is S. I. C. K." Hailey bugged her eyes with emphasis and Sam fought the urge to laugh.

"So, she had texted him she was sick, apparently thinking with his job and all, he'd want to stay away." She shook her head, a small smile dancing on her pink lips. "Boy, was she wrong. Dwayne came over and hovered. And when I mean he hovered, he hov-er-ed. He slept right beside her every night, made sure she stayed in bed, got her soup and orange juice, tissues, you name it. It was the most ridiculous thing she'd ever seen, from what she told me."

Hailey's smile grew, her gaze far off. She turned to Sam again. "So, make sure Uncle Chris spoils you, but be forewarned, these Gonzalez men have a problem with personal space when their women are sick, or in your case, hurt." She lifted a delicate shoulder. "It's kind of romantic when you think of it."

Behind Hailey, a snort sounded. Sam looked over her shoulder as Hailey turned to see Chris with a wide smile. "Don't listen to D, Hails. He has no sense of romance at all. Just ask your mother."

Hailey laughed and rose from the bed. "I think Mom would disagree with you there. But I'll get out of your hair. If you need anything," she said, and cast a glance at them both, "please don't hesitate to call. I have my phone on me and I'm only a short drive from the clinic. And before you say anything, I'll take Dad with me if I need to go by there."

Chris nodded and Sam murmured, "Thank you, Hailey. Have a good night."

"Sure thing," she said with a wave. "You, too."

Chris shut the door behind her and went to the bathroom. The water faucet turned on and off, the toilet flushed, and some rustling around sounded before he came out dressed in a pair of black boxers, a perplexed look on his face, eyes on the door Hailey just disappeared through.

"What's wrong?" she asked.

He didn't answer right away, and his brows turned down into a deep V on his forehead. The man was entirely too handsome for his own good. She couldn't help but unabashedly take him in standing there in all his glory. She'd heard soldiers were in shape, they had to be to do the work they did, especially Special Operation soldiers, but the defined, cut muscles on Chris took that physical fitness to a whole other level.

Wide shoulders gave way to arms molded with muscles. His stomach and waist looked as if he'd been carved from stone. Was some Adonis statue ready to be erected.

And speaking of erected … his package stood out in stark relief in those formfitting boxers, drawing her gaze more than probably polite.

Beautiful.

Of course, he probably would scoff at being

called beautiful, but that was how she saw him in her mind. And it wasn't just the outside that made him so. It was everything about him, his compassion, caring, and empathy he'd shown toward her and his dog. He truly cared about ridding the world of evil, and she'd seen that in everything he'd done over the past few weeks, from the interactions with his team, toward handling everything going on with her.

How she ever got so lucky to get him in her life, she'd never know. But what she understood now more than ever was she wanted to keep him. And she knew it was selfish, especially asking that of him, of taking in her and a child that wasn't his, but she didn't want to let him go. She wanted to make this decision for her, and her only. She wanted him … forever.

Everything was so new, though. Their relationship. They had known each other for a few weeks. How could she feel this connected to him? Was it all in her head? Was he a rebound from a bad relationship she just escaped?

She didn't want to think so and instead wanted to follow the warm, tingly feeling she got whenever she was in his presence. She wanted to chase this good feeling so she could continue having more of it. After everything she'd been through, didn't she deserve at least that?

"I don't know," Chris said, drawing her out of her musings, "but something is up." He shook his head and walked over to the bed, then lay next to her, tucking himself under the heavy covers. "I have more pills missing, and either I'm taking them and not realizing it, or someone is swiping them out from underneath me."

Sam raised her brows. "That's not good. Oxy, you said?"

He nodded.

"Those are highly addictive pills. How many were in the bottle?"

"Thirty. I have a prescription for one more refill, but I threw it away knowing I wouldn't use it. I don't like the way they make me fuzzy. And my mom had an addiction to drugs, if you remember…"

She nodded and curled up on her side, facing him as he settled in.

"I swear I've only taken a few, three at most, but nearly the entire bottle is gone."

"What do you think is going on?"

He stared at the door to his bedroom, a deep frown settled on his face. "I think I need to have a chat with D soon." He seemed to struggle on what to say next, but took a deep breath and faced her. "Hailey has been through a bit of a tough time."

Alarm coursed through Samantha, the implications of what Chris said hitting her. "You think Hailey is taking your pills?"

He nodded, a grim look on his face.

"Chris, that's a serious accusation. Even more so because she works in a clinic where there are controlled substances in abundance."

"But you have the key for that locker, right?"

She nodded.

He nodded back. "Good. Keep it on you for now. We'll do a count to make sure once we get back down there. But all I'm saying is what she went through wasn't easy. And whoever took her pumped her full of some drugs that left her completely out of it for long periods of time. Heroine. Heroine is what they filled her with. She couldn't function for a while after everything, and as far as I know, is still struggling with the withdrawal. It hasn't been that long since she's been back, and I know they are still doing counseling, but this is twice now she's been here and more pills have gone missing. I'm not saying it's her, but with her past and everything she's been through, all I'm saying is I think I need to have a chat with D about it. Just to be certain."

"It's a tough situation to be in, for all of you," she said.

His lips flattened and he pushed a tendril of hair behind her ear, the action so achingly tender her nose stung with tears. "Yeah, it is."

She captured his wrist and held it to her face before he could draw his hand away. "Chris?"

"Right here, Red."

Her stomach flipped with the urge to blurt out her feelings. Things were so very new between them. She didn't want to scare him off. But the urge to tell him refused to be delayed. She'd always been impulsive, but this was taking things a step further. They need to get everything out, to declare something between them. To have them both recognize it for what it was.

"I ... I..."

He drew closer to her and cupped her face until her gaze lifted to his. In the darkness of the night with the moon shining behind him from the window, he looked like a dark protector. A man who'd slay any dragon for her.

"I think I'm falling in love with you," she said in a rush, the words pushed out with such force that she had to draw in a quick take of air to prevent herself from passing out.

Chris froze, his entire being not moving at all. If she hadn't been sure, she would have suspected him of being that very statue she thought of earlier. Several seconds ticked by in utter silence and an uneasy feeling worked its way into her stomach. She'd said something too soon. She knew it!

She parted her lips to apologize, but found his mouth covering hers. He brushed his lips against her so tenderly, softly like a moth's wings. She pressed toward him, needing the contact of her body, and found his arm wrapped around her waist as he hauled her against him. The action was so unlike the kiss, forceful even, and she realized what he did. He kissed her with care as her mouth had a busted lip, but showed her with his actions just how much her words had moved him.

She parted her mouth and his tongue peeked out to claim hers, but still it was soft, hesitant almost, their tongues dancing to a tune as old as time itself. Their lips didn't touch, but they fused their bodies together, tongues wrapped around one another. She fell into his spell and let him show her what his words could not.

Chris broke away with a harsh growl. "You're hurt. Let's slow down."

She shook her head and rolled him to his back. He grunted and stared up at her, his eyes shining bright and round under the reflection of the moon. Silvery splashes of light played over his strikingly handsome features. The strong cut of his jaw, a dusting of a five o'clock shadow, and deep, wide-set, honey-colored eyes. He smelled of man with a hint of a spicy cologne she couldn't seem to get enough of. All of it combined drove her to distraction. She didn't want to wait. She wanted him despite being through her ordeal.

Heat settled between her legs and low within her stomach. She resettled over him, and her legs fell open to encompass his slim hips. Aligning them as she knew was a perfect fit, breath jumped out between her parted lips as her intimate parts came into contact with his dangly bits, only a thin barrier of their underwear the remaining obstacle.

"Red," he said, the growl echoing through the

room and causing a thrill to roll up her spine. He grabbed her hips, not to throw her off it seemed, but to hold her still. "Sweetheart." He tilted his head back as she dipped hers, then she ran her tongue along the length of his throat.

"I want you," she whispered. "Please."

A beat of silence, then he groaned and dipped his big hands under the elastic of her underwear to hold her ass in place over his hardening cock. His hips rolled, pushing against her most private part, held in place by his grip.

She curled her toes as pleasure washed through her limbs. Amazing that only hours ago she'd been in the clutches of terror, and now, she couldn't think straight for the warm tingles building within her.

His harsh breaths sounded in the room as she continued her onslaught of his neck, taking care not to stretch her lips too much. He didn't seem to pay any attention to her care, though, for his body started to get into the motion his hips led. His grip tightened, hands clutching for purpose.

Beneath her shirt, her nipples pebbled to hard rocks she wanted to scrap across his chest. Sweat dampened the skin behind her neck, and between her legs, she grew wetter. She could feel the material between them growing damper with each grinding movement of their hips against one another.

She could come just like this but wanted more. She wanted to feel him skin to skin.

Sitting up and ignoring the twinges in her back, she whipped the shirt over her head, taking a moment of victory at his desire-filled gaze on her body.

She'd done this. She gave him this reaction. Her confidence grew under his stare. Whereas she'd been a shallow creature led through the bedtime activities before, under Chris's attention, she wanted to lead them to pleasure.

Straddling him, she rolled her hips forward and back, her mouth parting as a new wave of pleasure washed over her body. The tingles made her scalp prickle, made her body beg to be filled by only what he could provide.

Chris clutched at her underwear, growling deeper in his throat until it sounded as if an animal had entered their secluded moment.

"Sweetheart," he said, the words sounding ripped out of him. "I need to be inside you. These"—he tugged at her panties on each side—"need to come off."

She didn't want to move from her position, but she wanted him inside of her. "Rip them off me," she breathed.

He paused and gave her an incredulous look. "Baby," he said through a short bark of laughter. "Trust me, that isn't nearly as sexy as it sounds." More laughter rumbled in his chest. "If you want me to give it a shot, I will, but I don't want to hurt you."

She met his grin with one of her own, shook her head, then flipped down beside him and whipped her panties over her hips and down her legs before the next breath. Then she turned to see his progress. He stared at her with wonder then flashed a blinding smile. She matched it.

He pulled off his boxers in record time then rolled atop her, his hips between her legs, their intimate parts lined up but him not yet inside.

His face hovered so close, his arms under her shoulders, and his palms holding the back of her head. She felt trapped … in a good way. Protected. Safe.

Then he shifted and pushed insider with one long thrust.

Her neck arched at the feeling of being stretched so full. His pelvis rolled against hers, rubbing along her clit in the most delicious fashion. Lids dropped halfway in pleasure, she tilted her head back and met his eyes. He held her gaze as if he were trying to solve all the world's problems.

"You feel so good, Red," he said with a growl. "Hot." He pulled out and thrust forward again. Her body jolted and her breath caught. "Wet." Thrust. "Tight." Thrust. "You grip me like a tight glove." Thrust.

His words pushed her higher and higher. His thrusts, followed by a roll of his hips, caused the tightening coil in her stomach to tighten.

"Come with me," he said and picked up the pace. One hand left from under her head and wrapped around the top, preventing her from hitting the headboard. They'd shifted on the bed under his thrusts. She didn't pay attention to any of it outside of how he made her feel.

The full feeling between her legs spread within her stomach until she reached for what he gave. It built and built, then hovered, suspending her for a moment where the world stopped spinning, her heart stopped beating, and her lungs ceased pulling in air.

Then she let go. "Chris!" she shouted. His hips pounded furiously, and he groaned, the sound bouncing off the walls. His hips dove between hers over and over, prolonging the pleasure until she couldn't take anymore.

She bit down on his shoulder and sucked the skin there between her lips.

He hissed and pulled her close, then fell to his side, bringing her with him.

"Jesus," he said, and she released the skin with a pop.

She smiled against his skin then gave in to the

exhaustion promising her peace. She closed her eyes and fell asleep with him still inside her body.

****

Chris lay awake long after Samantha had fallen asleep in his arms.

He couldn't dispute her feelings for him, that was certain. Falling asleep in his arms while he was still semi-hard inside her irrefutably knocked any argument out of his head with that.

He also couldn't deny things were moving really friggin' fast. Getting wrapped up in Samantha had done everything he'd always told himself he'd never do ... he had the starter family right here in his cabin he'd built away from civilization, intending to keep to himself, right on down to the kid on the way and the loving-family dog.

The side of his mouth kicked up despite his troubled thoughts.

He didn't think DA could be called a family-loving dog, but in his mind, that was exactly what he'd be to them. That was an irrefutable point he couldn't miss. His partner was one hundred percent attached to his doc, just as his handler could see himself doing, should he get his mind straight and figure out what he wanted. As it was, he was damn pleased at the protective nature DA had with Sam, especially since she was expecting. Almost like instinct. He also couldn't deny the connection he felt to her, but was it love? He didn't know. He'd experienced different forms of love in his short life, from the unending love of his adoptive parents, to that of his brothers—both in the service and within his adoptive family, to that of the love he had for his friends, Charlie being on that short list. But the love of a real relationship wasn't a feeling he'd ever experienced before, and he didn't know if this bone-melting need to be with Samantha at all hours of the day and night, of the need to protect her until his last breath, was something he'd call love.

Was it?

And the feeling that had screamed through him when he'd heard she was in the hospital—shit. He'd never had such an ugly emotion take root, never felt the dark danger of hatred as much as he had at the thought of another man putting his hands on Samantha, and in anger of all things. Even now, he tucked her closer as if to protect her in this house full of Spec Force operators and a trained military working dog.

He adjusted the both of them, slipping out of the heat of Samantha with a soft sigh then pulling her closer when she snuggled into him and closed his eyes.

It had been a day and a half with everything they'd been through and he was wiped.

After what felt as if it were minutes, a vision popped in his head of two little boys, both visions of what he'd been like as a child. The image faded in and out of his mind, but this time instead of fighting to discover, to see more, he relaxed and let the picture play out in his head.

"Hey, Cooper," he said.

His identical self looked back at him with a lopsided grin he'd grown accustomed to seeing in the mirror. "Do you think she'll bring home ice cream tonight?"

The little Chris shook his head, feeling an overwhelming sadness rise in his chest. A sadness built on hopeless dreams that they'd have a better life than this. What had they ever done wrong in all of their seven years of life to deserve such bone-wrenching hunger pains? "I doubt it. Want to see if we can find some coins in the couch and go down to the corner store for some candy?"

Cooper pouted. "But I really want some ice cream. She promised last week. Said she'd get us big scoops of chocolate ice cream this time."

This time, being yet another instance in which they'd gone over a week without their mother being around. She'd get like this every few months, slipping off to put that disgusting liquid in her veins and hang around with her latest boyfriend. Their father had been no better when he was around. The guy was always feeling up on other women other than their mother, sometimes right in front of her, too.

Chris tilted his head toward the living room, trying to get his twin's attention away from the darkening sky outside. He didn't think she'd come home tonight. She would have already been there. "Let's go search the couch. Maybe we'll find enough to get you an ice cream."

Cooper's lopsided grin grew. "Let's go."

They both scrambled up and made a dash for the living room. Turned out, they did find enough to buy Cooper an ice cream, but only enough for that. Chris ate a piece of moldy bread that night, his stomach aching with hunger and sickness after the meager meal. But he'd put on a brave face for his brother, who seemed to have a different outlook in their situation. One that was very childlike, very innocent. Chris saw through their situation for what it was ... their sad existence.

And that night, Cooper had fallen asleep with chocolate around his mouth. Chris didn't say anything. He didn't want to take this away from his brother. He wanted him to have something to look forward to.

Instead, Chris stayed up half the night listening for their mother.

He never heard her come home because she

never did.

Chapter Nineteen

Sam eyed her clinic as they parked across the street, wincing as she took in the black soot rising up and over her storefront sign. This would be a huge undertaking, cleaning up her practice and getting it ready for reopening. Thank God for insurance. She hoped it covered everything.

Chris shut off the truck just as his phone rang. "Gotta take this," he said, putting the device up to his ear. "D, what's going on?"

Biting down on her lip, she faced the dark building. She needed clothes, badly. Wearing the same pair of pants for the past few days left her feeling all kinds of disgusting. And despite Chris telling her she could borrow a pair of his pants to wash hers, with his team running in and out of the cabin, she didn't feel comfortable wearing sweatpants three sizes too big for her. She wanted her own clothing. And with everything happening, the fire, Manuel still missing … she needed that additional piece of comfort. Being in the early stages of her pregnancy meant she could only wear her pants for a few more months, but she'd take it for now.

"Listen," Chris said into the phone. "I have to talk to you about Hails."

Yikes, not a conversation she wanted to be around a second time. She eyed the front door, her mind spinning up a million possibilities of what could occur if she just darted inside and grabbed her things really quick. The sun shone above, bringing the misconception of heat because the wind and season had finally moved in. It was cold outside. Enough to cause her southern girl skin to prick with goose pimples every time she stepped outside.

The townsfolk walked up and down the sidewalk in front of her clinic, jackets in various forms of dark colors but scarfs as bright as the sun above. A police cruiser drove down the road, slowing as it came to a pedestrian crosswalk. Just a normal fall day in Nyack, N.Y.

She grabbed the handle and motioned to her clinic, catching Chris's gaze. He tossed his head toward Delta Alpha, who sat in the backseat, long pink tongue lolling out of his mouth as if he had not a care in the world.

She shook her head. Chris dropped the phone with a quick word to his brother. "Take DA, babe."

"The glass. I don't want to risk his paws."

Chris's lips tightened and he eyed the clinic and surrounding area. She could read his expression as if he'd spoken clear as day. He didn't want her going inside by herself, even with townsfolk all around and the peace of the day like a caress on her skin.

"Seriously, there's too many people around. I'll be fine, Chris."

He tossed her a look that promised retribution should she get even a scratch, then nodded and rubbed the back of his neck, his focus obviously on the conversation he had with his brother. "I'm not sure how to say this," he started and thinned his lips. Whatever else he had been about to get into got lost as she shut the truck door, shivering as a gust of cool air took its frosty swipe at her.

She jumped over the curb to the parking lot then darted across the street, checking for cars. Her hands shook and her body trembled in the cold as she fumbled with the lock to her front door. This season change had come out of nowhere, going from a balmy eighty degrees last week to fifty overnight, it seemed. Apparently, she needed to go shopping for some cold-weather jackets along with all that maternity clothing … and soon.

She shook herself as she stepped inside, brushing off the chilly weather. Inside wasn't that much better, seeing as she hadn't turned on the heat. It wouldn't do much good, though, since the front window of her shop only had a piece of plywood over it.

Taking an immediate right, she darted up the stairs, grabbed the smaller piece of her luggage, and tossed what she needed, along with a few extra pieces inside—a girl could never be too careful, before zipping it up and hauling it from the bed. It didn't do any good to focus on what had happened the last time she'd been there, and she pushed it firmly from her mind. This was her place, her home now, her future, and she needed to get over any hang-ups she had about it before she could move on. The best way to do that was plow right through it. At least, that was something her mama used to say.

She struggled to get the luggage downstairs but had a feeling that was more due to what she packed and how tired she was versus being unable to do such a task. Perhaps waiting for Chris would have been the thing to do so he could carry it down the stairs, but she was focused on being an independent woman the past few months. Carrying her own suitcase was something an independent woman might just do.

A light to the isolation room caught her attention at the bottom of the stairs. She frowned at it, wondering how long it had been on. Since she'd been there a few days ago, when the attack happened, and had left in an obvious rush to go to the hospital, perhaps she had left the switch on, but couldn't recall doing so.

Leaving the case by the front door, she skirted the front counter, took a few steps, and then stopped dead in her tracks as a man rounded the corner to the back room.

Her heart jumped right into her throat, pounding a fierce tune of fear.

Eyes the color of the night stared back at her with contempt. She took a step backward from the force of that look. There was no iris, no light shining there. Only pure death and hatred. His lips slashed across his face in a sneer, as if he couldn't stand the thought of being in her company for one additional second.

And he was the same man who had been in asking questions about DA last week. He took a step forward, showing signs of an old or new injury in his pronounced limp. In his hand, he held a lethal-looking black gun pointed at her.

For the love of—! She wanted to scream at the unfairness of it all, yell at the top of her lungs. Why her?

"What do you want?" she asked, proud that her voice didn't tremble. Her body shook, but she hoped it was only her that noticed.

His sneer grew more pronounced, curling high so she could see sharp incisors within his mouth.

"You walk around like it's your right." He limped closer and motioned at her hands, which she immediately raised, palms out.

"Who are you?" she tried.

"In my village, the women show respect, even cover their eyes. How dare you speak to me," he hissed.

She backed up for every limping step he took forward until her back met the ledge of the counter. Her mind spun with questions, but the anger and hatred in his eyes stopped her from asking questions. In almost a surreal state, she watched as if looking from above as this stranger advanced on her. She couldn't get her legs to catch up to her brain, screaming at her to run!

The man whipped out his arm, the force of his blow cutting across her cheek. She went to the ground as pain erupted. She'd been hit before, suffered abuse for years. Why did some men feel as though they had the right to hit a woman at will? Anger built like a balloon in her chest, causing her blood to boil until she felt ready to erupt with violence. At least DA hadn't come in with her. She tossed her head back and glared up at this stranger. "Who the hell do you think you are?"

He smiled then, a slow, alarming grin that spread over his face as if she had finally asked the right question.

"Not to sound cliché or anything, but I'm your worst nightmare. I will go down in history as one of the greatest."

She didn't see the needle until it was too late.

****

Chris opened the door to the clinic and stepped inside, his phone ringing in his pocket. Samantha. A little bemused, he answered it on the second ring. "Babe, I just walked in. Where are you at?"

"Sergeant Gonzalez," a familiar voice said down the line.

As if he channeled his partner, his hackles went up and his hand went for the Beretta at the small of his back. He ducked next to the counter as if he were taking cover, his instincts immediately kicking in. Crab-walking toward the partition that separated the waiting area from the back of the clinic, he scanned the area, looking for a threat. Because now he knew without a doubt. Months of suspecting, of sightings, of feeling it in his damn gut, he knew without a doubt Tayseer was in Nyack.

"What the hell do you want, you sick fuck?" he asked.

Tayseer tsked. "You Americans and your disrespect. Is that any way to greet an old friend?"

Having done a precursory check of the main floor

of the clinic, Chris rushed up the stairs to Sam's apartment. His heart pounded in his chest and the rushing beat filled his ears. Samantha wasn't here.

"Chris?" Sam's voice came down the line, her words slurred, as if she had just woken up.

"Sam! Sweetheart, are you okay?"

"She'll be fine, as long as you do what I want."

To think Sam was with him, within his clutches, put a horror through him he hadn't ever felt. "Where is she?" Chris took the phone away from his ear and pushed it against his leg, finding her apartment empty. "Fuck!" His shout bounced off the walls and echoed back to him. He smacked his face, urging the rising panic to go back down. He needed to keep his head, needed to think this through. Keep that level of calm that had always helped him in high-stress situations. But all he kept seeing were those pictures of what Tayseer had done to other families, the horrible blisters, the boiling skin. Except now, all he could see was Sam's face on each rotting corpse.

He took a deep breath and fought like hell to bring himself under control. Everything in him wanted to fight, wanted to tear this asshole on the phone to shreds. And he would. All he needed to do was get close enough.

Samantha…

He put the phone back to his ear, straining in the silence to hear everything. An engine hummed down the line. Sounded like they were driving somewhere. "What do you want?"

"Do you know how long I worked on it?" Tayseer asked as if this were a lazy day and they were two friends.

Chris fought to roll his eyes and curse again. The *it* in his question being the chemical weapon he'd worked on for years. And that was only from the intel they had.

Not necessarily the entire story. "There was no way that weapon could make it to the United States."

"That was not for you to decide!" A horn blared in the background. A thump sounded, as if someone dropped the phone.

"Tayseer!" Chris shouted.

"Pick up the phone, you bitch," he heard from what sounded far off. A loud smack came next. Samantha cried out and Chris growled.

"Your little bitch is finally following orders," Tayseer said.

"You lay one more goddamn hand on her," he started and didn't finish. He let it hang in the air, but in his mind, he thought of everything he wanted to do, everything he would do.

"Oh, I'm sure you won't do anything. You'll be too busy making a decision." An eerie laugh sounded as if pulled right out of an old Halloween movie.

He frowned. "I'm waiting, Tayseer. How about you stop talking in riddles and tell me what you want?"

"Ah, yes. What. I. Want." Tayseer didn't say anything for a few seconds, but the distinct sound of a blinker echoed in the background. Chris worked through his next steps once he got off the line, the first order of business being to get Sig to trace Sam's phone. Or Dwayne. Maybe Trent. Someone had to know how to track her.

"First, you will come alone. No police." Tayseer said, practically spitting that last word. Chris looked at Delta Alpha and couldn't help the surge of satisfaction in his gut that his partner had previously sunken his teeth into this bastard and had his fill. "You come with anyone and I'll take the choice out of your hands. Now, tell me you understand. Follow orders like a good little soldier."

He ground his teeth. "Got it."

"Oh, I forgot to ask … how are Karen and Daniel?"

Chris's spine snapped straight. "You piece of sh—"

"Ah, ah, ah," Tayseer cut in. "Don't forget your place, boy."

He squeezed the phone so hard it cracked beneath his hand. Rather than lose this lifeline to Sam, he forced himself to release the hard grip. "What did you do to them?" he asked after several moments of reconstructing his careful control.

"Why nothing," he answered in a mock-innocent voice. "But it's amazing how much information one can get on another online. Have you ever run one of those checks on yourself? There are a ton of websites dying to give information to anyone who pays for it."

"Get to the point."

"The point, Sergeant Gonzalez, is there is much I know about you. And I suspect I know more than you do."

Chris slapped the wall next to his head and dipped his forehead into the plaster, wanting to scream. "Stop talking in fucking riddles."

"There were two children born that night."

He blinked and pushed away from the wall, staring at the gray color but not really seeing it. Two children. Two. His dreams. The memories. What?

"Two children born the night you were born, Sergeant."

Air rushed out of his lungs in a rush.

Laughter sounded over the line and the road noise in the background changed, coming rougher somehow.

"Ask Karen if you don't believe me," Tayseer said. "And come prepared to make a choice, Sergeant Gonzalez. Meet us at the Bear Mountain Carousel. I'm sure you know the way."

The line went dead. Chris didn't even take a moment to think and rushed out of the apartment.

Chapter Twenty

Max "Sig" Carletto turned to Sergeant Davis with a raised brow, a chill unlike anything else skating down his spine. "You're never going to believe what I found."

Davis paused, a bottle of water halting at his mouth, and matched Sig's eyebrow raise, lifting off the couch from where he'd been watching last night's replay of the Yankee game. Sig had tuned it out. He was a Dodgers' fan through and through. A snap, crackle, and pop sounded from Davis's lumbering body and Sig muffled a laugh.

"Getting too old for this line of work, man," Davis grumbled, wincing as he rubbed a knee. "Whatcha got?" Davis bent over his shoulder and looked at the computer screen.

He turned back to his research and findings, an alarm building in his chest coming from somewhere he couldn't recognize. "Read this."

Davis read for a few moments, silent behind him until finally a curse sounded from his mouth, low and harsh. Just then, Davis's phone started ringing. Sig turned to him, waiting for their next step. Because there would be. A next step. What he'd found left no doubt about that.

"Davis here."

His sergeant listened for a few moments, his brows drawing lower and lower until alarm crossed over his face. "You've got to be shitting me." He looked at Sig. "Suit up. Now."

****

Chris and Delta Alpha crept up over the hill. A darkened carousel sat just above the rise like an abandoned building lost in the middle of the forest. Which, when he thought about it, with the carousel being far, far away from civilization and in the middle of a National Forest, it kind of was.

The sun had set, dipping behind the tall trees of Bear Mountain and casting the area into deep shades of black and grey. A cool wind gusted, causing trees to sway, leaves to drop, and critters to scurry, all the sounds reaching his oversensitive ears at once. Many complained about the noises of the city, honking cars, sirens, footsteps, and general living. But a lot of those people didn't know about the utter silence of the forest and how loud that quiet could become.

His hands shook with fear and adrenaline, wrapped around his M4 carbine. Millions of thoughts clamored in his head, trying to one-up another, endless possibilities for just what could go wrong here, why Tayseer had brought him to this particular carousel, and why this place seemed so familiar. With a quick glance at DA, he also wondered if he made the right decision bringing his partner along. After he'd parked some few miles back, he hadn't thought twice about bringing him along. But now, with the doubts about his own ability and decisions he had to make, he wondered if he'd made the right one with his dog.

Memories flicked behind his eyelids each time he blinked, pulling his concentration. Images of this same carousel, of another boy who looked like him, of their healthy mother before her body had been riddled with drugs. A moist muzzle shoved between his palm and the ground. Wet grass and dying leaves, a rotting animal not too far away all filled his nose, and combined with the too-loud whoosh of his heartbeat in his ears, his attention span turned to shit.

How was he supposed to help Sam, help his

brother if this was how he was? Distracted to the point of being worthless.

He gave a thankful pat on DA's head then crept along the tree line, keeping the darkened carousel in his sight when suddenly, the lights turned on and it began to spin. Between the loud music and glaring lamps, it took him a few moments to adjust. He was two hundred feet away, but it was a shock to his senses … again.

"Come on, Cooper," a younger him yelled over the music from the carousel, laughing, and holding the cone of his cotton candy tight as he tugged on his twin's arm, "it's about to start."

DA brushed along his side and Chris grunted under his breath, shook his head. Shit. Just a memory, but the feeling of holding his brother's hand felt very current. He resisted the urge to rub at his palm it had seemed so real.

He refocused on the carousel and squinted as something stood out. Two forms were tied inside against the poles, their lolling heads hiding their faces, but the unmistakable shade of red caused his gut to pull up tight. He darted out of the trees without thinking and pounded his way across the soft ground, his boots thudding with each contact. An echoing shot sounded out in the night, causing him to dive behind a wide oak tree closer to the carousel.

"Fuck," he said, panting and pushing his back against the trunk. Beneath his pants, the ground was cold and wet, liquid seeping into the backside of his jeans. DA had crouched low beside him. Chris took a moment to study his dog's reaction to the scene and the gunshot. There wasn't much he'd be able to do if DA showed signs of PTSD and fear, but he needed to make sure everyone made it out of this alive, and the first step of that was to make sure both he and his partner could handle the pressure.

DA seemed fine, ears perked up, body posed and at attention, close to the ground and ready for a command. It seemed his dog was in better shape than he for fear made his hands shake beneath the rubber grip of his gun.

The phone inside his jacket pocket started ringing.

He pulled it out and answered on a growl. "What?"

"Nice of you to join us, Sergeant."

"Oh, yeah? Nice way you have of greeting someone, asshole. I'm here, now what?" He winced as soon as the words left his mouth. He should probably be a bit more diplomatic, but he didn't take too kindly to having bullets shot at him.

"You know, you and I aren't all that much different," Tayseer said.

He scoffed. "Really? Are you seriously sitting here and telling me that a United States Special Forces soldier and a world-wide terrorist have something in common? Is that what I'm hearing coming from your mouth?"

Tayseer hissed. "What I mean, Gonzalez, is we both enjoy killing people."

His heartbeat thundered in his throat, threatening to break out of the skin. They were nothing alike, nothing. But with Tayseer mentioning killing people while he had his brother and Sam in his grasp left a foul, bitter taste in his mouth. "I don't know who the hell you think I am, but we are nothing alike. Nothing. You and I wouldn't even match up on Match.com we're so different." He winced again, unable to help himself with the smartass comments.

A sigh came in through his ear, the sound like

Tayseer had grown bored with their banter. "My work," he directed, bringing the topic back around to their earlier conversation, "is very important to me."

He said nothing, just listened while poking his head around the tree, trying to get a glimpse of Sam and Cooper. His brother. Christ! Everything within the last hour had changed. Everything. How could he have ever forgotten his twin? How crazy was it when the mind played such games?

"You and your team threatened that work," Tayseer went on. "But after tonight, they will remember me. I will show you all just what happens when you mess with me."

Chris took a deep breath and pushed back against the tree, rising to stand. Bark dug into his jacket as he inched his way up and his legs shook with adrenaline. Cooper had woken, lifting his head from the pole in which he was tied. Chris would recognize him anywhere. Hell, they were practically mirrored in looks. Cooper's hair was lighter than his own, but outside of that, it was like looking at his reflection.

"There is only one cure sitting here," Tayseer said, bringing his attention back to the phone. "Now you must choose."

Horror washed over Chris, sending needles of pain throughout his body. "You sick fuck!" he said, but the line had already clicked, indicating Tayseer had hung up.

****

Charlie hit the gas pedal, merging off I-287 and onto Palisades Parkway, her head spinning with the implications of what was occurring. A terrorist was in the United States and Chris was out in the middle of a forest dealing with the guy.

"Charlie, you need to wait for the FBI," Trent

said, his dark voice rumbling over her car speakers.

The panic that had been eating at her since she got D's call, him having been given a heads-up by Chris's team, hadn't lessened. No, in fact, it seemed to grow until it felt as if a monster had situated itself over her skin, eating at her.

Chris was like an older brother. Someone who had laughed into the dark night with her while they watched old eighties horror movies, making fun of the damsels in distress. Someone who had taken her to her eighth-grade dance because stupid Billy had said no boy would take her, and she wanted to prove a point, even if her date had been a sophomore in high school. Someone who had just a few nights ago picked her up and gave her a bear hug that almost squeezed all the air from her. He was family, and she was damned if she would wait for the friggin' FBI to take their time making their pretty, fancy-pants ways up to Rockland County when she could be there in mere minutes.

"As much as I love you, honey," she said, and Trent snorted at her endearment, "I have to do this."

"Dammit, Char—"

"He's family."

That shut him up.

"I don't like this. This Tayseer guy isn't one to play games with. The amount of intel coming in is highly disturbing." Trent's sigh rattled, and she had to force her rising guilt down. She got it. He was worried. About her. She would be in his shoes if the situation were reversed.

"I love you," she said again.

He cursed under his breath. "I love you, too. Don't get hurt."

An order. One she'd try to follow.

****

"One … two … three!" Chris rushed from his

hiding spot, sprinting across the remaining space between the tree and carousel. A ball of fur kept pace beside him, both of them working as they always had—like a well-oiled machine.

A shot rang out. Pain erupted in his leg, sending him stumbling forward. He fell into the side partition of the building where the carousel sat, catching his body before he smacked face-first into the ground. Rolling to his back, he breathed through the pain, sucking air between his teeth. There was no time to relax, though, for Tayseer had a gun and wanted him dead. Probably not as much as Chris wanted him dead, though.

He pushed to sitting and rested against the wood, ripping off his belt and making a field tourniquet around the bullet wound that would have made Doc proud. Even having a field tech assigned to the team, each of them had undergone the basic classes in the event Doc went down. It came in handy, like now.

His belt in place, he checked his M4 again and risked a quick peek around the partition. Both Cooper and Sam had their heads up. Blood ran in a red trail over his brother's head, coming over the gray sweatshirt he wore, but otherwise, Sam seemed to be unharmed.

He squeezed his eyes shut. That was, if one didn't think about them both being infected.

He shook his head, needing to push that next problem away. Staying focused was key to try to get them all out alive.

Shifting, he crept around and waited for the perfect opportunity to jump on the moving carousel. DA brushed along the side of his body. The air around them held its breath. He scanned beyond the moving floor, looking for any sign of Tayseer. Dimly, he heard a low rumbling of a voice, followed by a soft cry from Sam. That sound tore at his chest like mice threatening to tunnel inside, and DA growled low in his throat.

They hopped up on the machine.

Cooper's boyhood face flashed behind his lids.

Chris shook his head, brought the M4 up, and held the stock snuggly into his shoulder.

"You and I are the same, Sergeant Gonzalez," Tayseer yelled, the sound coming from the opposite side of the carousel. Sam and Cooper were only feet away to his left, their backs to him, tied to a pole, but Chris couldn't let his guard down, couldn't follow that basic instinct that screamed at him to go to them and make sure they were all right.

No, he had to hunt the SOB who threatened to bring down his world.

He brought his sights in line, keeping the muzzle raised in the direction of Tayseer's voice.

"You have death on your hands just as I do."

There. To his right. Chris spun, ignoring the twinge in his leg and fired off a burst of three rounds. The weapon vibrated in his hands. Bullets pinged off metal. Tayseer's face rose after the echoing shots, a gun raised and pointed at him. Chris dove for cover behind a bench on the carousel, diving out of the way just in time to hear the shot fired off.

He scrambled to find new cover, using the center platform as a pivoting dock. Now, on the opposite side of Sam and Cooper, he tracked forward, looking to come up behind Tayseer's last hiding spot.

A shot rang out and pain buffeted his shoulder, sending him spinning around to the ground. His head slammed against the hook of a plastic pony. Stars danced before his eyes, but he rose to his knees and scrambled for cover.

He looked around, searching for and failing to find DA. Where had he gone? Did he get scared at the gunshots? *Shit!*

"You and I. We're not good men, Sergeant Gonzalez. I know all about you."

More shots fired, but they seemed haphazard, as if Tayseer didn't know where he hid. Chris pulled back the flap of his jacket and winced at the perfect hole in his shoulder. Blood trickled down his chest and back, and his leg throbbed with pain. His vision swam, telling him how bad off he was.

Shit again…

"You left your brother to live a life of privilege. Your own flesh and blood, to live among the rich."

His adoptive parents had been anything but rich. Well off? Yes. They worked for their positions, but he wasn't about to argue with this mental case.

"You and I are one of the same, Gonzalez. We put ourselves before others. But that comes at a cost."

Sam cried out, and Chris resisted the insane urge to run in her direction. Instead, he peeked his head around his hiding place. Tayseer had her beautiful red hair in his fist and pulled her head back at an ungodly angle. His brother Cooper stared at Tayseer with rage.

"Tell him to come out of hiding," Tayseer said to her, his voice carrying only feet away from where Chris hid.

Sam pushed her lips together, refusing to give in.

"Tell him," Tayseer pushed, then leveled his handgun to Cooper's head. "Or I'll kill his twin brother."

His pulse ran up his throat as if it wanted to jump out of hiding. Before Sam could decide, Chris stepped off the middle partition and into Tayseer's view. "Leave them alone."

Tayseer smiled and pointed his gun at Chris. From this far away, it'd hit before Chris could react. "Drop your gun."

He didn't want to do it but was left with no choice.

Tayseer smiled as Chris tossed the M4 off the carousel. "There's a problem with people like us, Gonzalez."

Chris swallowed, forcing down bile. He shifted as the carousel continued to spin. The movement, along with his already dizzy head, made him sick. Blood loss and what he figured was a concussion weren't doing him any favors. He could feel his strength zapping out minute by minute.

"We're nothing alike," he said.

Tayseer fired, and another shot hit him in the same shoulder as before. Sam cried out, but Chris remained on his feet, turning back to Tayseer.

"When we die, there's no one left to mourn what is left of our pathetic souls."

Chris staggered forward a step, his gaze locked on Tayseer. "Let them go. I'm the one you want. They are nothing to you."

A shadow moved behind Tayseer, but Chris kept his eyes on him, wanting to hold his focus. "How did you do it? Track us down all the way back here?"

"I have … resources," he said. The mole in the CIA, he meant. Whatever they had promised the traitorous bastard, he hoped it was worth it. If Chris ever found out who it was, he'd make the mole's life a living hell.

Something moved to their right, pulling Tayseer's attention first. Charlie leveled her gun on Tayseer. "Police! Stop!"

Chris blinked, the world slowing to a mere crawl. In horror, he watched as Tayseer's gun went off without abiding by Charlie's command. He wanted to warn her that terrorists played by a different set of rules, that in his world as a Spec Ops soldier, you shoot first and asked questions later. Instead, all he could do was watch as her body shook with the force of the bullet and spun, falling to the side in the carousel, right at Sam's feet.

Someone screamed, and distantly, he realized it was him.

Another shadow jumped from behind Tayseer, and a dark muzzle latched onto the SOB's arm.

Delta Alpha!

Pulling every last bit of strength, he launched at Tayseer, diving over a bench and past a pony.

Spittle flew out of his mouth and landed on the man's face, the droplets fascinating him with his distorted attention span.

Tayseer's gun flew out of his hand as they all went down, then Chris rose above him and lashed out. Punched him in the face. Cartlidge crunched under his fist and pain blossomed from his hand. Blood flew to the side and dripped from him. So much of it, he couldn't keep track of the source.

Most of it had to be his.

DA continued to growl and yank at Tayseer's arm, but somehow, he lost purchase between one second and the next as Tayseer surged up and rolled them over, coming atop of him. His hands wrapped around Chris's neck and squeezed.

He tried to lift his arms, but they felt as if they were a hundred pounds each. His vision swam, black dots appearing. Shadows crowded in from the sides, threatening to blink out his existence. He fought to take in air but was cut off, unable to breathe.

Cooper would die most likely.

Samantha...

Her child she carried.

Tayseer cried out then and his body shook, as if

something had ahold of him and pulled with all of its might.

DA…

With one last surge of strength pulled from somewhere deep inside, Chris reached to his boot and yanked out his tactical knife, then plunged it straight into the side of Tayseer's chest, knowing it pierced his heart.

Tayseer's eyes widened then a peaceful look came over his face before he dropped to the side.

Chris rolled his heavy weight off him then pulled himself over to Charlie. He took in the status of Cooper and Sam, wanting to help free them but knowing he didn't have the strength to stand.

It was a little odd looking into a face that resembled his own so much, but that couldn't hold his attention long. He pulled up alongside Charlie and rolled her over, choking on his own saliva as she lay there so still. His fingers searched for a pulse and everything inside of him waited … waited … there! Her pulse beat fast and soft but was there. He tugged her up to his lap and rested against a bench. "I've got you, Charlie. Hold on. I've got you."

His vision swam and his head lolled, energy draining from his body like the air from a balloon. The carousel slowed and the world around him started coming into focus. Color drifted away, an oddity seeing as he had his eyes wide open.

A soft whine pierced his ears. He looked up at Sam and felt his heart flip. She stared back at him with tears in her eyes, her whole face awash in concern. DA sat at her side, his entire body trembling with the need to protect. "Chris," she said on a sob.

"I love you," he said to her now, knowing it was the truth. Her face crumpled even more. He looked to DA. "Good job, boy. Good job."

"Hang in there, Chris!" she screamed.

But he couldn't. His head weighed too much. His body was too weak. Nodding toward her, he squeezed Charlie to him again, shifting her bulk so she would know he had her. "I love you," he said again, his gaze on Sam as he rested his head against the bench. He couldn't keep his eyes open. Just as they shut, big figures clad in black uniforms rushed up.

Chapter Twenty-One

Samantha lifted her head from where it rested against her hand joined with Chris's. She'd dozed on and off over the past few hours, having only left his side to take care of the basic necessities after the hospital had released her, deeming her in good health. The past forty-eight hours had been one whirlwind after another, between the different questions she'd been asked by various individuals, the doctors checking and rechecking her health, the bloodwork submitted, and the all-clear that no unauthorized pathogens were in her body.

Chris had yet to regain consciousness, and despite being reassured by the nurses and doctors who watched over him, she couldn't help but see their worried expressions when they thought she wasn't paying attention. Her stomach twisted and turned each time the door to his hospital room opened, but the familiar and steady beep of his heart gave her a small measure of comfort, minuscule as it was.

Cooper entered the room, his tired gaze doing a quick sweep of Chris before landing on her. She shook her head to his silent question, the same they had stopped verbalizing over a day ago. Chris remained sleeping and unresponsive.

The sight of Cooper still jarred her, despite all the hours they'd spent together, despite having heard the story of him being Chris's twin. And he looked exactly like Chris, sans the hair color, but his features were remarkably the same. Had she seen this man on the corner of a street, she would have assumed him to be Chris.

Which could have been awkward, seeing how

close she'd grown to her gruff and loyal soldier.

Clicking sounds followed Cooper's entry, followed by the swoosh of the door as it closed. DA ambled up to her side, tucking close to her body, and stared at Chris. He'd stayed at her side since the whole scene at the carousel, despite the brief breaks he'd had outside.

"How is he doing?" she asked Cooper, stroking the side of DA's flank, assessing his healing body under her hands. DA's injuries were healing up nicely. His mind was another story and one they needed to monitor.

Cooper pulled a chair from the wall and up to the opposite side of Chris's bed, shrugging his big shoulders as he took a load off. Despite both of them being cleared and deemed in good health, she couldn't help but watch him for any twinges of discomfort, ready to call the doctors in the room at the first sign. She had grown protective of these two men, three if you included DA, within such a short amount of time. And a protector role was something she was becoming comfortable with.

"The nurses keep giving us the stink-eye every time we pass someone new, but one of the guys on Chris's team sweet-talked the head nurse, told them the whole story about how close Dumb Ass is with my brother."

"I didn't know they let dogs in a hospital, but I can't imagine him being anywhere else right now."

"With the number of different agencies running around and some full bird colonel swinging his weight, who knows why they turned a blind eye to it today." A few seconds of silence passed, the only sound being the heart monitor filling the room. Cooper cleared his throat. "He has a lot of people that obviously care about him out there."

Sam refocused, hearing a gruffness in his voice.

He didn't meet her gaze but instead stared at his brother lying so still. How surreal must this situation be between the two of them. The way Cooper had explained it, he and Chris had been separated by the state for several months before being reunited in a home together. A darkness had come over Cooper's face as he talked about the past, and something caused her not to pry too much into it. She didn't know if it was the shadows that crept behind his gaze, or the short answers he gave, only providing so much information as to get by. Whatever the case, it was clear there were some lingering issues that needed to be resolved there, but she didn't have the first clue how to help.

Trying to give a little to what felt like a horrible, helpless situation they'd found themselves in, one hopefully with a happy ending, she ventured and picked up the small bit of conversation he handed out. "From what I know of most of them out there is they are a great group of people."

Cooper nodded but didn't say anything.

She tried again. "You know, I'm an outsider here, too."

He turned his attention to her, one eyebrow arched.

She nodded. "I just moved here a few months ago. Have known Chris shorter than that."

His expression changed, growing almost incredulous. "You all seem extremely close. Hell, most of them out there seem as if they'd lay down their life for you from how they talk. Even DA," he said and gestured toward where DA's head rested in her lap, "seems very close to you."

She shrugged and ran a hand over fur as soft as silk. "We've all grown very close very quickly. But despite what you just said, many of them out there are practically strangers to me still. I think it's their loyalty to Chris that drives some of that protectiveness. Not me." She finished the last bit softly, almost hating to say those words, no matter how true they were.

She turned to look at Chris again, not wanting Cooper to see how much she wished the opposite to be true. How she longed for a family like the one Chris had, for her own.

"You're wrong," he said.

She looked back.

"Those men out there don't seem to me like people who would freely hand out their trust. Even with Chris and I being apart for nearly two decades, I don't think we're all that different. And I can tell you I wouldn't associate with people I couldn't trust. My brother is going to be much the same way."

Is going to be. Again, she couldn't get over how odd this entire situation had turned out to be. "When was the last time you remember being with Chris?"

Cooper released a sigh and looked up to the ceiling, running a heavy palm down his face. "God, when was that? All I remember the night I last saw him was I hadn't been feeling well. Was bed-ridden sick for a few days at that point. The place we were staying at had become dismissive about my illness. There are bits and pieces from that night that I can make out such as Chris arguing with the guy who ran the home, pleading with him to give me something to bring down the fever. I think I remember him throwing things around the room, too." Cooper shook his head and stared off into the distance, his eyes narrowing as if trying to get a clear picture in his head. "I think the guy ended up hitting Chris with something … a bat?" He shook his head again and refocused on her. "I can't really remember that part. Just remember waking up what seemed weeks later, but was only days, my fever broken, feeling sluggish but better, and Chris was gone."

"I went to get you medicine," a voice between them said, causing Sam to whip her head to Chris, who had his gaze on Cooper.

"Chris!" she exclaimed, jumping out of her chair and sending it flipping over. DA let out a warning *woof* beside her, but she was too overwhelmed to care. She dove toward him, taking his face in her hands as she stared down with happiness.

"Hey, Red," he croaked then cleared his throat. "Babe, can you grab me some water, please?"

A cup hovered next to their heads, held out by Cooper. Sam adjusted the bed so Chris could sit up in order to drink. He took small, cautious sips before draining the cup dry.

After handing the cup back to her, he grabbed her hand once she set it on the bedside table.

"How are you feeling?" she asked.

"Like I've been hit by a Mack truck." He winced, shifting on the bed, pulling himself up more. She helped rearrange pillows to make him more comfortable.

"I think I need to grab a doctor. Let them know you're awake," she said.

Chris shook his head, wincing with the movement. "No, wait." He grabbed her wrist before she could leave. "Hold on for a moment. How's…" He swallowed hard and grimaced. "How's Charlie?"

Sam's heart squeezed. The pain on his face was unmistakable. She rushed on to reassure him, settling her hand over his. "She's fine. A bit cranky with being in the hospital but your brother and Trent are watching over her, much to her annoyance." She couldn't help it. Her lips twitched. Annoyed was an understatement. The last time she went to the restroom, a bedpan had flown out of the room, barely missing Rossi's head.

Chris let out a heavy breath and squeezed his eyes shut. Clearly, he was in pain. He barely moved and dark shadows lined the hollows of his cheeks. "I think I should get the doctor," she said.

"Wait," he responded, his voice sounding as if it'd been run over gravel. "I want a few minutes alone with you before everything else takes over." He glanced between them. "I take it since you two aren't in isolation, you're fine?"

"Yeah," both Sam and Cooper said together.

Chris frowned, his face awash in confusion. "But Tayseer said…"

"Exactly," Cooper cut in. "And both Sam and I were given injections of something, but whatever was inside that needle was long gone once they ran the first blood test. So far, the other two follow-up tests have been clean, too."

"Jesus," Chris said, blowing out a huge breath. "And you two are fine?" He looked between Cooper and Sam.

Cooper nodded, and Sam followed suit.

"And the baby?" Chris asked.

Sam took his hand and placed his palm over her stomach, the tiniest of baby bumps visible. "The baby is fine, too."

His eyes grew bright, but he didn't say anything for a few beats. "Come here," he said gruffly.

She smiled and dipped her head, letting him guide her mouth to his with a hand on her nape. His lips were soft and warm, the touch sending tingles in their wake. A chaste kiss, but one she understood and that spoke of the happiness inside of him. That she was okay. That they were all okay.

"I'm going to…" Cooper started to say. He took a

step back toward the door to the room.

"No, stay here for a min … brother," Chris said.

Cooper's eyes closed as pain washed over his features. Sam tensed, her heart crying out for these two. So much anguish, so much loss. So much time wasted.

****

"I know you," Chris said, his words scratchy on his throat. "I remember you."

The pain in Cooper's face reflected like a hard blow to his chest, splintering out as if the emotion wanted to annihilate. The beeping in his room sped as he watched a lone tear track down his twin's face.

"I didn't know," Chris said, trying to make sense of why he didn't remember Cooper until that night. Why his memories had decided to flee. Forgetting about someone as important as his own flesh and blood made little sense. It almost seemed impossible. "I'm sorry. I know that's not much right now." He cleared his throat, grimacing as pain lanced his shoulder. "Had I remembered … had I known, I would have tried. I would have stayed." He let his head fall back on the pillow, at a loss for words. What could he say to fix this? To tell Cooper how horribly everything had gone? He had tons of questions about where Cooper had been, what had happened. Questions for doctors even to explain why someone so important, why events so important to him had been locked in his mind out of his consciousness.

Cooper lifted a hand to stop what was sure to be more apologies out of his mouth, then took one step, two, and leaned down to allow Chris to hug him. Awkward as it was with his big body sprawled out in a bed, he did what he could and held on to Cooper. A sense of peace settled inside even though the questions persisted. There was a lot to go over between him and his twin, but now that he'd found him, he sure as hell would take the time to get to know him again, and find out everything about what had occurred all those years ago.

Cooper stood again and subtly wiped his face with the back of his hand as the door behind him opened and Colonel Barber walked in.

While Chris knew he was in a hospital bed—and really, he needed to stop meeting his commanding officer while laid out in a bed—he had the urge to sit up at attention. Some habits died hard, and apparently this would be one he'd have to work on getting over, seeing as he'd made his decision. How Barber would take said decision was anyone's guess.

"How you feeling?"

Chris cleared his throat. "As well as one can be, I guess." He rubbed his chin, feeling the scratch of a new beard coming in. "Have you heard anything regarding Tayseer?"

Barber lifted a brow and settled beside the bed, hands held clasped low on his body. "Right to the point, huh?" He nodded. "All right, I have good news and bad news here. And rather than beat around the bush, I'm just going to go down what I know.

"Tayseer was killed. His body was picked up by some black ops group even I don't have a security clearance high enough to know their names."

Barber didn't look too happy about this, his eyes hard and mouth pinched with displeasure. Oh, boy.

"That's the good news. Bad news is I'm still stuck in the same place I was a week ago. No one seems to be returning my calls from the alphabet agency, and everyone else is playing a happy game of deflection. So, we're no further along in getting answers. We're still stuck at a mole being in the CIA and now said mole is out there somewhere running for their life. All they've told me is the right people—and son, I'm sure you can read between the lines on that—are hunting him or her."

"Jesus," Chris said and rubbed his head. "What a mess." He frowned, remembering something. "Wait, there were some guys out at the carousel…"

Barber nodded. "Said group I talked about earlier. The only thing they told me about them was about some PI with Off the Record. Andrew Cox or something. He left his card and asked that you give him a holler once you're up and moving."

Chris took the card Barber handed out and curled it in his hand. "Did he say what he wanted to talk about?" All of this seemed surreal. As if he were living in some Tom Clancy novel.

"Not a thing, but I think you know." Barber leveled his heavy gaze on him. "I'm almost afraid to ask because I already see the answer in your eyes, but I wouldn't be doing my duty if I didn't." He heaved a heavy sigh. "Have you given any more thought to what your plan is?"

His plan. The one Chris had been thinking on with whether or not to return to the military. A tough decision, but not much of one either. Hard to explain and adequately express what he wanted. The military had been all he'd known for so long, his family away from home. And that'd been the kicker the past few weeks. Realizing that Nyack, New York was his home. It was a place he'd never thought of in that aspect before. But surrounded by his brothers, his friends, and now Sam, he couldn't look at it anyway else.

Going back overseas to fight more wars and operations didn't hold the same appeal it had sixteen years ago. Sure, he still wanted to serve his country, but he also wanted to build his own life here with Sam. Build his own family. He had an idea on how to do that, how to get started, because civilian life was much more different from that of a military one. And with what he did in the military, there weren't too many career options that would transfer over. But he had an idea.

He met Barber's gaze and gave him a regretful smile. "I think you know, Colonel."

Barber sighed and held out his hand. "I get it. And I wish nothing but the best for you, son. Don't be a stranger, you hear?"

Chris nodded and shook his hand.

"I'm going to head out and get rolling on your separation paperwork. I'll be in touch. Glad to see you're okay."

With that, Barber left the room. The angst in his chest over this decision lifted. He felt as if he could breathe freely for the first time in years. As if someone had removed a plastic bag from his head, allowing him to draw in clean air, to see clearly. This was the right choice.

He was home … for good.

Epilogue

Three weeks later

Chris grinned at Matt, who tossed quick quips back and forth with Trent, both of them trying to one-up each other on which New York baseball team was the better, the Yankees or the Mets. Personally, he found the idea of baseball a bit too slow and instead rooted for football when the season was in play. Happened to be his favorite time of the year, too, with the fall leaves changing colors.

The past three weeks had passed with no drama whatsoever. An amazing difference, seeing as the past few months had led all of them on this roller coaster of emotions and activity. He'd spent forty-eight hours in the hospital before being released. If he never went to the hospital because of a bullet passing through his muscle again, it'd be too soon.

Delta Alpha had also been released into his care, having recovered from his injuries enough to allow him to come home just three days ago.

Cooper had also stuck around, spending a lot of time between Chris's cabin and his parents' house. That last bit had been an interesting development, one he could only assume meant good things. Ma and Pop were good folks, and upon meeting Cooper, they'd taken him under their wings with barely a minute pause. He could tell it affected Ma, learning there'd been two little boys and not one, for she'd excused herself shortly after meeting him only to return a few minutes later with glassy eyes and reddened cheeks. Her hovering and catering to Coop was something Chris would need to keep an eye on, just to make sure that relationship was healthy, but he had a feeling all would work out well.

The only thing that didn't quite sit right with him involved Sam still living above her clinic. They spent most of their free time together and didn't go a night without sleeping in the same bed, but he could almost picture that hand she still held in the air, hovering, pushing him back from getting too close. She hadn't brought up their relationship or discussed her future plans, especially when it came to the baby she carried, but every time he closed his eyes, their future together popped behind his lids.

He wanted her tied to him, wanted her to feel as if she could depend on him being there, and he'd been planning on how to make it clear, make sure she knew without a doubt that he wasn't going anywhere.

Between his team, his brothers who had dropped in, Trent, and Cooper, he hoped the secret he planned ended up being a good surprise for her.

After handing the grill off to Matt, he went in search of the object of his thoughts, finding her surrounded by Brooke, Hailey, Sabrina, a friend who'd come along with Matt, and Ma. Sam smiled as her gaze caught his, and the sight of it knocked into him as it did each time—like a bat against his body. He took a moment to catch his breath and once again thought about how much his life had changed in the short span of a half a year. The butterflies, the losing his breath, even the figurative hearts and flowers in his vision all sounded cheesy ... too soft and sweet for a soon-to-be former Spec Ops soldier.

Sunlight caused the deep red of Sam's hair look as if it were on fire, and he'd been right all those nights ago. It was extremely pretty in the light of day, something he knew he'd never get tired of. There'd been more times than not that he had lost himself to the fascination of her hair while they sat outside as the sun went down, her attention on the changing sky before them, his on his fingers within her shimmering copper strands.

"*Mijo*," Ma said, drawing his attention. "Please tell me you did not leave the grill to your father. That man has no sense of time when it comes to grilling meat and will burn each piece until the steaks break your teeth."

Charlie snorted and Chris laughed. "Ma, seriously. You're killer on a man's ego. He's not that bad."

She just gave him a look, a slight pursing of lips and head tilted down so she peered up at him from under heavy lashes.

With a smile, he shook his head then held his hand out for Sam. "No, Matt is manning the grill. Mind if I steal Red here for a minute?"

"Just a minute? Is that all it takes?" asked Charlie.

"Charlese Lopez!" Ma yelled.

Sam laughed as his pseudo-kid sister buckled over. He kept shaking his head but laughed with them, feeling a sense of home deep inside.

This was what it was all about.

"What?" Charlie asked as Sam slid her hand into his, her palm so, so soft. "You're the one who assumed that's what I was talking about."

"Pfft," Ma said and grabbed another bell pepper. "I've got my eye on you, young lady. We all know what you mean. My oldest baby would never—"

"Ma!" he said, jumping in before he could figure out a hint of where she would go with that line of thinking. He didn't want to hear it, didn't want to know.

"What, *mijo*?" she asked, a mock innocence in

her dancing eyes.

He mimed zipping his lips but pulled a smiling Sam toward the hallway that led down to the two attached rooms of the cabin.

"I know it doesn't take Trent just a minute," Charlie said under her breath, and Brooke laughed.

The sounds of their laughter grew muted as he drew Sam to a stop in front of the second door in the hall.

"I love your family," she said, eyes alight with humor.

"Eh, they're all right." A lie, but it was fun to tease. "It'll be nice when the rest of the crew drops in later this week. Jake, Luke, and Mike are completely different from the ones you've met so far."

She tilted her head. "Bad different or good?"

Chris shrugged, unable to explain. "Not bad or good. Just different. You'll see." He pulled in a deep breath, and his nerves took flight like a thousand moths in his stomach. "I have something to show you."

A smile played on her pink lips and curiosity sat behind her beautiful sea-green eyes. He shifted his stance and took both of her hands in his, wanting to get this right.

"Chris? What is it?"

He shook his head again, not wanting her concerned. "It's okay. I'm just—I want to get this right."

Her grip tightened on his fingers and she sucked in a breath, eyes wide. All at once, he realized what he sounded like. What she thought he was about to do.

Way too fast. Way too soon.

"Whoa, whoa, not that." He paused. "Well, yes that. But not right now. Later. Not too far later, though."

Her cute face scrunched up. "Ummm."

"I'm jacking this up," he said and shifted to the door, settling his hand on the knob. "How about I just show you, then we'll talk about it."

"Okay," she said hesitantly.

"The guys, well, everyone helped out with this, but no pressure. You can say no. But we hope … I mean, *I hope* you say yes."

He opened the door.

"Oh!" Sam gasped and stepped inside.

The light-gray painted walls offset the rustic barn-wood shiplap accent wall with a soft charm. Hailey had found a stencil of the forest deep within the woods and painted one wall in a darker shade of gray than the rest. On the floor, they'd removed the old carpet and put down a large fluffy white rug to help protect feet from the cold winter nights, or knees and hands as they began to crawl around.

A dark maple crib sat in the corner, one he'd built with his team, and on the opposite wall was a six-drawer dresser stained to the same shade.

A nursery. For Sam and her child, should she choose him.

He stepped up behind her and ran a hand around her hip, coming to rest over her belly button and the ever-growing bump within.

"I don't know what to say, Chris."

He used his chin to brush hair away from her neck then kissed the fluttering pulse that marked her heartbeat. "Say yes. Move in with me. Let me take care of you."

Within his arms, she went stiff, then faced him, her expression pained.

Her soft palms cradled his cheeks. "Hear me now, Chris," she said, her words gentle. So gentle, a ball of unease started to coil within him. "I can take care of myself. I can even take care of myself and my baby. We are not your responsibility."

He opened his mouth, ready to disagree, but she cut him off.

"For far too long, I had to rely on others to get by. Never learned to be my own person. I can't allow that to happen again. I won't allow it. Especially now that I'm about to bring another life into this world."

And he got it. He completely understood. He remembered feeling helpless and at the mercy of others, knew that while her situation had been different, the feelings within would have been much the same.

"Yes," she said, her eyes bright. "We'll move in. But we'll all take care of each other. No one person or puppy will have more responsibility than the other. We'll all carry the same and give the same."

He doubted he'd ever be able to give her as much as she gave him. Hope. Love. Family. There was too much she'd helped him see. Things that had been in front of him for years, but things he'd been blind to.

He wrapped his arms around her, crushing her to his chest. "Jesus, Red, do you realize how much of a heart attack you were about to give me? I thought you were about to say no."

She laughed and pulled back. "Me? I thought you were about to propose!"

He snorted. "Nah, we're going to get married. That much I know for sure. Just not yet."

Her adorable nose scrunched up, fine little wrinkles making him want to kiss her all over again. "Ummm, shouldn't that be something you ask me, rather than tell? I'm not one of your military boys to boss around, you know."

He hooked an arm around her neck and tucked her close as if he wanted to give her a noogie, then groaned. "You are a killer on a man's ego. Just like Ma."

She giggled.

"Men, we're men, Red. Not boys. Soldiers, if you can help it."

She pushed at his stomach, digging those beautiful fingers right into the tickle spot at his side. He released her, jumping back a few steps, then grabbed the knob, intent on joining the party again and checking on the grill. Matt may have taken his strict instructions with a serious nod of his head—they all knew Pop was a man who couldn't be helped on the grill—but he was also a man who gave in to their pop more often than not.

A quick rap sounded on the other side and Chris opened it.

"Hey, I'm sorry, man, I have to head out. A big bust just happened down at JFK and the main guy on call is tied up on another case. They need me to head in and take a look," Matt said, an apology on his face.

Chris caught the hand he held out, slapping the palm before shaking it in an age-old way they'd done since they were kids. "Don't be a stranger, you hear?"

Matt lifted a brow. "Shit, I have to be hearing things if you're telling me to not be a stranger."

"Ha, ha," he responded, feeling Sam slide her palm against his. He pulled her into the hallway and followed his brother out from the back of the house. "Who's on the grill?"

Matt winced and Chris wanted to cry. His mother would have a conniption. "Dude, you're in so much trouble if he messes anything up."

"He can't be that bad," Sam said beside him.

He just gave her a look.

"Shit," she said under her breath. "Maybe I should go check on the grill."

"You man the grill?" Matt asked, both brows raised to his hairline as if the thought of anyone else being able to man the grill was some state secret.

She laughed. "I also know how to pour a beer."

Matt clutched his chest as if he were having a heart attack. "Be still my heart. Marry me, Samantha. I'll give you the world."

She shook her head, her eyes lit with delight as she headed toward the back door. "Sorry, I've already been told I'm marrying Chris."

"What's this?" his mother asked, coming from around the corner while his brother looked at him with comically wide eyes.

"Shit," he said, reading the look in his mother's eyes. "Ma, don't start."

Thunder moved over her face and she cocked a hip, a sure sign she was about to light into him. "First of all…"

"Dear God, there are parts," Matt said next to him.

"You don't tell a woman to marry you. You ask."

"She's got a point."

Chris gave his brother a narrowed-eyed look. "You're not helping."

"Second," his ma continued, "you've been dating her for all of, what, three months? I get she's beautiful and I would be more than happy to have her as a daughter, but she needs to be taught. I need to teach her how to deal with you so you don't walk all over her."

Matt barked out a laugh, then shut up as Ma narrowed her eyes at him. "And you…" she started.

"Me, yes," Matt said and leaped over then leaned down to plant a loud kiss on her cheek, "I must be going. Duty calls."

Within seconds, Matt had bounded out of the room, the door closing before Chris could take another breath. He looked back at Ma, seeing the gray at her temples, the fine wrinkles lining her eyes. Love surged in his chest along with a sense of time slipping by way too fast. He couldn't imagine his life without her and didn't want to consider it now. "Ma," he said, keeping his voice soft and full of meaning.

She opened her mouth, then shut it and folded her hands across her stomach. "Do it again, Christopher. She deserves better."

He smiled. "You're right, and I plan on it."

"Good." She clapped her hands. "Where's your father?"

He winced. "You see…"

Her eyes widened. "Oh, no! *Dios, mijo!*"

****

Three hours later…

Chris dropped into his chair and crossed his booted feet over one another, taking in the roaring fire inside of the pit they'd built just outside of his tree line. Embers rose into the air as if dancing with one another until disappearing into the blackened sky. The aroma of roasted marshmallows and beer filled the air, the two scents somehow working with one another to create a peaceful evening.

Ma and Pop had left just minutes ago, him walking them out to their car and seeing them away. Now, all who remained were Trent, Cooper, Dwayne, Brooke, and Hailey. He was happy to note Charlie and Sam were giggling to themselves, talking about something that had them looking over at him suspiciously. Doc and Sig sat on the other side of Charlie, watching the women's antics with secretive smirks of their own. Delta Alpha lay to the side of Sam's chair, eyes closed and face as peaceful as he'd seen in a long time.

The conversation with a detective down in some small town in Georgia had been enlightening. Seemed

Manuel's body had been found in a hotel room and from what Detective Lawson had said, the entire scene had been clean except for the body, which sprouted nothing but black, blue, and purple bruises across every inch of skin. Manuel had been tied to a chair, sitting in the middle of the room, and an anonymous caller had given the police instructions on where the body was and who to call—that who being him.

He didn't know who had offed Manuel, but he wasn't too worried over it. As far as he was concerned, that person had given Sam and him peaceful nights and minds.

The only thing that struck him as odd about the whole thing was the phone call made to him and the similarities between Luke's stepfather's death and that of Manuel's...

One of the women snorted, drawing his attention to them again. They both had their laughing gazes on him. His heart turned over in his chest as worry gnawed there. After the conversation he had with Dwayne about Hailey possibly being the one who took his pills, he wanted to hover over her and watch every move she made. She'd been through so much that none of them would hold it against her, but the last thing he wanted to do was push her back into a corner after everything. D had told him he'd handle it and Chris had to trust his brother would do the right thing ... and soon.

"Okay, I give," he said. "What's going on?" He took a long pull of his beer, drawing the amber liquid in with deep gulps. It seemed as if he'd been moving and going all day.

Samantha smiled and the sight of her dancing eyes and happiness caused something in his chest to shift, as it always seemed to do when she did that. He decided right then and there that his new mission in life would be to keep that smile on her face for the rest of their lives.

The snort sounded again, originating from Charlie. He cocked his head. "Seriously, Charlie, what's up?" he asked.

She grinned wide. "I have a few theories but I can't seem to make a decision."

He glanced around the circle, trying to see if anyone could give him a hint. Everyone looked as bemused as he felt, with the exception of his two teammates.

Very suspicious.

He narrowed his eyes as Sam let out another giggle next to him.

"What are these theories?" he asked, wondering if he'd regret playing along.

Charlie's lips twitched again. "Could it have come from you tripping over something?"

"What?" he asked, lost.

She tilted her head to the side. "Nah, that can't be it. You're the most sure-footed guy I know." She tapped her chin, then held up the same finger. "Did you try drugs at some point?" Almost before the question was out of her mouth, she shook her head. "Nah, that can't be it either."

"For fuck's sake, Charlie," he started, but she talked over him.

"Maybe fall into a wall?"

Sam giggled again.

He opened his mouth, ready to shut this down but once again, Charlie talked over him.

"No, no, that can't be it. Maybe," she said and sat up straighter, held that same damn finger in the air, and took a deep breath. And he knew. He cut a glare at his two teammates who were doing their best to avoid his gaze. "Maybe you bent over wearing your flight suit and just so happened to split the suit right up the back on a laundry day and thus, had no underwear on beneath. That *has* to be it!"

"Damn it, Sig," he barked, just as the man in question fell from his chair howling with laughter. Others joined in on the action, all having apparently been having a conversation about how he'd obtained his team nickname.

Across the fire, he met a gaze so similar to his that it still startled him. Cooper laughed along with everyone else and some of the strain around his eyes had eased. Warmth suffused his chest, and along with the sound of his family and friends laughing, the sight of his healing dog by his future wife's side, and her safe and sound beside him, all was right in his world, for he was finally home.

The End

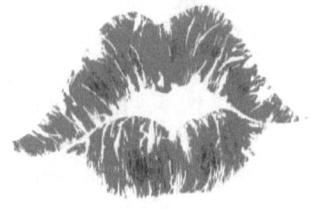